MARKED!

"The tall feller in the gray suit. That's Ferguson, all dressed up like he does when he's in town. Get ready for him, Teal. He's comin' this way. Get ready, Teal. For God's sake, don't miss."

"Don't be a fool, Mose. I can't kill him like that. Not with the Mexican patrol men and those three cow-punchers watching me so close. This smells to me like a grand set-up."

"Ya ain't gettin' scared, Teal?"

"Scared?" Teal's lips parted in a snarl. "No, Mose, I'm not scared. Neither am I so damned foolish as to shoot Add Ferguson here and now. I'll take my own time and pick my own place. . . ."

Other *Leisure* books by Walt Coburn:

BORDER WOLVES

WALT COBURN

LEISURE BOOKS NEW YORK CITY

LEISURE BOOKS ®

June 2004

Published by special arrangement with Golden West Literary
Agency.

Dorchester Publishing Co., Inc.
200 Madison Avenue
New York, NY 10016

ISBN 0-8439-5368-3

The name "Leisure Books" and the stylized "L" with design are
trademarks of Dorchester Publishing Co., Inc.

Printed in the United States of America.

Visit us on the web at www.dorchesterpub.com.

BORDER WOLVES

Table of Contents

The Block K Rides Tonight!

Following his enlistment in the U.S. Army during the Great War, Coburn tried writing and for a year and a half he wrote and wrote, earning endless rejection slips. Then one day Bob Davis at *Argosy-All Story* accepted Coburn's short story, "The Peace Treaty of the Seven Up". From then on Coburn would try to write at least 2,000 words a day, never rewriting, six days a week, with Sundays off, never working more than four or five hours a day but also never taking a vacation of longer than two or three days once a story was completed. It would be daunting to list Walt Coburn's contributions to *Star Western* since he had a story in almost every issue for nearly a decade and a half. This short novel first appeared in *Star Western* (7/39). "Pat," as Walt called his wife Mina, was the inspiration for many of his heroines, including Kathleen Mavourneen Kilgore in this story that also served as the basis for THE RETURN OF WILD BILL (Columbia, 1940), the first of a series of "B" Westerns starring Bill Elliott in the rôle of Wild Bill Hickok.

1

"Return of a Feudist"

Old Mitch was drunk when he set the shotgun trap at his big pole gate. If the old rascal had been sober and hadn't whiskey-fumbled the contraption, Cole Griffin's head would have been torn off by its double charge of buckshot as he leaned from his saddle and yanked out the long wooden gate pin. The string that was tied to the gate pin was attached to the triggers of the double-barrel shotgun.

The roar and flash of the ten-gauge shot was terrific. The heavy buckshot tore through the air a few feet above Cole's head. He was off balance, his weight all in his left stirrup, the twenty-inch gate pin gripped in his right hand, bridle reins held loosely in his left hand. Cole's big bay horse whirled, twisted, and pitched. He was thrown heavily, landing on one shoulder, his head hitting the hard ground with a *thud*.

Cole was dazed, scared, and bewildered. For a moment he lay there on the ground. Then instinct worked swifter than any actual co-ordination of mind and muscle. He rolled over and over, landed in a patch of sagebrush, clawing for his six-shooter. He threw the gate pin away with a muttered curse and pulled his gun.

In the moonlight he saw the door of the log cabin open and someone run outside. He crouched behind the patch of sage-brush and thumbed back the hammer. His horse had quit bucking and was standing, stiff-legged, facing the swinging gate. The spooked horse was whistling through widened nostrils. The running figure looked more like a boy than a man, small and slight.

"Pull up, you would-be murderin' son-of-a-bitch!" Cole

10

shouted. "Reach for the moon, or I'll gut-shoot you!"

"Oh!"

The running figure halted abruptly. A pair of arms reached high. In one hand a long-barreled six-shooter was pointed straight up at the stars.

"Drop that gun!" Cole rasped.

The big six-shooter dropped to the ground. The hammer must have struck a rock, for the gun exploded with a roar, its recoil sending it spinning through the air. Its loud echo was stabbed by a woman's shrill scream. The lifted hands dropped with a womanish gesture to cover her eyes.

Cole swore softly and grinned. "You kin take your hands away from your eyes, lady. Nobody's hurt."

From inside the lighted cabin sounded a man's bellowing voice. "Lemme up! Lemme outta here! What in hell's tarnation's a-goin' on out there? Git me outta this mess, Sammy Lou, and gimme my gun!"

Cole looked around. Save for the girl, dressed in overalls, shirt, and boots, standing there now with her hands raised to the level of her shoulders, nobody was in sight, and the bellowing man in the cabin seemed to be the only other human on this little ranch. Cole stood up, his gun in hand, still shaken and hot with seething anger. He stared hard at the girl.

The man's voice inside the cabin was cursing thickly, but the girl didn't seem to hear. Her face was white and her eyes were wide with fear. Her hair was a thick mop of black curls that had been cut off like a boy's for convenience rather than any attempt to set a style. She might have been fourteen, or she could have been half a dozen years older. But she still looked like a small, slim boy who was badly scared. She was staring at Cole, her eyes searching for some sign of gunshot wounds.

"Are you hurt?" she asked in a small, scared voice.

"No. I'm not hurt!" Cole shouted. "But that ain't your fault, nor his. Tell him to stop that roarin' and cussin'. You'd think he'd have more respect for a female. Tell him to dry up, or I'll bend a gun barrel acrost his murderin' head."

"Sammy Lou! Dagnation, gal, why don't you . . . ?"

"I'm all right, Mitch!" the girl called. "I'm comin'!"

"Who's shot? Who got 'er, Sammy Lou? If it's Jake Kilgore, let 'im lay there. Git these ropes off me an' I'll tend to his carcass!"

"Mitch," the girl said to Cole, "is gettin' over a bad 'un. I always tie him up till he quits seein' things. I'd better get back to the cabin before he goes hog wild. Put up your horse, mister. You're sure you're not hurt?"

"I'm not hurt. And before you go runnin' back to the cabin, let's git one or two things straightened out." Cole's searching eyes had discovered the sawed-off shotgun trap. He walked over to it and kicked down the ten-gauge. "Are you alone here? Don't lie to me, young lady. I ain't in any humor for lies or any more gun jokes. Who else is hid out around here?"

"Nobody. Old Mitch is there in his cabin. I rode over to get him sobered up. If you weren't a plumb stranger, you'd know that without askin'."

Cole caught the note of bitterness in the girl's voice. Her features were far from beautiful. Her nose was too short and her red-lipped mouth was a trifle too large. Her chin was firm and slightly cleft and her smile was as infectious as a small boy's. She smiled at him now, her dark eyes crinkling almost shut. Her strong white teeth showed for a second or two.

"I'd better take Mitch his six-shooter . . . if you'll let me pick it up."

"And let him finish the job that his shotgun trap bungled?"

"Don't worry about it. He probably set it for Jake Kilgore.

12

They've been at it for years."

"Been at what?"

"This gun business . . . feudin'. It started before I was born, back in the old vigilante days here in Montana. My daddy was mixed up in it. He was killed. So were some others. If you crossed the Missouri River at Rocky Point or Cow Island, you must have heard tell of it."

Cole Griffin nodded. He picked up the big six-shooter and handed it to the girl. "So you stay here and ride herd on that old warthog, Mitch, while he's soberin' up after a big drunk. Some job for a girl, that is! I'm takin' you up on that invitation to stay over night. What was it he called you?" Cole nodded toward the cabin where old Mitch's voice was subdued now to unintelligible mutterings.

"Sammy Lou Sorrels." Her tone was defiant.

"Then your father, like as not, was Sam Sorrels."

"Yes. The vigilantes hung him for horse-stealing and murder. See that big lightning-blasted cottonwood down in the lower pasture? That's the tree he was hung from. They strung up five from the same tree. Mitch was the man who cut 'em down and buried 'em. Jake Kilgore and another man rode up on him. Mitch shot Jake Kilgore's gun arm off and killed the other man. That's the story, if you haven't heard it before." The tremor was gone from her voice now.

"I heard it for the first time only a few months ago, down in Texas. I'll put up my horse and go on to the cabin. If your friend Mitch is able to savvy what you're sayin', tell him Hank Griffin's son sprung his shotgun trap. I'll be along directly."

The girl's dark eyes stared hard at him now. "Hank Griffin was one of the men. . . ."

"Hung from the same tree with Sam Sorrels about eighteen years ago. But you don't look old enough to have been livin' then."

"I was three months old. Then your name is Cole. Mitch made you a saddle for your sixth birthday. Your mother took you and disappeared. She left the country with Grant Kilgore."

"You shore know your history." Cole's faint smile was grim and his eyes were icy blue in the white moonlight.

"It's all I do know," she told him. "I've been raised right here on the banks of the Missouri River in the badlands . . . the orphaned kid of a hanged outlaw. Figure it out for yourself, what kind of a chance I've ever had to become a lady. My mother was a half-breed Sioux. She'd gone to the government school and taught me to read and write. I sent off for books. All the books I could get. A captain on one of the riverboats always stops at our place to load on cordwood for his steam engine. He brings me books. He left me a trunk full of his daughter's clothes last summer. I wore the prettiest dress to the Christmas dance at Rocky Point, and Kate Kilgore laughed at me. I grabbed a butcher knife and tried to kill her. Then I rode back to the ranch and bawled like a kid. And I'm not ashamed of it!

"I'm a river 'breed, and my father was hung for a rustler. The man who hung him and Hank Griffin and three other men was Grant Kilgore. He was head of the gang of murderers who disguised themselves as vigilantes. Your mother ran off with Grant Kilgore. You were raised as Grant Kilgore's son. Your name was changed to Cole Kilgore, wasn't it?" Her dark eyes blazed hotly. Her voice was a little shrill with hatred and contempt. "Wasn't it?" she repeated, her hand gripping the big six-shooter.

Cole's face had whitened under its deep coating of tan. His ice-blue eyes matched hers for cold fury. "You know too much," he told her, holding his voice steady. "You know a couple of facts, and then you make your own story to fit 'em."

"Your mother ran off with Grant Kilgore. She was ashamed to let her son keep his real father's name. Your mother was a white woman. They called her the most beautiful girl in Montana. But she was. . . ."

Cole's hand was across her mouth. His other hand gripped her slim shoulder, shaking her roughly. "Leave my mother's name alone." His fingers tightened on her shoulder.

The girl winced; her white teeth bit his hand. He jerked it away, blood trickling from his thumb. "It's too bad," she panted, twisting out of his grip, "that Mitch's shotgun missed. Damn you, ride on to the Kilgore ranch where you belong!" She twisted away and ran back to the cabin.

Cole saw the door bang shut. He stood there, breathing hard, scowling. Then he suddenly relaxed. He looked at his bloodstained hand and grinned. "The little wampus-cat," he muttered, and walked over to his big bay horse.

As he picked up the bridle reins, he heard the clatter of shod hoofs. His right hand dropped to the butt of his six-shooter and he stood there in the gateway, watching as three riders approached.

The man riding slightly in the lead of the other two had a heavy gray mustache and square-cut beard. His left arm was a stub with the heavy flannel sleeve cut off and sewed shut. The rider at his right had a drooping black mustache. The third, several years younger, was clean-shaven, but both had the same hawk-beaked nose and the high cheek bones of the older man. They were, Cole guessed rightly, Jake Kilgore and his two sons, Bart and Sid. They pulled their horses to a halt, the two sons with their hands on their guns. Jake Kilgore acted as spokesman.

"We heard shootin'. What was it about, and who are you?"

"Old Mitch was shootin' at snakes, but he didn't kill any. Ketch me over on your Block K range and mebbyso you'll have a right to ask questions. But this place belongs to Mitch. I don't figure that my name is any of your particular business tonight."

"I've seen you before," said Jake Kilgore, leaning across his saddle horn, his bleak eyes studying Cole's face.

"Yes?" Cole's tone was flat.

"Yeah. I don't fergit a face."

"Me 'n' Sid," said Bart Kilgore, "could make the feller talk. For a stranger in a strange land, he acts too high an' mighty. If me 'n' Sid was to. . . ."

"Dry up," snapped the elder Kilgore. "I'll recollect where I've seen this jasper's sign."

Cole wondered if he resembled his dead father. Perhaps that was what was giving Jake Kilgore the notion they had met before. Cole's hat was pulled down to throw the shadow of his hat brim across his eyes. If old Jake Kilgore recognized him as Hank Griffin's son, he might make a gun play.

Mitch's double-barrel shotgun lay behind the sagebrush within easy reach. The gun was empty, but they had no way of knowing that. A sawed-off double-barrel shotgun at close range is a weapon that few men will tackle. Cole took a step toward the sagebrush and stooped over with deliberate unconcern. When he straightened up, the sawed-off shotgun was covering the three Kilgores. The twin hammers *clicked* back under the pressure of his thumb.

"I'm tellin' you peacefully to ride on down the road. If any of you claws a gun, both barrels of this scatter-gun is goin' to explode. I ain't aimin' to miss. Now git goin'."

"He might mean it," said Sid. "Hell, let's git away from here. Let 'im alone, Paw. We'll take care of 'im another time."

"Dry up," snapped Jake Kilgore. "You figger on hangin' around these parts, mister?"

"I aim to locate here. Are you goin' now or are you stallin' to ketch me off guard?"

"Not with that thing pointin' at us. Come along, boys. We'll take care of this gent some other night."

Jake Kilgore and his two sons rode on, and Cole Griffin watched them out of sight.

Sammy Lou Sorrels came suddenly into view from a patch of willows. She carried Mitch's six-shooter. "I slipped back when I saw 'em coming down the road. I heard everything you-all said. I saw you run that bluff on 'em with the empty shotgun. I was going to do something about it, if the bluff didn't work."

"Somethin' like shootin' me in the back?" Cole grinned, ejecting the empty shells from the shotgun.

"We didn't part exactly friends, did we? I'd like to hope I was all wrong about . . . about your mother."

"You were," said Cole. "I didn't know that was how people like Mitch or you felt about the way she left Montana. Up until a few months ago I didn't know my father had been hung as a horse thief and cattle rustler. That's what fetched me back to Montana. I came to learn the truth about my father, to find out the things Grant Kilgore left untold when he died."

"Grant Kilgore . . . dead?"

"I killed Grant Kilgore at El Paso . . . four weeks ago," Cole said flatly.

11

"A Coyote Dodges the Wolf Pack"

Old Mitch was a huge man, powerful in spite of his years. When he was sober, his gray-blue eyes were as clear as the

Montana sky after a spring rain has washed the alkali dust from the air. His hair was thick and white and a drooping white mustache hid the humorous, firm, square-cornered mouth. He was somewhere around seventy, but his big white teeth were as intact as those of a youth. His surname was probably Mitchell, and no doubt he had a given name of some sort, but his given name had been lost during the years, and the Mitchell had been whittled down to Mitch.

He had a standing bet that he could fist-whip or wrestle down any man along that strip of the Missouri River badlands. He made the best corn whiskey in that part of the country, but he never sold a drop of it. He drank it himself, averaging a quart a day, and gave it to his friends. Mitch was a rip-snorting, profane old hellion with a heart as big as a bucket. Loyal to the men he called friend, he was bitter in his hatred for men who had incurred his enmity.

Sammy Lou had him tied down to his bunk. The sight of the huge bulk of a man with arms and legs spread-eagled and tied with ropes to the four heavy pine posts of his bunk reminded Cole of a picture he had once seen in some child's book of the giant Gulliver tied down. Sammy Lou looked very small as she stood beside the bunk. Cole closed the door behind him and stood there, a slow grin spreading his lips.

Mitch's bloodshot eyes stared hard at the tall cowpuncher. A stubble of sand-colored whiskers marred the clean, blunt line of Cole's jaw. His straw-colored hair needed a barber's shears. Dust powdered his tanned skin. His eyes were as blue as clear ice. His grin widened and Mitch broke the tense silence.

"You got her hair but that grin and them eyes is Hank Griffin's. Sammy Lou tells me you run off the Kilgores. That'll help wipe out the Kilgore name you bin a-usin'. See if you kin untie the knots the young 'un put in these ropes. She

18

wet 'em like I told her, and they're tighter'n a miser's wallet strings. She used two ketch ropes, and I don't want 'em cut. I always git her to hog-tie me thisaway when I'm gittin' over a bad 'un . . . because once, when I was locoed drunk, she got in my way and I slapped her. Like to kill her, savvy? I'd sooner have a whole herd of Kilgores a-standin' over me and hackin' at me with dull knives than to hurt that young 'un, understand?

"Untie them knots, young Cole Griffin. We'll have a snort of the best likker that ever washed the dust out of a man's windpipe. Sammy Lou says you're all right to tie to. Your daddy and Sam Sorrels was as good friends as I've ever had. They died a-fightin', and the vigilantes under Grant Kilgore strung 'em up to my big cottonwood as a warnin' to scare me outta the country. But I shot the gizzard outta the Kilgore top gunman, and I shot the gun arm off Jake Kilgore. Git me untied quick, young Cole Griffin. This talkin' gits a man's tongue dry. Did you come back to whup the men that hung your daddy?"

"Somethin' like that," said Cole, untying the last knot.

"Sammy Lou tells me," said Mitch, swinging his big legs over the side of the bunk and flexing his stiffened muscles, "that you killed Grant Kilgore. The news ain't reached this far yet."

"It will," prophesied Cole grimly. "Grant Kilgore was goin' under another name at the time I shot 'im. He called himself Jake Grant."

"Usin' his brother Jake's name." Mitch reached under the bunk and brought out a jug. The girl was making fresh coffee and biscuits.

Cole said: "There were three of the Kilgore brothers. Grant was the oldest. Then Seth, then Jake. I heard Seth was shot down on the street in Fort Benton. That left Grant and Jake."

"Drink?" Mitch asked.

"I'll wait for the coffee," said Cole. "I'm scared of whiskey."

Mitch nodded, and tipped up the jug.

"Take it easy, Mitch," said Sammy Lou. "Hungry, Cole?"

"I shouldn't be." Cole grinned. "I ate yesterday."

Mitch chuckled. Sammy Lou smiled and shoved the pan of biscuits in the oven of the little sheet-iron stove. Then she began slicing thick steaks from a large chunk of loin beef. Cole saw that the hands of the battered alarm clock on a shelf above the bunk pointed to midnight.

"What fetches the Kilgores out this time of night?" he asked.

"They might be after cattle. Of a moonlight night they might pick up a few head of wild stuff that bush up in the day-time and slip down outta the brakes to water at night. Them cattle is wilder'n blacktail deer. Some is in the Kilgore's Block K iron. Some belongs to other men. The Kilgores claim Hank Griffin's old HG brand. They got Joe Colter's Figger Eight iron. Likewise Pete Master's Triangle brand and the JB that belonged to Jim Blake. After them fellers was hung, the Kilgores grabbed their ranches and what livestock they had. Hank Griffin's widder had done gone down the Missouri River on a steamboat with Grant Kilgore. I wonder how she cleaned her conscience when that steamboat passed my place where Grant Kilgore and his vigilantes had hung pore Hank."

Cole's face went white. His hand dropped to his gun. He faced Mitch who sat on the edge of his bunk with the wicker-covered demijohn.

"My mother was the finest woman that ever lived. Don't talk that way about her unless you back it up with a gun. She was in Fort Benton when my father was hung. Grant Kilgore told her that the vigilantes were goin' to kill her and her small boy. That was me. Grant Kilgore did a lot of smooth lyin'. The newspaper at Fort Benton printed the story that Hank Griffin and the others were an organized band of rustlers and killers. My mother and father had quarreled a year before. Separated. She had been a singer in a river showboat company when my father married her. For a year she had been earning her own living, singing and acting with a troupe at the Fort Benton Opera House. Grant Kilgore was a big, handsome, smooth-talking man. He had money and posed as a government cattle and horse buyer.

"She didn't find out he was a tinhorn gambler until long after she married him at Saint Louis. When she found out the truth, she left him. Just before she died, she told me that he had headed the vigilantes who hung my father. I had my own cow outfit on the Río Grande in Texas. I sold out and picked up Grant Kilgore's cold trail. I cut his sign in an El Paso gamblin' house. He recognized me and shot first. His bullet parted my hair. Mine tore out his black heart. That's the story. I'll kill the man who says anything against my mother. Is that plain?"

"It's plenty plain, young Cole Griffin. And I'm proud to hear you clear the name of the purtiest woman I ever laid eyes on. You're right. She wasn't meant for ranch life. Her and Hank both made a big mistake when they married. They was never happy together here on the river. They agreed to call it quits. That's when Hank Griffin begun drinkin' hard. Whiskey was rank poison to Hank. You got a right to be scared of the stuff. Me, I'm different. I git snakes in my boots when I'm gittin' over a big 'un. But outside of that, likker is food an' drink. I make my own likker and I drink it. Look sharp, young feller. Somebody's a-comin'. Bar the door an' put out the light, Sammy Lou, and git into the cellar. If that's

21

the Kilgores a-comin', me 'n' young Cole Griffin will deal 'em misery."

"Mitch!" called a voice outside the cabin. "Open the door, Mitch! You gotta hide us!"

"It's Frank!" cried the girl. "He's in trouble, Mitch!"

"Let the young 'breed coyote in," growled Mitch, cursing softly as he shoved the demijohn back under the bunk.

Sammy Lou pulled back the heavy wooden bar and opened the door. She gave a startled little gasp as a tall girl in leather divided skirt, beaded buckskin blouse, and tawny braids stumbled into the cabin. Behind her, shoving her inside, stood a tall, handsome, black-haired young cowboy wearing bearskin chaps and a buckskin shirt. His face was tense and grayish under its natural swarthy color. He had a six-shooter in his hand. His eyes were a yellowish gray. He shut the door behind him and stood with his back against it, breathing hard.

The girl with the yellow hair was looking at Cole. She had fair skin that was freckled across her aquiline, thin-nostriled nose. Her lips twisted in a forced smile. The look of fear left her eyes slowly as she smiled faintly at Cole. He flushed a little under her bold scrutiny.

"Jake and Bart and Sid are huntin' us!" panted the tall cowboy who was obviously part Indian. "We gave 'em the slip, but if they pick up our sign. . . ."

"They'll shoot you down fer a coyote," growled old Mitch, "and, if I had my say, they'd shoot *her* before she gits any more damn' fools killed along this river. Damned if I'm a-runnin' ary hide-out fer Jake Kilgore's she-whelp and her sheep-brained fellers! Clear out, Frank Sorrels. Your daddy must be a-turnin' over in his grave right now. His son a-gallivantin' with Jake Kilgore's. . . ."

Sammy Lou's hand was across Mitch's mouth.

"Look out he don't bite," Cole could not help but say, holding up his left hand that was crusted with dried blood.

"If the Kilgores are hunting her," said Sammy Lou, ignoring Cole's grin, "they'll never look for her here. Frank's my brother, Mitch. I've helped you. You've got to hide him and Kate in the cellar!"

"Hide him!" said Kate Kilgore, her large eyes still looking at Cole. "Coyotes always hunt a hole when a wolf shows up. I'd rather be horsewhipped than stay in this whiskey shack. It was his notion, not mine, that fetched us here."

Her hands, covered with Indian-tanned buckskin gauntlets, coiled the heavy plaited braids that came below the level of her beaded belt. She bunched the braids in a coiled knot at the nape of her white neck and put on her wide-brimmed black hat. She was by far the handsomest girl Cole Griffin had ever seen in his life. Even her throaty, husky voice had a charm that made a man shiver a little. She possessed that indescribable magnetism that is given to few women, and she knew how to use it.

Her straight height dwarfed little Sammy Lou and her white-skinned, tawny beauty made the little quarter-breed girl look shabby and uncouth. She had courage and vanity and selfish pride. She was made to wear silks and velvets and jewels.

"Take good care of the coyote," she said, opening the door. "The wolves are on the prowl tonight." Then she looked boldly at Cole. "Why don't *you* ride on to the Block K Ranch with me? Or are you also afraid of wolves?"

"Is that an invitation or a challenge?" Cole had difficulty in keeping his voice steady under the direct gaze of her long-lashed yellow eyes. Cole, his eyes on Kate Kilgore, was unprepared for Frank Sorrels' swift attack. He felt a hard fist crash against his jaw and saw the glitter of a long knife blade. He was thrown against the wall. The knife missed his throat by a scant inch as he ducked. Then Cole swung a vicious, looping left into the distorted face of Frank Sorrels. He followed it with hard, smashing rights and lefts that drove the quarter-breed backwards. A swing that had all his weight behind it dropped Sammy Lou's brother in a limp, battered, bloody heap at her feet.

"The next time you pull that pig-sticker on me, you damned 'breed, I'll carve my name in your yellow hide!"

Sammy Lou, her face white with rage, stooped to grab the hunting knife from her brother's limp hand. Cole pulled her back and picked up the knife. Mitch took Sammy Lou in his big, powerful hands and held her as she kicked and fought like a little wildcat.

"Git that buckskin-maned Kilgore female off this ranch," growled Mitch at Cole. "I'll have the young 'un cooled down by the time you git back. Git 'er off the place, Cole! Take your time a-comin' back. Looks like you done broke Frank's neck."

III

"At the Hangman's Tree"

Cole had a white man's loathing for a knife and contempt for the man who would pull one in a fight. The swift, blinding rage, that sears a man's brain when he kills, was slow to cool. That anger now included the sister of the man who lay as if dead on the cabin floor. She was trying to fight free. Cole saw her blazing eyes flick a sidelong glance at the butcher knife she had been using to slice the steaks. He still had her brother's bone-handled hunting knife. He drove the blade deeply into the log wall and snapped it off at the brass hilt, tossing the bladeless handle on the floor. Even the drunken Mitch was included in his blind anger.

"Shotgun traps and knife-fighters!" He grinned twistedly at Sammy Lou and big Mitch. "Mebby you were right when you said I belonged with the Kilgores. At least, they pack their guns in their hands and they don't jump on a man's back with a knife. You're damn' right I'll take my time comin' back. I still don't know where *you* were, Mitch, when the vigilantes hung Hank Griffin."

"You better clear out," said Mitch, the whiskey now firing his blood. "You're crowdin' your luck. Me and Sammy Lou has got along plenty many years while Hank Griffin's son was wearin' the Kilgore name. You string your bets with them and yourn will be just one more Block K hide to hang on the fence. Take that yaller-eyed Kilgore wench an' git off my place!"

Cole backed out the door and closed it. He hardly glanced at Kate Kilgore as she mounted her horse. A few minutes later he had saddled his horse and rode off into the night. Kate Kilgore, riding alongside him, was wise enough not to break the silence. She was smiling faintly, her yellow eyes covertly watching him.

"I hope," she said, "that old Mitch will send for you and bury the hatchet when he gets sobered up. You may need him for a friend if you stay in this part of the country."

"What makes you say that?"

"Paw and my brothers were not at the ranch today when one of the hands fetched the mail from Rocky Point. There was a letter that had an El Paso postmark and the return address was marked the sheriff's office. Female cat curiosity prompted me to open it. It was a sort of formal routine notice that said my father's brother, Grant Kilgore, had been shot and killed by Cole Griffin, alias Cole Kilgore."

Cole shifted his weight to one stirrup, turning in his saddle to look squarely at the girl who rode alongside him. When he spoke, his voice was firm. "I shot Grant Kilgore. I only wish I'd gotten the job done many years ago. But I was too little then to aim a gun. Grant Kilgore was a snake. He needed killing plenty."

"So I've heard my father say. But blood is, as the saying goes, thicker than water. Jake Kilgore won't be pinning any leather medals on your shirt for killing his blackleg brother, Grant. If you have any real common horse sense, you'll keep right on riding till you're out of this part of the cow country. The name Kilgore should be spelled with two l's. They run this country around here."

"Are you tryin' to throw a scare into me?"

"Perhaps I am. I don't want to see you killed. I got you into a mess back yonder. I lost you a friend . . . two friends, if you count the little 'breed girl. Maybe you killed Frank Sorrels on my account. He dropped like a shot beef. But if you didn't kill him, you made a bad enemy. Drunk or sober, Frank's treacherous. I got you into that mess. I'm trying to keep you from tangling with my father and brothers. This is not safe range for the man who killed Grant Kilgore. You just left the only place where you'd find a safe hide-out from the Block K outfit. The Rocky Point Crossing on the Missouri is only a few miles up the river. The horse I'm riding is fresh and he's as good a horse as you'll find in Montana. Let's swap horses here. Go back to Texas, or wherever you came from. Or better yet, take me with you. I'll go down the trail to Texas with you, Cole Griffin."

Kate Kilgore's husky voice was steady. Her yellow eyes shone like smoldering lights in the moonlight. She was looking at him squarely, the smile wiped from her lips.

"I don't understand. Go to Texas with me? Why?"

"Why? Because it would be adventure, danger, excitement. I'd be riding with a man who would fight to keep the love I could give him. What is there here for me, shut in by the same skyline day after day and night after night? Listening to the same talk day in and night out. Women slaving over stoves and washtubs, wearing cheap cotton dresses they get from mail-order houses. Men smelling of stale sweat and barn stalls asking you to waltz to the squeak of a two-bit fiddle. Listening to the Kilgore men brag about their toughness. Watching the river steamers go by on their way back to Saint Louis where there are lights and music and white tablecloths and real silver. In my room at the ranch is an old theater poster. It has the picture of one woman who ran away from here because she felt the same thing stifling her heart. That woman was your mother. Grant Kilgore was a blackguard and a gambler, but he had been to big cities and he had a college education. Grant Kilgore offered her an escape from the slow suicide of ranch life here in the badlands. She was billed at the Fort Benton Opera House as Kathleen Mavourneen. My mother named me after her. Kathleen Mavourneen Kilgore . . . Kate Kilgore.

"There's no love involved here. But I could learn to worship the man who took me away from here. You're different from any man I have ever met. You'd never be content to bury yourself in this god-forgotten place. Would you be sheep-brained enough to slave away the finest years of your life building up a cow outfit here? Fighting the heat and mosquitoes in the summer. Snowed in from November till May? Take me with you. I'll share every hardship along the trail. I'll sleep on the ground with a saddle blanket for cover. I'll go hungry and thirsty. I'll take a gun and help you fight. I'll go through hell with the man who will take me down the long trail and I'll help him fight to get the things that can make us

27

both happy. I'd help him rob trains or hold up banks and win a South America stake to live in a city like Buenos Aires. We can get fresh horses at the Block K horse camp across the river. I'll go down the outlaw trail with you, Cole Griffin. If they trap us, I'll die fighting beside you!"

They had pulled up now, off the road and in the shadow of a giant cottonwood. Overhead was the moon. The stars were like millions of white diamonds in a black velvet sky. Cole's blood was pounding hard in his veins. He knew that there was no other woman on earth like this white-skinned girl whose eyes were golden pools in the shadow of long, thick, black lashes. Her husky voice thrilled him until his nerves tingled. She had taken off one of her buckskin gauntlets and her long-fingered hand was on his arm. Their stirrups touched.

Some wild thing in the brush made a noise, and Cole's head turned quickly. His eyes, still a little hypnotized by hers, saw five grassy mounds marked by five weather-beaten wooden slabs. This was the Hangman's Tree. One of those graves was that of Hank Griffin. The answer that he had been about to give the daughter of Jake Kilgore died unspoken. He took hold of the white hand that was on his arm, gripping it tightly.

"My father was hung from this tree. He's buried in one of those graves. I'd never find happiness anywhere if I ran off now like a coyote in the night. I rode up the trail from Texas to fight it out with the men who hung Hank Griffin."

Two drops of scarlet blood showed on her underlip that she had caught between her white teeth. Her golden eyes were almost black now. She jerked her hand free and pulled on her glove with a vicious jerk.

"You're no better than the Kilgore men!" Her voice was almost a whispered snarl. "You're no better than that drunken beast back there in his cabin. I thought I had found a real man, but instead I've been wasting breath on a stupid clod. I hope the Kilgores hang you, like Grant Kilgore hung the man who made a prisoner of your mother!"

She swung her rawhide quirt down on the rump of her big black horse and was gone before Cole could find any word or gesture to stop her. Something white had fluttered from her skirt pocket and lay now on the ground. It was a large envelope folded in the middle.

Cole Griffin swung from his saddle. His hand was a little unsteady as he picked up the envelope. It was addressed to Jake Kilgore and in the upper left hand corner was printed, **Sheriff's Office, El Paso, Texas.** He read the brief notice of Grant Kilgore's death and shoved the letter and its envelope into the pocket of his chaps.

He walked over to the five graves. He found the slab with Hank Griffin's name burned deeply into the pine wood with a branding iron. His hat in hand, Cole Griffin stood there in the shadow of the giant cottonwood that had been struck by lightning and remained now with a charred rip up the base of its heavy trunk, its thick branches leafless, like the fleshless arms of a skeleton.

"I was a long time gettin' here," he said aloud. "I'll pay off your debt or die a-tryin'."

He got on his horse and rode off alone into the black shadows of the broken badlands.

IV

"The Midnight Branding"

There must have been fifty head of cattle in the bunch that milled in the two corrals that were connected by a short chute and a squeezer gate. Three steers were held in the chute. A fourth was held in the pressure of the big, flat-sided squeezer. There was a branding fire that heated half a dozen irons. Some gunnysacks soaked in a wooden trough near the branding chute.

Bart Kilgore and Sid were doing the branding. The gray-bearded, one-armed Jake was bossing the job.

"Wring that sack more dry, Sid. Damn it all, won't you never learn nothin'? Git a sack too wet and all it does is cool off the iron. It's gotta scorch plumb through. Through the sack and onto the critter's hide. Now bear down, Bart. Shove that iron hard and steady. Git that brand on right or I'll peel your hide off with a jackknife. *Hard,* dammit! Put your weight ag'in' it!"

Sid held the damp sacking against the steer's hide. Bart shoved the bar iron hard. There was the *hiss* and white cloud of steam. Then the smoke of burning, wet hair. Bart, hat pulled slanting across his eyes, leaned his weight against the branding iron.

"Take it away!" snapped old Jake.

Bart stepped back, holding the iron. Sid jerked the sack away. There was a four inch strip burned out of it.

Jake Kilgore brushed the altered brand on the steer's hide with one gloved hand, leaned closely to examine the job. He straightened up, then bent over and picked up a handful of loose dirt, rubbing it over the brand. He nodded curtly to Sid and Bart.

"That makes that Slash steer one of our Triangles," he said. "Let 'im go."

Sid released the long pole that held the squeezer. Old Jake swung open the little chute gate. Bart prodded the steer with its newly altered brand into the far corral that held about half the cattle the Kilgores penned at their hidden corrals.

The chute gate shut. The next steer was prodded into the squeezer and Sid fastened the long pole with a rope. Jake climbed the corral and, mounting a saddle horse inside, crowded the cattle against the opening of the chute until another steer was reluctantly crowded into it. Bart closed the gate at its rump. The chute again held four steers, one of them gripped fast by the squeezer. Another wet sack. The steer wore a big S brand. Bart picked up a cherry red quarter circle branding iron. Jake cussed him.

"'Tain't hot enough. White-red, I told you so many damned times you orter sing a song about it. Make a clean-lookin' Figger Eight outta that S or I'll take a blacksnake to your back. Damn it all, Sid, use a fresh sack. They cost two-bits, that's all they cost, unless you stole 'em fer nothin'. And a blotched brand costs us mebbyso a stretch in the pen. That Wyoming buyer is gittin' spooky about blotched brands. You heered him say he was turnin' back everything that was blotched or new-lookin'. I kin learn Kate to do a neater job than you two done on some of that last bunch we turned out."

"Kate, hell!" snapped Sid hotly. "She's moonlightin' right now with that damn' Frank Sorrels 'breed."

"You're damn' tootin' she is," snarled the gray-whiskered Jake. "Them's her orders. She's keepin' that quarter-breed away from here and scarin' the guts outta him by makin' him think we might ketch her with him. Kate's got more brains than a corral full of things like you. And another night soon she'll be holdin' hands with that Wyoming cattle buyer, Dude Krebbs, down on the Little Big Horn."

"And holdin' out one of her lily white hands," put in Bart sourly, "for a share of the money we git for these cattle."

"She earns it, just as much as you two whelps earn yourn," said Jake Kilgore. "And she banks it. She don't go blowin' it fer booze or losin' it to tinhorn gamblers. She's buildin' herself a stake."

"Yeah. A gitaway stake," blurted Sid. "The high-toned lady! She'll wind up in a Saint Louis honky-tonk. . . ."

Old Jake Kilgore reached his younger son in two long-legged strides. There was a short prod pole in his hand. It struck Sid alongside the head with a dull, sickening crack. Sid's long legs buckled at the knees and he went down, the wet sack slipping from his hands.

"You hadn't oughta done that," muttered Bart, stepping away from his one-armed father. "You might've killed him."

"Slap him alive with a wet sack," growled the elder Kilgore. "He's too ornery to die natural, thataway. It'll learn him an' you both to treat your sister fer what she is. A lady, by grab, and don't you ferget it!"

Cole Griffin slipped farther back into the black shadows of the brush. He worked his way back cautiously to where he had left his horse. He had seen all that he needed to learn about the hidden corral he had located by the bawling of cattle. His horse needed rest and feed. He was half starved himself and needed some sleep. He had a sack of salt and a butcher knife in his saddle pocket. He would rope and butcher a calf and build a fire after daylight in some remote part of the badlands. The Kilgores were delivering their bunch of re-branded cattle down near the Wyoming line on the Little Big Horn River. With a pair of horse clippers he would erase the wet sack brands they were sweating and losing sleep to make. He would have a law officer with him when he rode up while the Kilgores were making delivery to their crooked cattle buyer. Rustling was punishable by a long prison term.

Cole Griffin had used a gun on Grant Kilgore, and now he

was going to smash the Block K outfit. He'd send Bart and Sid to the pen and buy their outfits that would be confiscated and put on the auction block at a sheriff's sale. Cole Griffin's job here in the badlands was finished for the present. He was going to Fort Benton next to have a talk with the sheriff and the cattlemen who were forming a Livestock Association, tell them what he knew.

Before daylight Cole butchered a Block K calf and hung the meat to cool. He dared not risk building a campfire until after daybreak. The light of a fire might attract unwanted visitors. He was camped at the head of a little creek not more than a mile above the old deserted Hank Griffin ranch house that the Kilgores now used for a winter line camp. He staked out his horse and tried to sleep, but his eyes would not close. He lay on his back and watched the moon. He kept thinking of the little quarter-breed, Sammy Lou, who had only once worn a woman's dress. Of Kathleen Mavourneen Kilgore who had a picture of Cole's mother in her room at the Block K Ranch. Kate Kilgore helped her father and brothers rustle cattle by making dupes out of men like Frank Sorrels and the Wyoming buyer. She was banking her money to build up a getaway stake.

Cole wondered if Kate Kilgore had told her father and brothers about the letter from the El Paso sheriff. She had been plenty mad when she had left him sitting his horse by the lightning-blasted Hangman's Tree. If she had the sort of vindictive nature that would nurse a grudge, she'd tell Jake Kilgore about the lost letter and put the Kilgores on his trail. On the other hand, she might be playing a more clever and subtle game. Kathleen Mavourneen Kilgore had brains and a daring brand of courage. She had contempt for her father and the two gun-toting brothers whose lives were bound by the badlands horizon. From what she had said and the things she had left untold for him to figure out, she parried and blocked their uncouth, clumsy abuse with a sharp-edged, stabbing wit and intolerance that galled her brothers and won the secret admiration of her cattle-stealing, hard-bitten father.

Kate Kilgore had opened and read the letter from El Paso. News of that shooting of Grant Kilgore would be slow to travel this far north. The sheriff down yonder had fulfilled his duty by informing the closest relative of the dead gambler. Only by accident would further notice or information concerning Grant Kilgore's death get to Jake and his two sons. But Kate Kilgore knew. And if she kept her secret, she was armed with a weapon she could use on Cole Griffin if he stayed in this part of the country. Cole reckoned that it would be more in keeping with her nature and temperament to keep her secret. She was not done yet with the man who had humiliated her, hurt her pride and vanity.

She had bared her heart and soul to him. Certain of her beauty and her strange power over men, she had offered herself to a man she had known less than an hour. And he had refused to take her. That must have hurt her far worse than anything she had ever suffered at the hands of any man. She had not been playing with him as she did with fools like Frank Sorrels. She had been hurt badly enough to have killed him. And she was not going to let any man wound her pride and vanity like that and get away unhurt. She was a Kilgore. If she had chosen any other spot than that Hangman's Tree, Cole might have yielded to the seductive beauty of the yellow-eyed, tawny-haired adventuress. But she had halted there in the shadow of that stark tree. She must have purposely chosen that place. She was too clever to make a big blunder.

She had gambled on her charms being stronger than any

feud code that bound Cole Griffin to his hanged father. There was something a little splendid about Kate Kilgore's courage. She wanted no weakling for a mate. She wanted a man who was willing to make a big sacrifice for her. She was not selling herself cheaply. She had stacked the odds against herself and then made her splendid play. Kate Kilgore had lost, but she would get her revenge.

Even now, as the day began to brighten, the memory of her beauty quickened Cole's pulse. His life had been packed with danger, adventure, excitement. He, too, felt all the impulses Kate Kilgore had in her heart. But he was a cowpuncher. No big city could ever hold him longer than a few days or a few weeks at the most. He needed the freedom of open ranges, the untainted air of mountains and deserts and rolling prairies. Cities like St. Louis were all right for a week or two—a cowpuncher's spree in town, lights and music and gaiety for a few nights. Then he had to ride away from it and get back out to the cow country he loved.

Kate Kilgore was willing to risk the rigors and dangers of the outlaw trail. But not for long. At the end must be that dazzling goal of some big city. She was the most beautiful and fascinating woman Cole Griffin had ever met, ever hoped to meet. He did not fool himself by pretending that he was not sorely tempted to find her again, and ride away with her. He had gotten a good price for his outfit down on the Mexican border. He did not need to rob banks or hold up trains to get a South America stake. He could give Kate Kilgore all those things that meant so much to her. But he could not share that gay city life with her and find happiness. Their dreams of high adventure were much the same, but their ultimate goals lay in opposite directions.

Cole wanted to meet Kate Kilgore again. He wanted, somehow, to heal the wound he had made in her woman's heart. He wanted to tell her that she was the most beautiful woman in the world, the bravest girl he had ever known. He wanted to hold her in his arms and tell her that. Then he wanted to say good bye forever. He hoped that he had the strength to do that. But he was more than a little afraid of himself.

He broiled strips of fresh veal over a little fire and ate until the gnawing pain in the pit of his stomach was gone. He let his horse graze at the end of a picket rope while he bathed in the creek and shaved the heavy stubble of whiskers from his jaw. He spent the day lazing in the shade, his saddle cinched loosely on his horse, always alert and ready for flight or a gunfight if he was attacked. Because he felt half ashamed of his hot-tempered break with old Mitch, he made up his mind to ride back there and make peace with the old cowhand who had been his father's friend. He hoped, for Sammy Lou's sake, that he hadn't broken her brother's neck. He felt sorry for little Sammy Lou who thought herself just a little river quarter-breed and whose only friend was whiskey-soaked old Mitch.

V

"Cole Rides Out"

At the Cow Island Crossing, Cole had heard about old Mitch. Men called him a dangerous old rascal who openly defied the big Kilgore outfit, butchered Block K beef when he needed meat, and let all manner of renegade outlaws use his place for a way station along their dim trail to nowhere. Mitch was a tough old son, they said, the last of the little ranchers who had not been wiped out by Jake and Grant Kilgore. Since his five partners had been hanged, Mitch had carried on a single-handed war against the Kilgores.

"Ol' Mitch," said the man who had a little trading post at the Cow Island Crossing on the Missouri River, "has them Kilgores ridin' in bunches. They none of 'em has the guts to ride alone past Mitch's ranch, day or night, drunk or sober."

Old Mitch had plenty of courage. They let him alone. Even tough old Jake Kilgore with one arm shot off had respect for the old rannahan. Cole had taunted him with the question about where he had been the night Grant and Jake Kilgore and a bunch of so-called vigilantes had hung Mitch's five partners. It had been an unfair question and Cole was heartily ashamed of it. He'd had no right to hint that Mitch had hid out somewhere, afraid to fight. He was going to ride back there and make peace with old Mitch, and he was going to tell that little Sammy Lou that he didn't think of her as a moccasin quarter-breed. He hoped he hadn't killed Frank Sorrels even if the young knife-slinger did deserve killing.

It was dusk when he kicked dirt on his little fire and tightened his saddle cinch. He headed along a dim trail that would meet the river road just below Mitch's ranch. The trail took him through rough, broken country. He rode down a little cañon toward the river. Then the ugly *whine* of a rifle bullet jerked him out of his musing. The bullet nicked the crown of his hat, struck a rock, glancing off with a *pinging* whistle. Cole jerked at his saddle gun as he jumped his horse off the trail and into a patch of buck brush. He saw the telltale puff of gunsmoke on a rim rock two hundred yards above him. The echoes of the shot crashed in the little cañon. The would-be bushwhacker kept shooting. Bullets droned like hornets, clipping the branches of the thick brush. The man on the rim rock was hidden from sight as he lay flat on his belly and sent down his deadly hail of bullets.

Cole and his horse were hidden by the thick brush. There was no sense in wasting bullets shooting at the man on the rim rock. The smoke of Cole's carbine would give away his exact position. In half an hour it would be dark enough down here in the cañon to make a run for it. Cole swung from his saddle and stood crouched, his carbine ready for a snap shot if the bushwhacker on the rim rock moved into sight. Then, booming through the echoes of the rifle up on the rim rock, came the roar of a heavier-calibered gun. There was a quick movement up on the rim rock. The roar of the big-calibered rifle crashed again. Behind its echoes came the bellow of old Mitch's voice, hurling profanity.

"The next time, you bushwhackin' snake, I won't be shootin' to scare you! I'll blow the brisket plumb outta your damn' hide!"

Mitch's voice and the roar of his gun came from somewhere not far down the cañon. Cole got back on his horse. He still had his carbine in his hand, and now, as he sat on his horse, he caught sight of the man Mitch's bullets had driven from the rim rock ledge above. Cole's carbine raised to his shoulder with a swift, unbroken movement. His sights were lined on a man wearing a black hat, riding a bay and white pinto horse.

It was an easy shot for as good a marksman as Cole Griffin. The spotted horse had to travel at a walk on a narrow strip of trail that skirted the side of the rim rock. Cole had seen that paint horse the night before at Mitch's place. It was Frank Sorrels's horse. Sorrels had worn a big black hat and his neck had not been broken. The big young quarter-breed had made a bushwhacker try at revenge.

Cole lowered the carbine, letting down the hammer with his thumb. He worked the gun lever to drop the cartridge out of the barrel into the palm of his hand. He shoved the cartridge into his chaps pocket and slid the carbine into its saddle scabbard. Emptying his gun barrel of a loaded cartridge was a safety precaution that any man but a greenhorn always took. But quite another motive prompted him to put the brass cartridge in his chaps pocket rather than shove it back in the gun's magazine. A faint grin twisted the corners of his mouth. Then he rode on down the cañon. When he had traveled a little way, he pulled up and raised his voice to a cautious shout.

"Hi, there, Mitch! This is Cole Griffin! How about . . . ?"

"You needn't be hollerin' your name to the wide world." Mitch's big voice sounded so close that Cole jumped a little. Mitch came from behind a patch of heavy chokecherry brush, a long-barreled .45-70 rifle in the crook of his arm. "I figgered it might be you," said Mitch, "that Block K bushwhacker was a-foggin'. I hoped to cut your sign. I bin up here in the cañon, runnin' off the last of the drippin's from as purty a batch of sour mash corn as ever was 'stilled. Sammy Lou's a-cookin' us a son-of-a-gun in the sack. And I'm tellin' you, son, you never tasted a real son-of-a-gun till you've throwed your lip over a bait of hern. We might as well git on down to the ranch."

That was old Mitch's way of letting Cole know that he was holding no grudge. Cole grinned and took the cartridge from the pocket of his fringed, round-legged shotgun chaps. He held it in the palm of his hand.

"This cartridge was in my gun barrel and the hammer was cocked, Mitch, when I lined my sights back yonder on Frank Sorrels."

"I kinda hoped you'd believe me when I let on that it was a Block K man that was shootin' at you. Not on his ornery account. He's a bad 'un. The sooner somebody kills him off, the better. But don't judge little Sammy Lou by her brother.

Her heart's as white as yourn. The Injun in her is good Injun. Frank got his bad streak from travelin' with bad company and drinkin' the wrong brand of likker. Though even good whiskey is bad medicine to ary Injun or 'breed I ever knowed. Injun blood and hard likker don't mix. There's no sense in lettin' Sammy Lou know that Frank was layin' up on that rim rock."

"That's right, Mitch." Cole shoved the cartridge into the magazine of his saddle gun. "I'm pullin' out for Fort Benton. I want to have a medicine talk with the sheriff. I spent half the night watchin' the Kilgores workin' the brands on some big three- and four-year-old steers they're deliverin' to some gent named Dude Krebbs."

"The hell you say! You mean you wasn't moon-ridin' with that buckskin-maned Kate Kilgore?"

Cole felt his face grow hot, and he was glad that it was dusk and old Mitch couldn't notice. He went on quickly, giving Mitch no time to express his vitriolic opinion of Kate Kilgore. "They were sack-brandin' stuff into the Figure Eight, Triangle, and JB irons."

"Them's the remnant brands they still use. They're almighty keerful not to mess with Jake's Block K. Them remnant brands is registered in Bart's and Sid's names. So if there's ary slip-up, it'll be the boys, not old man Jake, that gits jailed. That ol' he-wolf is plumb cautious thataway."

"They work the S iron into a Figure Eight," said Cole. "The Slash brand goes into the Triangle iron. They make their JB connected out of some gent's Pot-Hook."

"The S is the Sorrelses' brand," said Mitch. "The Slash belongs to Bob Means on Telegraph Creek. The Pot-Hook is owned by a dude feller named Parkes over on Beaver Creek. Except for the S stuff, them steers has come from a long ways. Strays that the Block K cowhands has bin throwin' back where the Kilgores kin pick 'em up handy. You watched 'em brand out them steers?"

"I heard cattle bawlin' and cold-trailed 'em to some brandin' corrals back in the badlands. From the way they talked, it was the last bunch they had to brand. They're holdin' a herd somewheres across the river and they start trailin' 'em for the Wyoming line tonight."

"Sellin' the cattle to Dude Krebbs, you say?"

Cole nodded. "Know him?" he asked curiously.

"Plenty. Dude is Kate Kilgore's fancy man. One of them blackleg college fellers that was sent out West. Remittance man. He got out of Fort Benton on account of a crooked beef contract him and an Army officer was workin'. The Army officer blowed his brains out. Dude Krebbs hightailed it before they could git enough on him to send him to the federal pen. He's smart as a fox and a bad man in a gun scrape. One of them range dudes that has a squaw sew a buckskin seat in his britches. Packs a white-handled gun and curls his mustache. Krebbs ain't his real name. His old man is some big toad in the Washington puddle, they say. He'd be a hell of a lot fu'ther away than Wyoming if he wasn't plumb stuck on Kate Kilgore. Dude Krebbs sided me once in a bad tight. Supposin', Cole, we leave the Fort Benton sheriff outta this deal? I bin fightin' the Kilgores a long, long time and I ain't never asked fer no law help yet."

"Just as you say, Mitch."

"If Dude is mixed up in this," said Mitch, "it's on account of Kate Kilgore. And the pen is a hell of a place to send even a man like Dude Krebbs. I seen one of them tigers once that was locked up in a cage. One of them zoo places at Saint Louis. I stood there a long time, watchin' that tiger walk back and forth, staring through them steel bars. As handsome a wild thing as ever I seen. I stood it as long as I could. Then I slid my six-shooter out and shot that tiger square between the eyes. It cost me all the drinkin' money I'd fetched along to paint Saint Louis red. But I'd want a man to do the same fer me if I was locked behind jail bars. I reckon Dude Krebbs would feel likewise."

"We'll keep the law out of it," said Cole.

They mounted. Mitch broke the short silence as they reached the wagon road and were riding side by side. "Me 'n' you kin handle the Kilgores," he said simply, and Cole smiled faintly at the old hellion's confidence in himself and the son of Hank Griffin.

"They'll have cowpunchers helpin' 'em with the cattle," said Cole, weighing possible odds they'd be up against, "and there's Dude Krebbs to handle."

"That don't sound much like Hank Griffin a-talkin'," growled Mitch.

"Hank Griffin got hung," Cole reminded him grimly.

"None of them five would have got hung if they'd done what I told 'em to do. They was drinkin' rotgut whiskey . . . not my likker. Grant and Jake Kilgore and their hired gun-toters they called vigilantes had all the bulge on Hank and Sam Sorrels and the others when they jumped 'em. But them gunslingers that Grant had hired around Fort Benton is dead or quit the country years ago. Jake will have his two sons, Bart an' Sid, a-backin' him. Two, three cowpunchers, mebby. Most mebby, though, there'll be just the Kilgores handlin' them cattle. Jake don't trust nobody outside his own kin when he's handlin' stolen cattle. Like as not Kate will be ridin' up on the point with Jake. She's as good a cowhand as Bart or Sid. Dude ain't takin' up no gunfight fer the Kilgores. I tell you, son, me 'n' you is men enough to git the bulge on 'em and whup 'em."

"All right, Mitch." Cole let it go at that.

They rode on in silence, each busy with his own thoughts.

Cole was dreading this meeting with Sammy Lou. He was relieved when they reached Mitch's place and no light showed at the cabin.

Sammy Lou was not there. The son-of-a-gun in a sack, no more or less than a tallow pudding cooked in a flour sack, stood on the back of the stove. But the fire in the stove was almost cold. Mitch looked in a crevice between the logs, lifted out a piece of wooden chinking, and reached into a small cavity behind where it had been. He took out a folded piece of paper and scowled over the note she had left him.

"She's pulled out," Mitch said, his voice edged with worry and anger. "That no-account brother of hern has bin here again. She's gone off with him somewheres. It would have bin better all around if you'd broke his damn' neck last night."

"What does the note say, Mitch?"

Mitch reluctantly handed Cole the note. The rounded letters on paper stood out accusingly at him.

Good bye for a while, Mitch. Frank needs me worse than you do now. I can straighten him out. Take care of yourself. Don't trust that Cole Griffin. Kate Kilgore put the Block K brand on him last night. Sammy Lou

"She slipped off early this mornin'," said Mitch, "and rode off to the Sorrelses' ranch before breakfast, then come back to my place. I rode past the Sorrelses' place on my way to the still. She'd burned up that trunk of fancy clothes the river captain give her."

"Got any idea where she went?"

"No. She's gone off into the hills with her brother. He must have took the short trail here after he quit the rim rock. No tellin' what kind of a whiskey lie he told her. He's bad medicine. He was all right till rotgut whiskey an' the Kilgore

43

gal made a plumb fool outta him. There's no use in tryin' to locate 'em now. They know every hide-out in the badlands. Only thing to do is fergit her till she shows up again."

But Cole knew that old Mitch was worried. They ate supper in silence. Mitch lit a blackened corncob pipe and pulled slowly at the tooth-scarred stem, exhaling blue clouds of strong smoke.

Cole kept thinking of Sammy Lou's burning up the trunkful of clothes. White woman's clothes. The dress she had worn to the Christmas dance with moccasins instead of high-heeled slippers to match. The poor little kid. Cole reckoned he'd hurt her a lot more than his fists had hurt her brother, Frank, when he had knocked out Frank Sorrels. It made Cole feel almighty cheap and cowardly. Finally he got a sheet of paper from the writing tablet Sammy Lou kept at Mitch's cabin when she did her written lessons from her schoolbooks. He whittled the lead of a rifle cartridge to a point and used it for a pencil. It took half an hour and he wasted several sheets of paper before he got a note composed. It was a clumsy effort, but it was the best he could do. He read it over, frowning.

Sammy Lou,
It was just plain childish of you to burn up your pretty clothes. Don't ever let anybody or anything make you feel like you don't belong in those kind of clothes. You're not a common little river 'breed. It looks like I'll have to get you a new outfit and take you to the next dance to prove it. How about a red silk dress and slippers to match it? Unless a better man beats me to it, I'm taking you to the next Christmas dance. You've got to believe that I am your friend.
                                          Cole Griffin

He gave it to old Mitch to read. Mitch nodded his approval and Cole felt a lot better.

"Put it in behind the hunk of loose chinkin', Mitch." Cole took his hat and saddle gun from the deer antlers above the door where he had hung them.

"Where you goin'?" questioned old Mitch.

Cole grinned faintly. "The Kilgores don't know who I am or where I come from. I'm ridin' over to the Block K outfit and hirin' out to Jake Kilgore for a tough hand. That note of Sammy Lou's gave me the idea. Unless my luck spoils, I'll be ridin' on the point or slappin' the drags with my rope when that cattle drive reaches the Little Big Horn on the Wyoming line."

Mitch could find no argument to stop him. When the old rannahan found out that Cole was determined to throw in with the Kilgores, they made their plans accordingly.

"But unless you got a trick up your sleeve, son, you're a-gone goslin'. You're bluffin' with a bobtailed flush."

"Mebbyso I've got the joker buried, Mitch. I'm gamblin' on my hole card bein' the right color."

"That hole card," guessed Mitch shrewdly, "wouldn't have yaller hair, by ary chance?"

"By ary chance"—Cole grinned, his face flushing a little under the older man's keen scrutiny—"she just might."

"Then you'll find that Dude Krebbs is twice as dangerous as ary one of the Kilgores. He's a coiled rattler."

"I'll be keepin' that in mind," said Cole.

"I'll be cold-trailin' you," Mitch reminded him. "You know how to signal me. I won't be too far off."

Cole left old Mitch cussing softly, there at the barn, and rode alone down the river. He had a good idea where he would overtake the Kilgores and the drive of stolen cattle. He was gambling that Kate had kept her secret about the letter from the sheriff at El Paso.

VI

"Signed On to Die"

The Kilgores were traveling with a pack outfit and a small remuda of top horses. The outfit was eating a daybreak breakfast when Cole Griffin rode up. Sid Kilgore was with the herd. The remuda was penned in a rope corral. Jake Kilgore, Bart, and Kate were squatted around the little campfire, their plates loaded, their coffee cups filled.

Cole rode up, whistling the dismal tune of the "Cowboy's Lament". He kept his hands clear of his guns. Bart's six-shooter covered him. Jake's big hand was on the cedar butt of his long-barreled Colt and his bleak eyes were sharp with suspicion.

Cole looked hard at Kate Kilgore. She smiled faintly and lifted her big tin cup of coffee in a sort of salute. Cole's nerves relaxed a little. He knew that she had kept her secret about his identity and the killing of Grant Kilgore.

"I sighted your camp," said Cole, "and remembered I was hungry. I've been ridin' all night."

"Then supposin' you keep right on ridin'," said Jake Kilgore. "I'm particular who eats at my camp."

"Or fill your hand with a gun," said Bart Kilgore who was on his feet now. "The last time we cut your sign, you had a shotgun in it."

"Dry up," snapped old Jake Kilgore, getting slowly to his feet. "We don't want no killin's along the trail. Keep a-driftin', mister."

Kate Kilgore put down her coffee cup and deliberately walked between Cole and the two Kilgore men. "Did I get you in bad with old Mitch? I didn't get a chance to thank you before, mister, for taking my part. Get down and rest your saddle." Kate turned to her father, ignoring Bart's ugly scowl. "I didn't tell you, Dad, because I didn't want to get you all in a lather. Frank Sorrels spooked the other night and made me run with him to old Mitch's place. This man was there. Mitch was drunk and ugly. Frank was showing the coyote. This man took my part. Frank Sorrels tried to knife him and he beat the 'breed senseless and dropped him at old Mitch's feet. Then he cussed Mitch out and got me away from there. He rode a mile or two with me to see me safely on my way. He's some man who was riding the outlaw trail and using Mitch's ranch for a stopping place along the way. If he got into a ruckus with you at Mitch's ranch, I reckon it was because he didn't want strange company bothering him there. He got me out of an ugly tight. If he's not welcome here, then neither am I. If this man rides on, I'm riding with him."

"Another of her fancy men," sneered Bart. "She's. . . ."

"Dry up, Bart," said Jake Kilgore. "If you guessed right as many times as Kate does, you'd amount to somethin'. You and Sid said you sighted Frank Sorrels at the Cow Island whiskey camp and his face looked like he'd tackled a grizzly. Fill that mouth of yourn with grub, then git out to the herd and relieve Sid." He looked hard at his daughter. "You might've told me about the ruckus at Mitch's place."

"And have you and that drunken old hellion locking horns? We've got these cattle to move. We're short-handed as it is, without you gettin' laid up and calling a doctor to pick buckshot out of your hide."

Jake Kilgore grinned. "Long-headed and close-mouthed. If you'd bin born a boy, I'd have had a son to brag about. If you say this jasper helped you out of a tight, then I reckon he's worth feedin', anyhow. Git down, mister. I've cut this feller's sign somewhere before we run into him at Mitch's. I'd give a purty if I could place 'im. Did Mitch call him by name?"

"Now I remember," said Kate Kilgore, her golden yellow eyes looking at Cole with tantalizing mockery. "I think Mitch did have a name for him."

Cole's right hand was near his gun as he dismounted, putting his horse between him and Jake Kilgore. Bart had mounted his horse and spurred off at an angry lope, leaving his breakfast half eaten on his tin plate.

"Mitch called him Cole," she said, her husky voice almost purring, "Henry Cole."

Jake Kilgore's hard eyes stared at Cole. "Never heard of him. But a man's name is easier to change than his looks. Tie into some grub, mister."

Cole was riding his horse with a hackamore instead of a bridle. He led the horse to where the grass was tall and loosened the saddle cinch, removing his carbine from its saddle scabbard. "Just in case he takes a notion to roll," he explained, leaning the gun against a rawhide-covered kack box. "I had the stock broke off a saddle gun thataway once." Cole filled a plate with steak and fried potatoes and Dutch oven biscuits and filled a tin cup with strong black coffee. He sat on the ground between Kate Kilgore and her father, and began eating.

"Which way were you headed," asked Kate, "when you sighted our camp?"

"South. Mexico is south, accordin' to my geography."

"Traveling light," she went on, her eyes challenging him. "Are you in any particular rush?"

"There's nobody hot-trailin' me, if that's what you mean." Cole met her challenge with a fine grin. "Unless it's that 'breed gent. He took a bushwhacker shot at me yesterday evenin'. The light was kinda bad and mebby he was too drunk to shoot straight. Anyhow, he missed."

"Did you?"

"I let him get away. There was no sense in clutterin' up my back trail with a killin'."

"And, besides"—Kate smiled—"Frank's sister is a mighty pretty girl . . . for a 'breed."

"I reckon mebbyso that did have somethin' to do with it," Cole agreed frankly.

"That damn' 'breed Frank Sorrels," put in Jake Kilgore, "must have gone on the warpath plenty. He shot one of my men at the Cow Island whiskey camp early yesterday mornin'. Crippled him in one laig."

"And left us short-handed," said Kate. "I was coming to that. Cole could ride his string, Dad. We'd make better time with the drive. Nobody's crowding his trail."

"I'd have to talk it over with the boys. Bart don't like him. He'll rib Sid. Nope. Can't put on a stranger, nohow."

"Better a stranger than some home range cowboy that gets loose-tongued the first saloon he finds. Bart and Sid can't tell a real hand from a range tramp. It was one of their sidekickers that got shot by Frank Sorrels. I saw Cole take a knife away from Frank and wipe up the cabin with him, then challenge Mitch. That's more than any of your Block K men would tackle."

"Sounds like you're dead set on hirin' this Cole feller."

"You're a smart man, Jake Kilgore." She smiled at her father. Then she looked squarely at Cole. It was a direct challenge. "There's a job for you, Cole, if you have the nerve to tackle it."

"You've hired a cowhand." Cole's eyes were icy blue, belying his easy grin.

So Cole Griffin was firmly, dangerously established in the

camp of his enemy. It would need but a word from Kate Kilgore to wipe him out with a deadly hail of bullets. Bart and Sid were open in their enmity and suspicion, and Cole was a good enough judge of men to know that old Jake Kilgore was more dangerous than his sons because he was disguising his suspicion behind what seemed to be a gruff tolerance of a man who had pleased his daughter's fancy.

Sid's attitude was insolent and Bart's was surly, as they broke camp. The remuda and pack horses were trailed along with the cattle. Kate and her father rode up on the point, on opposite sides of the strung-out cattle. Jake put Cole in the swing across from Bart. Sid was bringing up the drags and cussing his job.

When the cattle were strung out, Kate Kilgore dropped back to where Cole was riding. "Whatever your name is," she said, her voice no longer soft, "it's not going to win you anything but a lonely grave."

"You said you hoped I'd hang. I'm obliged to you for not telling Jake Kilgore my right name. For not mentioning the letter."

"Perhaps I'm not quite as obvious as your little 'breed girl. But don't forget, even in your sleep, mister, that I'm what the old saying calls 'a woman scorned'. You followed us. You knew whose camp it was you were riding into. Perhaps I'm clever enough to know that you gambled on getting this job I gave you. I'm wondering if you're fool enough to think I'm going to swallow any other excuse for your being with this drive of cattle. I was fool enough to throw myself at your head the other night. Now I wouldn't marry you for all the gold and diamonds on earth. So don't waste time playing any love games."

"You didn't need to remind me of that, Kathleen. I rode away from that Hangman's Tree just as badly hurt as you were. I don't ask you to believe that, but it's the truth. If I made love to you, I'd mean it. If you were fool enough to marry me, we'd bust up quicker than my mother and Hank Griffin did. I'm a cowpuncher. I'll never be anything else."

"A cowpuncher," she caught him up quickly, "is supposed to be loyal to his outfit. That's part of a real cowpuncher's code. Only a low-down snake breaks his own code. You just hired out to the Block K."

"I hired out to Kate Kilgore. I intend being as loyal as I know how to be. You're my boss. I never had one I'd sooner fight for. I'm not goin' to let you down."

"Save the rest of it till tonight when the herd is bedded down. You'll go on guard with me at midnight. I'm curious to hear just what's in this speech you've been rehearsing to yourself. Bart looks like he might take a shot at you, herd or no herd. Better drop back to the drags and send Sid up on the swing. I can't tell you how thrilling it is to have Cole Griffin riding with this drive of stolen cattle. It breaks the monotony of the trail. And don't let Sid get you on the prod. He's just a mouthy kid. Keep your hand off your gun or you'll be acting out the lead rôle in that song you were whistling, about 'bury me not on the lone prairie.'"

VII

"Bushwhacker's Showdown"

Sid and Bart Kilgore were planning to crowd Cole into going for his gun. Sid was the worst with his ugly taunts that hinted Cole was Kate's lover. When they got too nasty, old Jake would stop it with his wolfish: "Dry up!"

Kate would sit cross-legged, her yellow eyes watching the

dangerous play. Once or twice, when she saw Cole's jaw muscles quiver with the effort to keep cool, she had gotten between him and her brothers. Her eyes would silence even the loud-mouthed Sid.

Five days and nights of it had worn Cole Griffin's nerves raw. He wanted to ride away from the outfit, or signal to old Mitch who was cold-trailing them. Bart was letting up some the past day or two, a fact that made Sid even more antagonistic and ugly. Cole wondered if he could stand it much longer. His hands ached to get at Sid's throat.

Now and then, during the day, Cole sighted a lone rider somewhere along the distant skyline, sometimes behind, sometimes ahead of the herd. Yesterday he had sighted three riders. He reckoned that Mitch had located Sammy Lou and her brother Frank. Because Mitch mistrusted Frank and loved Sammy Lou, he was keeping them with him.

If Jake Kilgore and his two sons suspected that they were being followed and watched, they gave no outward sign. But Kate Kilgore, standing night guard with Cole, taunted him about it openly.

"I might have known you weren't playing it lone-handed. Is it that whiskey-soaked Mitch and a couple of his beef-butchering neighbors that you have trailing us, or did you soften up and call on the law to help you hamstring the Kilgores? I forgot to tell you that I know you watched some of these steers get branded. I was trailing you when you located the branding corrals that first night we met and you spurned my brazen hussy advances. I was curious to see if you'd go back to Mitch's cabin. You didn't. You heard cattle bawling and watched my dad and brothers do a little fancy brand work. I don't blame you for getting help on this job. You'll need it if you call for a showdown, if you live long enough to make your big play. You're not wearing a law badge pinned to your undershirt by any chance?"

"No."

"It wouldn't do you much good, anyhow. The Kilgores haven't the proper respect for the law. A tin badge doesn't mean a thing to Jake Kilgore. As for Bart and Sid, it would make them that much more ornery. You've taken just about all you can stand from them, haven't you?"

"I can stand it," said Cole grimly.

"We camp tomorrow evening on the Little Big Horn. That's where Dude Krebbs takes delivery. I thought maybe you'd like to know. Bart and Sid are getting spooky. I'm not the only Kilgore that's caught sight of those skyline riders. I wouldn't buy your chances, mister, for a lead dollar. Why don't you ride away from this herd right now?"

"With you?" Cole grinned.

"Not with me, cowboy. I gave you your chance back at the Hangman's Tree on the Missouri. If you were playing a lone-handed game, I might be tempted. But you're just the monkey that's going to try to pull the hot chestnuts out of the fire for old Mitch. I tell you, Bart and Sid are going to crowd you tomorrow night at supper. Nobody can get there in time to side you when they make you pull your gun. Please, for my sake, Cole, ride away from here right now!" Kate's voice was soft, husky, vibrant.

"For *your* sake?"

"If you're killed, I'd feel like your murderer."

"Your brothers call me your lover. It's when Sid starts dirtying your name that I can hardly stand it. It's goin' to be a pleasure to tromp the head off that young sidewinder. He's as mangy a whelp as ever I've had the bad luck to meet. Tomorrow night can't come too quick to suit me."

"I thought it was Jake Kilgore you were after. The boys were too young to have any part in the hanging of Hank Griffin."

"Compared to Sid," said Cole, "Jake Kilgore is a gentleman."

"It was Jake Kilgore," said Kate, "who told me to get rid of you tonight. He told me that Bart and Sid were going to jump you tomorrow night at supper. After his own fashion, he thinks a lot of me. He shares the boys' opinion that I'm in love with you. He told me to get rid of you, even if I had to run off with you."

"Your father knocked Sid down at the branding corrals for an ugly crack the young whelp made about you. I've watched him when Sid was draggin' your name in the mud to git a rise outta me. I got the notion he might even side me in a gun fight."

"You're wrong. Blood is thicker than water. Jake Kilgore's not siding Hank Griffin's son against his own two boys."

"But Jake Kilgore"—Cole smiled—"doesn't know I'm Hank Griffin's son."

"No? You're a little stupid. He's known it for two days. When he got me off to one side to warn me, I told him I'd known it from the start. He turned gray. You'd have thought I'd stuck a dull knife in his heart. You think you were in danger when Sid and Bart crowded you. You were never closer to death than you were at camp night before last when I told Jake that I'd known your name was Cole Griffin. I thought he was going to kill us both."

"What stopped him?" Cole's throat felt as dry as dusty flannel.

"I lied to him. I told him you followed me here because you loved me. I told him he'd better kill us both. I didn't think I'd lie that much for any man. That's why, tonight, I hate you. Can you understand, Cole Griffin, that I hate you?"

"You told Jake Kilgore that I loved you and that you were in love with me," said Cole. His face was almost as white as hers in the white moonlight. His voice was no more than a croaking whisper.

"I lied." Her lips barely moved and her voice was so low-pitched that he sensed, rather than heard, her words. "I hate you."

Cole Griffin leaned sideways in his saddle. His arms were around her, locking her in an embrace she could not break. She fought wildly for a minute, then her mouth was against his and her arms were around his neck.

Neither of them saw or heard the approach of the tall, black-mustached man who rode up behind them. His voice, deadly calm, tore them from each other's arms.

"I thought Frank Sorrels was lying when he told me I'd ride up on something like this. Mitch tells me you're Hank Griffin's son. Your father ain't alive to play his hand. I'd turn the job over to Mitch if you weren't trying to steal something I claimed. You're either double-crossing Mitch or you're playing a damned blackguard trick on Kate Kilgore. In either case, mister, you're a sneaking, yellow cur-hound. We'll meet over in that cut coulée. Have your gun in your hand when I sight you."

He reined his horse around and rode off at a lope. Cole and Kate Kilgore stared after him. They looked at each other, both still dazed. Then Cole Griffin laughed as heartily as if he had just watched some comedy trick on the stage.

Kate Kilgore smiled. Cole edged his horse closer and reached for her hand. His laughter faded to an easy grin. He dropped his bridle reins over the saddle horn and his free hand groped in his pocket. He brought out a little buckskin sack, loosened its string with his teeth, and took out a rather heavy gold ring set with a large emerald. He slid it slowly down over the third finger of her left hand.

"It belonged to my mother, Kathleen. The only bit of jewelry she ever wore on the stage. She'd want you to have it. I wanted to give it to you that first night, there at the Hangman's Tree. No matter what happens, I want you to wear it . . . always."

Tears welled to Kate Kilgore's golden yellow eyes as she leaned from her saddle and kissed Cole. Then she read something else in his eyes and her arms tightened around his neck. "Cole! You're not going to shoot it out with Dude Krebbs!"

"So that's Dude Krebbs! I thought so, from the way he talked about claimin' you. I've got to knock his horns off. You wouldn't be proud of a man that'd take a cussin' like that. For four days and nights I've gritted my teeth and grinned when I wanted to knock the heads of your two brothers together till they cracked and rattled like gourds. This purty gent is no kin of yours. He prodded me where it hurt. He's halfway right about my double-crossin' of Mitch, and not playin' out Hank Griffin's hand."

"But he lied when he said he had any claim on me," Kate said slowly. "You're the only man I've ever kissed in my life!"

"And I'll come back to claim you for keeps. The shootin' will spook the cattle, so watch out. I reckon this is goin' to spoil the sale of these steers, so you might as well let 'em scatter and drift. I'll meet you at camp. I've got to talk to Jake . . . tell him I'm marryin' you. Then I'll give Bart and Sid a fistwhumpin' they'll remember, and have a showdown with Mitch. My night's chores are shore laid out. I'm commencin' right now with Dude Krebbs."

Cole rode off, his six-shooter in his hand. He knew now what old Mitch had done. The old rascal had ridden ahead and contacted Dude Krebbs. He had made some kind of a dicker with the crooked cattle buyer. Krebbs had mentioned Frank Sorrels. Frank and Sammy Lou were with Mitch.

Ahead, not more than two hundred yards, was the coulée.

Its black shadows hid Dude Krebbs from sight, but Cole would be plainly skylighted against the moon. Dude Krebbs was a killer. He was in love with Kate Kilgore. Cole knew the breed of swaggering gunslingers well enough to feel sure that the blackleg Dude was going to take any advantage that came his way. Cole pulled his hat down across his eyes and gripped his gun tighter.

His teeth bared in a mirthless grin, he raked the big Block K horse with his spurs. He topped the rim of the coulée with his horse at a run. From the shadows below he saw the flash of a gun. A bullet nicked his shoulder. He shot at the gun blaze as the running horse went down the steep slant. He saw other guns blaze swiftly—one to his right, the other ahead and below. It looked like he had ridden squarely into an ambush. The thought came to him that old Mitch and the quarter-breed Frank Sorrels were siding with Dude Krebbs.

Cole was going down the slope with the breakneck, reckless speed of a Pony Express rider carrying the mail. He shot at the gun flash on his left, threw a second shot toward the shadowy outline of a rider to his right, and rode headlong at the blaze of the gun ahead and below him.

"You yellow-backed, bushwhackin' coward! If there's any guts in you, Dude Krebbs, ride out in the open!"

Dude Krebbs spurred his horse from behind the shadow of some buck brush. Krebbs was shouting something Cole couldn't make out. Their guns blazing, the cattle buyer could not get out of Cole's path quickly enough, and the two horses and men piled up in a wild tangle.

Cole jerked his feet free of the stirrups and let himself get catapulted through the air. He landed in the heavy buck brush that broke his fall. Shaken, his face and shirt ripped, he scrambled to his feet. He saw the two horses untangle themselves. He made a leaping lunge at Dude Krebbs's horse when he saw that Dude, limp as a sack, dead, perhaps, had a foot caught in the stirrup. He grabbed the bridle reins of the lunging, rearing horse.

Old Mitch came up, his horse on a run. Cole clung to the reins of his frightened horse with his left hand. His gun swung toward old Mitch. "Throw away your gun, you bushwhackin' old son-of-a-bitch, or I'll shoot the bell off you. Your pardner's foot's hung in the stirrup. His neck should be hung in a rope. Yours likewise. Get 'im loose!"

"Loco!" growled Mitch, quitting his horse with a speed that was almost miraculous for a man of his age and heavy build. Mitch got Dude Krebbs's foot free of the stirrup, laid the limp form on the ground, and bent over him.

"Shot twice," he muttered, "neither wound bad enough to hurt. Knocked his head on a rock or got kicked by a horse. He's a hell of a long ways from dead, to my way of thinkin'."

Old Mitch looked up. Cole's six-shooter was covering him. The young cowpuncher's eyes were blue ice.

"You had to bushwhack me. Dude Krebbs wasn't man enough to play a lone hand. He had to have you and his 'breed pardner side him. You got a gun in your hand, you old hellion. Stand up and use it like a man!"

Old Mitch dropped his cedar-handled six-shooter as if it was the wrong end of a hot branding iron. He straightened slowly, his hands in the air. "You ain't gone loco, have you, young Cole? I was acrost the ridge and heard shootin'. That was the signal me 'n' you fixed that was to fetch me with my gun in my hand. I find you swingin' onto Dude's horse and a-cussin' me. I ain't fired a shot tonight. I found Sammy Lou an' Frank afore I left home. Kep' 'em with me. I located Dude this evenin' and we made medicine. Dude said he might scout the Kilgore camp some. I wake up and find I'm alone. Dude ain't come back. Frank's gone. Sammy Lou's gone. I swaller me an eye-opener and fork my horse. I hear shootin' and come a-foggin'. But my gun ain't bin fired . . . yet!"

"Three men were shootin' at me when I rode down off the rim." Cole's hot temper was cooling quickly. There was no doubting the truth of old Mitch's words. Mitch, for all his shortcomings, was no liar. "Pick up your gun, Mitch. I'm wrong and plumb sorry. Somewhere in this coulée is two bushwhackers. Krebbs is comin' alive."

Mitch picked up his gun. Cole found Dude Krebbs's white-handled six-shooter. As Dude sat up dazedly, Cole tossed the gun toward him.

"Just you and me this time, mister. When your eyes and brain are clear, pick up your gun. I want to see how tough you are."

VIII

"Feud Trail's End"

Old Mitch stooped and grabbed the white-handled gun. His growl was like that of an old, cranky grizzly. "Cool off, you two young roosters! There's bin too much of this damn' nonsense a'ready. Cole just saved you from bein' drug to death, Dude. And what's this about you and two more gents bushwhackin' Cole?"

Dude Krebbs got to his feet. He wiped the blood and dirt from his bruised face. His left arm was wounded and a trickle of blood came from a bullet nick along his ribs. "I suppose it did look like a trap," he said. "But it wasn't. I rode back here to wait for Cole Griffin. I saw Frank Sorrels ride into the coulée. He must have followed me. Then, before I could send him away, I sighted another rider. It looked like Sid Kilgore. Just as Cole Griffin topped the rim and came down the slope like a bat out of hell, Frank and Sid sighted one another and opened up. They were shooting at each other, not at Cole Griffin. Griffin rode through their line of fire and came at me. We were shooting at each other when he rode me down. I'm no bushwhacker, Griffin. Give me my gun, Mitch."

"And let you shoot a man that just saved you from gittin' your head kicked off? I'll whup you both, directly, if you don't git some sense. It's that yaller-eyed, buckskin-maned. . . ."

"You're talkin' about the girl that's goin' to marry me, Mitch," said Cole hotly.

"Keep her out of it, Mitch," added Dude Krebbs. "That girl is aces. Looks like you win there, Griffin. I'd be a cheap sort of sport if I couldn't wish you both luck. You can give me back my gun, Mitch. I'll need it to side Cole Griffin when he breaks the news to the Kilgores that Hank Griffin's son is marryin' Kate. You and Kate would be wise to hightail it right now, Griffin. Mitch and I will take the news to old Jake."

Mitch was staring hard at Cole. He talked as if he were musing aloud. "Looks like I might have bin wrong about her, all along. There ain't a weak point about either of you gents. You couldn't both be plumb wrong about her. She's got nerve. She's got more nerve than ary one of the Kilgores. Dude's right, young Cole. Let me take this hunk of news to that ornery Jake."

"Jake Kilgore knows about it already."

"The hell!" Old Mitch's voice lost its mirth. "Me 'n' Dude will go along, anyhow. You seen anything of Sammy Lou, Dude?"

"Didn't she stay back at camp?"

"She was gone when I woke up from a little dozin' spell. Let's git goin'. No tellin' what she's got into."

They got on their horses. They saw two riderless horses on the slope of the coulée. Frank Sorrels and Sid Kilgore were both dead. The two had fought out a lifelong enmity and died with their boots on and their guns smoking. They laid the dead enemies side by side and covered their faces. Then they rode on toward the Kilgore camp.

Jake looked up, his bleak eyes fixed on old Mitch. A faint, grim smile twitched the bearded corners of his mouth. "Git down. Kate, it looks like you'll have to patch up Cole and Dude. Git off your horse, Mitch. And don't git gun jumpy. I'll handle Bart an' Sid when they show up. This coffee won't poison you, Mitch, no more than the Block K beef you bin eatin' fer years."

Old Mitch untied a bulky sack from his saddle and produced a jug. He grinned as Kate put her arms around Cole and kissed him. "Reckon you need somethin' stronger'n coffee to stand that, you ornery ol' hellion." He chuckled.

"And you'll need a jolt of forty-rod when you read this." Jake Kilgore set down his cup and brought a piece of folded wrapping paper from his pocket. He handed it to Mitch who took it warily and unfolded it as Jake emptied half the coffee from his tin cup and filled it with whiskey. Mitch read the penciled scrawl and cussed softly. Then he glared at Jake Kilgore.

"How long has this bin goin' on?"

"That's the first I heard of it. Bart wrote that note an' left it in one of my boots sometime durin' the night. It kinda accounts for times that Bart rode off from the ranch alone."

"And fer the times Sammy Lou pulled out and never said where she had bin keepin' herself."

"The note says they're ridin' to the nearest town to find a preacher, and, when they come back, it'll be too late fer me to do a damn' thing about it," said Jake. "Says they'd have got hitched long ago, except fer you ridin' herd on Sammy Lou."

The twinkle came back into old Mitch's eyes. "I knowed Sammy Lou wouldn't run off without leavin' some kind of word."

"I don't know," said Jake Kilgore, "how Frank Sorrels and Sid will take it."

"Frank," said old Mitch, "is dead. So is Sid. They locked horns tonight."

Jake Kilgore took a stiff drink of his coffee and whiskey. Kate knelt beside him and put her arms around him.

"Bart will come back," Kate told her father. "And if you need me, Dad, I'll come back."

Jake Kilgore nodded. He got to his feet and the bleakness was gone from his pale gray eyes. He was looking at old Mitch. "Mitch, I always aimed to tell you, that time when me and Black Jack rode up on you when you was diggin' them five graves. You killed Black Jack and shot my arm off. And after that the grudge between us was too deep to git acrost. I had no part in the shootin' and hangin' of Hank Griffin or the rest! Me and Grant Kilgore split fer keeps before Grant organized what he called them vigilantes. I heard about the hangin' of the five men. I got it outta Black Jack. I made him go along with me to your place to have him tell you I had no part in it. I aimed to do the right thing. You never give me the chance, and I never quit hatin' you fer it. Not till right this minute.

"I was waitin' here to tell Cole Griffin what I just told you. I wanted him and Kate to know, so they'd be happy together. I was tellin' Kate about it when you fellers rode up. Tellin' her I'd swore to kill my half-brother, Grant Kilgore, on sight if ever I cut his sign again. She told me that Cole had killed Grant Kilgore. I hold no grudge ag'in' Cole Griffin. Him and Kate will always be welcome at my place."

Old Mitch picked up the wicker-covered demijohn in his left hand. His right was held out toward Jake Kilgore. "I never figgered this time would come, Jake. But now that it's happened, I'll be damned if I ain't almighty glad. It's bin twenty-five years since me and you got drunk together. That was afore me and your other half-brother, Seth, shot 'er out at Fort Benton and started the feud between the Kilgores and us other fellers. And up till now I never admitted it to no man that there was times when it was almighty hard to keep on a-hatin' you. I'd kill a Block K veal and then leave a big keg of good likker where I knowed you'd find it." He turned to Cole. "And that shotgun trap that you rode into, Cole. Wasn't there a sign nailed to the post gate warnin' the Kilgores and anybody else who come past that there was a scatter-gun trap planted inside the gate?"

"Frank Sorrels tore the sign down right after you put it up," said Kate.

"Frank," said old Mitch, "was ornery. Sammy Lou's got all the good Injun there was in that family. Kate, I bin shore wrong about many things. Sizin' you up wrong was the worst mistake of 'em all. And it's no time now to be askin' favors. But if you and Cole have a weddin' here, if you'd sort of ask Sammy Lou, and make her wear a dress and slippers. . . ."

"I'll dress that youngster up till she'll be the best-looking girl there," Kate said. "Dude, will you dance with her?"

"Every dance that I can take away from Bart and Cole Griffin. And I hope it's at Fort Benton. I've paid off my debt there . . . down to the last dollar. Cleared Major Smith's record, to boot. Perhaps I robbed Peter to pay Paul," he added with a faint grin.

"Let's me 'n' you," said old Mitch to Jake, "take along the jug and gather them cattle. If we sell 'em under the right brands, mebbyso honest Dude'll take 'em off our hands."

Jake Kilgore was about to agree when he saw Mitch pick up the short-handled camp shovel. They had two graves to dig.

Kate, fixing strips of bandages and heating hot water, saw Jake and Mitch ride off with the demijohn and the shovel. Tears stung her eyes. She had never loved Sid as a sister should, but, now that he was dead, sorrow pinched her heart. She was remembering the tune Cole Griffin had been whistling when he rode up to the Kilgore camp, "The Cowboy's Lament". It had seemed prophetic then, and now a verse of the old trail song came back to her. "For I'm a wild cowboy, and I know I've done wrong. . . ." Kathleen Mavourneen Kilgore was to sing it at sunrise as she stood by the two open graves and tarpaulin-wrapped forms. She was destined to sing her songs where the lights shone with extravagant brilliance, standing alone on a raised platform, but Cole was to hear her sing more often as they rode, side by side, around their own beef herds that were bedded down on the wide prairie under a canopy of stars. Because Kate Kilgore loved the lonesomeness of the big cattle country she had been born to, even more than she could love the false gaiety of the crowded cities. Kathleen Mavourneen and Kate. Cole Griffin was marrying them both.

Rusty Rides Alone

Walt Coburn had become something of a fixture at Street & Smith's *Western Story Magazine* by early 1924 when Jack Kelly came to California to see him. Jack Kelly and J. W. Glenister owned the Fiction House chain of pulp magazines that Kelly edited. Kelly offered Coburn 3¢ a word and would feature a 25,000 word novelette every month by Coburn in *Action Stories*, providing Coburn with cover billing. In a way, Kelly's offer was fortuitous because it brought Coburn financial stability. He was paid $100 a week by Fiction House and at the first of every month he was sent a check for the difference between the $750 owing for the month's 25,000 word story and what had already been paid to him. "Rusty Rides Alone" first appeared in *Action Stories* (3/31). In the early 1930s Columbia Pictures purchased film rights to several of Coburn's stories for use in their series Westerns starring Tim McCoy. "The Secret of Crutcher's Cabin", collected in THE SECRET OF CRUTCHER'S CABIN (Five Star Westerns, 1999), served as the basis for SILENT MEN (Columbia, 1933) with Tim McCoy. RUSTY RIDES ALONE (Columbia, 1933) with Tim McCoy was based on this story, a particularly strong entry with Wheeler Oakman as Poe Powers and Dorothy Burgess as Mona Quillan.

I

"Riders in the Night"

A dozen or more men crept through the night's shadows toward the small cabin where a light burned behind heavy burlap curtains. These men were all heavily armed. Their horses were hidden back in the brush down the creek, guarded by two men.

Closer and closer the circle of men drew in toward the cabin. Always they kept to the blackest shadows, crouching by the stable or the horse corral, slipping across to the pile of cordwood stacked beside the shed near the house. Now, at a whistled signal that might have been the call of an owl, they closed in. A big, wide-shouldered man pounded on the door.

"Come in," called a man's voice from the interior of the rough building.

The big man shoved open the door. There was a sawed-off shotgun in his hairy hands. He and the men with him had masks made of black cloth tied across their faces.

Inside was a single man in jumper and Levi's, a red-haired, freckled, blunt-featured cowboy who grinned amiably as he raised his hands above his head. He wore no gun that was visible to the intruders.

A growled oath came from the big leader of the night riders. "What kind of a game you playin', anyhow?" he snarled through the black mask. "Where's Bob Harlan?"

"That," replied the red-haired cowboy easily, "is just somethin' else I don't know. I never heard of Bob Harlan."

"Don't lie, red feller. This ain't no Sunday school picnic. We want Bob Harlan. Where is he?"

"If you was to pull the trigger on that scatter-gun, mister, I

66

would still have to give you the same answer. I don't know no Bob Harlan and I don't know where he is."

"Then what are you doin' in his cabin?"

"Just washin' up the dishes I dirtied when I ate supper. I'm ridin' the grub line through this part of the country and I stopped here to git the wrinkles outta my belly. There wasn't nobody home, so I put up my pony and pack mule and kinda made out to rustle me some supper. Up in my country that's kinda the custom."

"And just where is your country, mister?"

"Montana, till I quit there. I aim to stay here somewheres in Arizona, if I kin land a job with some spread."

"Montana, huh? That's Bob Harlan's old stompin' ground. Sounds almighty queer. Damned if I ain't got half a notion to gut-shoot you where you stand."

"That," said the red-haired cowboy, "is plumb up to you, I reckon. I've done you no wrong, but I ain't gonna stand here an' beg like a dog." A hard glint crept into the steel gray eyes of the red-haired cowboy and his wide mouth tightened into a thin line. He faced the men without flinching.

As the cabin filled with masked men, there was the odor of whiskey. One of them who was a little unsteady on his feet laughed harshly. "He's a game devil, Jude."

"Shut up," growled the big man. "Keep your drunken gab shut." He stared hard at the red-haired cowboy. Above the black mask showed a pair of squinted, pale gray eyes, one of which had a slight cast in it.

"What time did you ride here, red feller?" he growled.

"Just about dusk."

"Where from?"

"From across the Blue Mountains. Stayed at a horse camp there last night. The boys there told me I'd find work here in Apache Basin. They claimed the outfits down here was payin' top wages. So I come on down. My grub had run out and I stopped here. Now if you're gonna kill me fer that, have at it. My arms is a-gittin' tired up there in the air. Holdin' your arms up thataway is bad fer the circulation."

"So is a handful of shotgun slugs." Without taking his eyes from the red-haired cowboy, he called orders to his men. "I'm lettin' this cuss stay alive. He ain't harmed us. Start goin', boys. The night's gittin' on an' we got a few more calls to make."

The red-haired cowboy lowered his hands. The big man stepped closer, his bloodshot eyes slitted. His breath smelled strongly of corn liquor. His voice was a snarling growl.

"Come mornin', you drag it fer another range. We ain't welcomin' no strangers in Apache Basin. Don't go doin' ary ridin' till sunrise or you might have hard luck. But come sunrise, you be on your way."

The red-haired cowboy made no reply. The big man turned toward the door where a lanky man stood with a six-shooter in his hand.

"How about leavin' a man or two here to wait, in case Bob Harlan shows up?" asked the lanky one.

The big man shook his head. "Cain't be splittin' up the boys. May need every man afore mornin'. Harlan will keep. Let's git goin'."

The door banged after them. The red-haired cowboy picked up the dish towel he had been wielding when he was so rudely interrupted. There was a humorless grin on his wide mouth as he resumed his task.

Nice little crowd of boys, he mused. *Pleasant, just like a pack of timber wolves. I smelled the stench of somethin' bad when I rode down from that horse camp. Fellers I met sized me up like I was some breed of skunk. Only pleasant gent I met was that tow-headed cowboy on his way to town. I asked him where is the nearest ranch. He sent me here. Said I was plumb welcome to what I kin find. I reckon that'd be Bob Harlan. Well, I almost found a belly full of buckshot. I wonder if he knew that those jaspers were a-comin' to get him?*

II

"Red Chips"

Sunrise found the red-haired cowboy loading his bed on his pack mule. He now wore a filled cartridge belt and a six-shooter, and his carbine leaned against the corral. As he worked, his eyes kept watch in all directions.

The cabin was in a clearing on the bank of a running creek. Beyond were scrub junipers spotting low, rolling hills. There were patches of brush that might easily hide a man. The red-haired cowboy grinned crookedly and whistled tunelessly through his teeth. He watched the ears of his saddled horse, as he jerked the pack rope tight on the squaw hitch that held his tarp-covered bed.

Now the ears of his blue roan horse twitched forward. In a flash the red-haired cowboy was crouched in behind some cedar posts, his carbine ready. His eyes watched the direction indicated by the blue roan's ears.

A man on horseback came into view, a tall man on a bay horse. He rode at a brisk trot and there was a carbine across the saddle in front of him, ready for use. When he sighted the laden pack horse and the saddled blue roan, he called out.

"Hi, there, red-headed feller!"

"Hi there yourself, tow-headed feller!"

"Nice mornin' after a dark night, ain't it?"

"It is," said the red-haired cowboy, rolling a cigarette. "It

69

is, for a fact. It's kinda good to be alive on such a nice mornin'."

"You said a lot then. In any big rush?"

"Not exactly. Personal, I'd kinda like to linger around this Apache Basin range, but somethin' tells me I better be ridin' along."

"I thought," said the tow-haired cowpuncher, "that mebbyso you could lend me a hand for about ten minutes."

"Shore thing."

The tow-haired cowpuncher, without dismounting, led the way to the cabin. He dismounted stiffly and stood leaning against his horse, hands gripping the saddle horn. His face was gray with pain. The red-haired cowboy said: "Hell, man, you're hurt!"

"Bullet in my laig. I thought mebbyso you'd he'p me git the dang' thing out."

"You bet I will, feller."

Inside the cabin the red-haired cowboy played surgeon: clean dish towels for bandages, corn whiskey for antiseptic, a pocket knife for a probe. Crude surgery but the towhead was game. When the job was finished and they had each taken a pull at the jug, the wounded man held out his hand.

"My name's Bob Harlan. I'm plumb grateful. Now you better be ridin' along because you might git into trouble. I got some enemies here in the basin, and, if they thought you was my friend, or if they even ketched you here, they'd kill you. Better be ridin' on, cowhand."

"My name," said the red-haired waddie, grinning sideways, "is Jim Rust. Rusty for short. I met those enemies of yours last evenin'. They paid me a visit."

"Hell they did!"

"Yeah. And the big 'un called Jude gimme my travel orders. But you ain't in any shape to be left alone. And anyhow the more I been ponderin' on how that Jude gent treated me, the more ringy I get. I reckon, if you don't mind, I'll stay a spell."

"Nope. You ride on, Rusty. No use draggin' you into this dirty mess. There's a war a-startin' here in Apache Basin. There was three men killed last night over on Cowhide. We gave Jude Quillan and his gunmen a game. I was over on the Cowhide on a horse deal with the Ellison boys. About midnight we heard the dogs bark. When they rushed the house, we took 'em on. Come daylight, they drifted and I started home. Some skunk took a long shot at me as I rode along the trail. Hit me in the thigh. I'll be all right, pardner, in a day or so. You pull outta this while the goin' is good. There's gonna be war."

Rusty shook his head. "You ain't in any shape to be left alone. You're from Montana, so the Jude wolf said. Me, likewise. I worked for the Circle C, the Bear Paw Pool, the Circle Diamond, Shonkin, and Square. Born at the foot of the Little Rockies."

"I'm from the other side of the old Missouri River," said Bob Harlan, his eyes lighting up. "Man, it's good to meet up with a cowboy from that country. I worked for the Two-Bar on the south side of the river. Some with the F outfit on Sun River and the Staple outfit. Repped with the Circle C and the Square."

"And so wouldn't I be a fine son-of-a-bitch to lope off an' leave you in a tight? Ever meet the Harkers? They live somewhere in this part of the country? Babe and Frank Harker?"

Bob Harlan gave Rusty a quick look. "Babe was killed here in the Apache Basin two months ago. Some of Jude Quillan's skunks did the bushwhackin'. Frank was with us last night at the Ellison ranch. I'll tell a man I know 'em. The whole family. Dad Harker and his missus and Margaret. Finest folks

71

in the basin. Their place joins the Ellisons' on the Rawhide. Margaret teaches school."

"Then I reckon I kin talk, Bob. Here's the reason for me bein' here." He handed Bob Harlan a frayed letter.

"From Margaret," said Bob. "Tellin' about Babe bein' murdered."

"Me and Babe Harker were pardners since we were kids," explained Rusty. "He was younger than me but he always kinda follered me around and I thought a heap of him. When my dad died and I was left an orphaned, wind-bellied kid, the Harkers took me in an' raised me till I was old enough to rustle for myself. So when I got Margaret's letter, I quit my job as ramrod of the Bear Paw Pool and I headed for Apache Basin. I came here to do a little gun throwin' myself. So I'll jest unsaddle and fetch my bed in here. And when this Jude Quillan lay-out shows up again, my guns will be where I kin get to 'em. I'm buyin' a few chips in this game."

III

"Bloody Wool"

"What started this war here in Apache Basin?"

"Jude Quillan started it, Rusty. He wants the whole valley for his stinkin' sheep. Us cowmen here was in his way. None of us has any cattle to amount to anything. Just small cowmen. The Ellisons are the biggest spread. We run a pool wagon and kinda look after one another's interests. Over on the rim there is more cowmen but they shore drag hungry loops. There're a renegade pack that's bin run outta Texas, the same as Jude Quillan. You must've come past some of their ranches up on the rim of the Blue Mountains. They got a horse camp there."

"I stopped there. I kinda sniffed somethin' wrong about that spread, though they treated me all right. They had a jug that had good likker which passed around frequent."

"They peddle corn likker in town as a sideline. There's a few good boys up there, for all they trail with a wolf pack. Boys that is on the dodge, mostly. I know two, three that has bin good friends to us boys. But Poe Parsons and that gang that trail with him are snakes. They whittle on our cattle aplenty. In the cedar breaks it's hard to work the range clean of mavericks. Poe and his boys ride good horses and they're all crack ropers. Poe is always in the first money at the rodeos. He might've bin at the horse camp when you was there. Tall, black-headed dude with a little black mustache and eyes like an Apache. They claim he's quarter-blood Apache. A good-lookin' rascal and a killer. Always dresses fancy."

"He was the gent that told me they was a-payin' fancy wages down here in the basin. Does he trail with Jude Quillan's night riders?"

"Not him. I'll say this for Poe Parsons, he does his shootin' in the open and on the square. He's plumb fearless and quick as hell with a gun. And for all he's a rustler and handles wet cattle and horses, he'll sometimes ride down to my place or the Ellisons' or Harkers' or one of the other ranches and do a man some kind of an unexpected favor. I've knowed him to pay off a man's note at the bank when the bank was goin' to foreclose. I've knowed him to ride forty miles to fetch a doctor when one of the Ellison boys took sick with pneumonia. Once, when I busted a laig at the Prescott show, Poe sends two of his men to take care of my stock and he told 'em if they stole so much as one calf, he'd handle 'em plenty rough. That's Poe Parsons, the big boss of the wolves that live up on the rim."

"How does he stand with Jude Quillan?"

"Nobody kin give you the answer to that but Jude Quillan and Poe Parsons, and neither of them is much of a hand to run off at the head."

It was getting dark now in the cabin and Rusty had dressed the hole in Bob's leg. The door was barred and a blanket hung across the window of the cabin. Bob's wound, while painful, was not serious. A hole in the thigh muscle. Rusty fed him whiskey to ease the pain.

They talked on until bedtime, then Rusty rolled his bed out on the floor, and pulled off his boots.

Both men slept lightly. But Rusty was snoring gently when the nicker of a horse sounded out in the darkness. Rusty was up from under his blankets like a cat springing. His carbine was in his hand.

"*Shhh!* Quiet, Rusty." Bob Harlan sat up on his bunk, gun ready. There sounded the *thud* of horses' hoofs. Now a voice, hailing the cabin with bold tone.

"Hello there, in the cabin! Are you there, Bob Harlan?"

"It's Doc Newton and a deputy sheriff. Heard you were hurt and came to patch you up!"

"What in hell's the deputy for?"

"Protection, Bob. Let me in."

"Ride straight to the door," called Bob Harlan grimly, "and git off." He said to Rusty, "Light the lamp after they git inside."

Rusty, at a peephole beside the door, saw two men ride up. They dismounted. His six-shooter ready, Rusty let the two men in, barred the door, and stood to one side. In his sock feet he made no noise.

"The deputy," said Bob, "will light the lamp."

A match flared, revealing a short man with a drooping sandy mustache. Under that mustache was a grin.

"You're gettin' almighty cautious, Bob," he said as he lit the lamp.

"Howdy, Dave. Didn't know it was you. Howdy, Doc. Danged white of you to come. Rusty, you needn't watch Dave, he's all right. When the time ever comes for Dave Jones to arrest me, he'll do it open, not by a trick."

"I hope, Bob, that day will never come. But things look snaky. I don't know how you got hurt. Don't give a damn, much. Only what does the other gent look like?"

"Never even ketched sight of him, Dave, but it was a good five, six hundred yards from where he lay up in the rim rocks and I was movin' along at a trot. A mighty hard target. Unless I'm a-guessin' all wrong, it was young Wes Quillan. He's the best shot in Apache Basin."

Dave Jones and the doctor exchanged a quick look. Then the doctor commenced his work.

"Whoever did this job of patching you up, Bob, is no slouch at first aid work. With what he had to work with, I couldn't have done better myself. Stay off this leg for a week and you'll be all right."

"I'll be here to take care of him," said Rusty, and the way he said it brought a faint smile to the lips of Dave Jones, deputy sheriff.

"Say," asked Bob Harlan suddenly, "who told you I'd bin hurt? Nobody but the man that shot at me and Rusty here knew about it. Who took word to town to you, Doc?"

"That," said the grizzled country doctor, "is something I can't tell you, Bob. I was sworn to secrecy, after a fashion. It was about an hour before daylight when somebody rapped loudly at my door. I lit my light and answered the summons. Nobody there. Just a note written in a disguised hand. The note said you were wounded and needed me. But I was to burn the note and say nothing to anybody. But I fetched Dave along partly for company and partly to lend me a hand in case some gentleman tried to prevent my coming to your place."

"A note," mused Bob Harlan, frowning in a puzzled manner, "that's odd. Shore odd. . . . Dave, you understand I ain't preferrin' ary charges ag'in' nobody on this. What happens in Apache Basin, us folks that live here has to settle amongst ourselves in our own way. The law stays outside the corral. We'll brand our own mavericks."

Dave Jones nodded, pulling at his sandy mustache. "I ain't at all anxious to mess into this war, Bob. But if I'm ordered to, I'll have to buy chips in the game. You know how I hate Jude Quillan. He's made the brag that he'll put his oldest boy Zeb in as sheriff next election. If Zeb gets in, it will be Quillan law from Apache Basin to the far end of Mormon Valley, and from the Blues to Bitter River. The town of Rim Rock will no longer be fit for decent women or honest men. It'll be wide open and the sky the limit. Whiskey and bad women. Gamblin' and shootin'. It'll be Jude Quillan's town. He'll be king. Zeb and Luke and Wes, his three whelps, will carry out his orders. Ma Quillan and her daughter Mona will be wearin' diamonds and silk."

"Can't imagine Mona in anything but overalls and chaps and boots," put in the doctor. "Don't think I ever saw her in anything else." He chuckled as he taped the last bandage across Bob's wound.

"I'll never forget the day she slapped that drunken rowdy that tried to kiss her there in front of the Lodge Saloon. She slapped him half a dozen times and every time she made contact you could hear the sound of it half a block away. Then she walked away as if nothing had happened, and Poe Parsons kicked that cowboy halfway across the street."

"Her and Poe make a shore handsome pair," said Bob. "I bet a hat she runs off someday and marries Poe Parsons."

"I'm no gambling man, Bob," said the doctor, "but I'll call that bet."

IV

"The Bushwackers"

Bob Harlan's leg healed rapidly. There had been no threats of night raids on the part of the Jude Quillan outfit. Bob was able to ride again and he had taken Rusty over his range. It was a cowman's paradise and the thought of it being sheeped out made Rusty's blood boil. Grass and water in abundance, at the edge of the basin were the juniper hills to shelter the stock from storms.

"Yonder," said Bob, pointing to the broken skyline that lay to the eastward, "is the Bitter River country and Mormon Valley. Mormon Valley got its name from the old Injun days when the Apaches was on the rampage. They wiped out a Mormon wagon train on the banks of Bitter River. It's cow country now, same as this. The N-Bar is the biggest spread but they don't run much of a wagon. It's mostly small fellers like us that's in here now. It's as purty a range as this, almost. Then over west lays Rawhide Crick. The town of Rawhide is in under them two sharp pinnacles. The Harkers and Ellisons live over on the Rawhide. I reckon, Rusty, that you're right anxious to visit the Harkers."

"I'd kinda like to ride over there."

"I'm all right now. You kin pull out any time. After that lickin' we give that bunch of skunks, I don't think Jude will try anything for a while. Him and his boys are busy movin' some sheep into the mountains, anyhow. They've got no time to go gunnin' for folks. If you start now, you kin make the

Harker place by dark. It lays in that notch between them twin buttes. They'll be shore proud to see you, pardner."

"Sure you're all right, Bob?"

"Shore thing. I'd go along, only I got a few chores to tend to. See you when you git back, Rusty."

"I'll be back in a day or so, Bob. So long. Take care of yourself."

Rusty rode away, whistling. He was anxious to get to the Harker Ranch. Anxious to meet his old friends. More than anxious to see Margaret Harker again. Margaret, brown-eyed, brown-haired, soft-voiced, with her quiet little way of doing things for a man that most girls would never think about. A girl in a million, Margaret Harker. It was worth the long ride from Montana to Arizona to hear her voice. Rusty hummed a song and smiled at the blue sky. Love? Gosh, a drifting cowboy can't afford to fall in love. Love is for those who have something to offer a woman. A cowboy takes his loving out in campfire dreams. His home is where he spreads his bed. But Rusty would be almighty glad to see Margaret.

Rusty might not have given himself to his dreams had he known that, from a high butte, two men watched him with field glasses. They lowered their glasses and grinned at one another.

"It's the red-headed cuss, Wes," said a short, blocky, unshaven man whose paunch lapped over the lacing of his bull-hide chaps. "Reckon he's quittin' the country?"

"If he was," said the tall, slim-waisted cowboy whose age could not be more than nineteen, "he'd have his pack mule. Where's your brains, Ed? You must've washed 'em away with that corn likker last evenin'. The red-topped gent is either goin' to town or he's headed for the Ellison place or mebbyso the Harker Ranch. Jude done tol' him to quit the country and he ain't done it. I reckon we'll mosey on down an' 'tend to the sorrel-headed jasper." His face was hostile.

"You mind Jude's orders, Wes? He said no killin's."

"Who said anything about a killin', bonehead? There's other ways of handlin' such fellers. Come on, you pot-bellied specimen."

They mounted the horses they had hidden in the junipers and took a trail that would cut that of Rusty's. Half an hour later that red-headed cowboy was looking from under his hat brim at the two men who leered at him.

"Whichaway, red top?" asked Wes Quillan, youngest of the Quillan tribe.

"Near as I kin make out," said Rusty calmly, his gray eyes watching the two, "the direction I'm headed for is called west."

Wes Quillan's thin mouth writhed in a snarl. "That'll be all the comical cracks we want outta you, sorrel head. You're headed for Rawhide Crick and we know it."

"Then what was the idee of askin' a man somethin' you already knew? Supposin' I am, slim feller, what of it?"

"You was told to quit this country. Why ain't you made tracks?"

"Well, young 'un, I kinda like the looks of this range. You kin ride back and tell your boss that I aim to stay here. I'm ridin' now to the Harker Ranch. Babe Harker was a pardner of mine. Some skunk killed him from the bush. I rode plumb down here from Montana to git the skunk that killed Babe Harker. Roll that up with your next smoke, young 'un."

A gun suddenly showed in Rusty's hand. It seemed to cover both men. Rusty smiled and thumbed back the hammer. Wes Quillan and the stocky-built man looked a little startled, and neither of them made a move to draw their guns.

Rusty grinned widely. "The other evenin', when you boys

called my hand, you had all the aces. Now it's my turn to rake
in the chips. If either of you would-be tough gents makes one
little move that I don't like, it'll be the last one you'll ever
make on this earth. Fatty, it's shore a temptation to puncture
that paunch of yourn just to hear the wind whistle out. And
I'd like to see if I could send a slug through that skinny kid
without bustin' a bone. They're shore temptin' targets.
Dunno when I bin so tempted to pull a trigger.

"Besides, I don't like the color of Fatty's shirt, and this
slim kid is too mouthy. I hate mouthy kids. Gun-packin' kids
that tries to build a tough rep. Where I come from, they quirt
such ideas outta their boneheads. I wish one of you two harmless thugs would make some kind of a break because I ain't
tried out my gun for a couple of weeks. I'll give you your
choice, gents. Either use them guns you pack, or throw 'em
on the ground. I'm givin' you a fair chance. You may git me,
but I'm gittin' both of you. Commence!"

"You got us covered," growled the fat one. "We ain't got a
chance."

"You got as much chance as your tribe give Babe Harker.
Damn you, commence!"

Rusty's eyes were slits. His grin had twisted into a snarl.
The gun in his hand seemed to spew flame.

"You got us foul," said Wes Quillan, his face gray under its
bronze. "We'll lay 'em down."

"Toss your guns on the ground, then, you two skunks.
Make it quick."

Wes Quillan and the man called Ed dropped six-shooters
and carbines on the ground.

"This means your finish, red top," threatened Wes
Quillan, his eyes red with hate. "You can't pull a thing like
this and win a thing. We'll git you."

"Your squeaky voice grates on my nerves, young 'un. Shut

80

up. Ride off and ride far. Go to Jude Quillan and tell him that there's one more cowboy that he's got to kill before he's the main boss of Apache Basin. Tell the man that bushwhacked Babe Harker that a cowboy from Montana named Jim Rust, better known as Rusty, has ridden plumb from Milk River to Apache Basin to kill him. Tell him that I'll meet him alone any place, any time, and at any kind of a game he wants to deal. Now hit a lope, you two mangy coyotes, and don't look back or you'll git a bullet between the eyes."

"We'll go," said Wes Quillan, white under the verbal lashing Rusty had meted out to him, "but before we go, I want you to know who I am. My name is Wes Quillan and I'm a-goin' to kill you someday."

"If ever you kill me, you skinny coyote, it'll be from the brush. Hit the grit, you sheep-stinkin' lice!"

Wes Quillan and his fat companion rode away at a lope. Rusty grinned mirthlessly as he heard them arguing, blaming one another, no doubt, for their humiliating misfortune. When they had gone a safe distance, Rusty quickly took their guns apart and shoved the various parts of gun mechanism in the sand. Then, whistling tunelessly through his teeth, he rode on toward the Harker Ranch.

He had gone probably five miles and was fording a shallow creek flanked by brush when a throaty, husky voice challenged him.

"Reach for the big blue sky, cowboy, and no foolin'!"

"Your deal," said Rusty, his hands going skyward.

From the brush across the creek rode a tanned, black-haired girl in cowboy garb. In her hand was a .38 gun. Rusty looked into a pair of smoky gray eyes and grinned.

"I bet you're Mona Quillan," he said.

"You win that bet, but you won't win any more. Come

81

across the creek and get off that horse. Shed your gun. You won't be needin' it any more from now on."

V

"The King's Whelp"

Still grinning, Rusty stepped off his horse and unbuckled his gun belt. Then, as if he were not under the cover of a gun, he fished tobacco and papers from his shirt pocket and rolled a cigarette.

"Where's your sheep hook, ma'am, and your band?"

"You think that's a joke, I reckon, don't you?" she flared. She was a remarkably good-looking girl, dark, raven-haired, straight-featured. Her smoky gray eyes at times seemed almost black. Perhaps a trace of Indian blood, for her cheek bones were high and she had that fiery, unconquerable nature that belongs to the Indian. Cherokee, Rusty guessed.

"I was just tryin' to make conversation. This is the first time I ever saw a good-lookin' girl throw down a gun on me. Just why are you stickin' me up, anyhow?"

"I was watching through my glasses when Wes and that fool Ed cut your trail. I saw what you did to 'em. I'm just payin' you off in your own kind of money."

"I could've killed 'em both," said Rusty. "They began it. I finished it. You're the first girl I ever saw that wore her hair cut off thataway and wore man's clothes and still looked like a million dollars."

"I'll get along without the compliments, cowboy. You can't soft soap your way out of this tight, so don't waste time tryin'."

"That wasn't my aim, lady. Just what are you a-goin' to

do with me, anyhow?"

"Take you in to our ranch. Dad will do the rest of it. It'll be plenty, don't worry."

"I hope he doesn't stake me to a band of woolies to herd, that's all."

Mona Quillan almost smiled.

Rusty went on amiably. "I rode herd on a band of three thousand sheep once, up in Montana. The herder had died in a blizzard, and the coyotes and wolves were bad. It was three days before the camp tender showed up and I never was gladder in my life to turn loose of anything. But I got to be right fond of the two dogs that belonged to the dead herder. They were smarter than a heap of humans I've known. They seemed to know I was plumb ignorant about sheep. Must've smelled the cow on me, I reckon. So they did most of the work. Nights, when we drifted with the storm, I laid out. When the camp tender, a-follerin' my trail, ketched me, I'd drifted that band of woolies within gunshot range of the Circle C bunkhouse. I was workin' for the Circle C at the time.

"Come daylight, there I was. I figured I'd sneak aroun' and come into the home ranch by another direction but my luck turned sour. Yes, ma'am, luck was shore ag'in' me. Just as that fool camp tender comes a-drivin' up with his buckboard, here comes the old gent from the ranch, a-whippin' down the hind laig. I started away from him. But here comes that fool camp tender and I'm ketched, you might say, between two fires. So I gave up the game an' pulled my head down low, turtle-like, into the collar of my coonskin. But the old gent knows the horse I'm a-forkin'.

"'What in the name of this and that and thus,' he bellers, 'are you a-doin' herdin' this bunch of stinkin' sheep?'

"'I won 'em off Ole Nelson,' says I, 'in a stud game at

Malta. I'm just driftin' 'em on to their winter range. How many sheep do you want to let me pass through the Circle C ranch?'

"If the old gent had bin subject to apoplexy, he'd've died right there. As it is, he fired me. Then up comes the camp tender. He's a Swede that's only bin in Montana forty years and don't speak good English yet. He's all blowed up like a toad because he thinks I've stolen the sheep. The old gent, recollectin' a few of the times I bin in jail fer this an' that, figgers I got drunk an' stole the sheep. The only friends I got is them two dogs.

"'Git off that Circle C hoss,' says the old gent, 'and walk to the bunkhouse. No red-headed idiot is gonna git away with a job like this.'

"Which I did. But my feet didn't track and I fell down. They're some froze up to my knees. Then things kinda commence goin' around in black circles and I wake up in the bunkhouse with the cook and the old gent and Ole Nelson himself a-workin' on me. Nelson, who owns the woolies, has found the dead herder where I put him in his sheep wagon, and he finds the note I left.

"Ole Nelson, for all he's a Swede sheep man, is a square feller. He gimme a check for a thousand dollars then an' there, and the old gent produces a quart of his private stock and hires me back with a ten dollar raise.

"But I had to quit there. Yes, ma'am, had to pull out. Them knot-headed cowhands jest hoorawed me until. . . . Sorry, ma'am, but I need that cannon!"

With a swift leap, Rusty had grabbed Mona's wrist and flipped the gun from her hand. He picked it up off the ground and recovered his own gun. Mona sat her horse, breathing hard, her eyes smoldering, her red lips twitching.

"Sorry, ma'am. First time I ever mistreated a lady. But I

just couldn't stand the smell of that sheep ranch you wanted me to visit."

Suddenly Mona Quillan spurred her horse forward. Hung by a thong around her gloved wrist was a heavy rawhide quirt. Before Rusty sensed her intention, the wicked quirt was ripping at his face. He threw an arm up to protect himself. The girl was like an infuriated wildcat. Again and again the quirt lashed the man. Her horse reared and shied, but she handled the animal with the skill of a broncho rider. Crowding the horse against the man, she slashed, the quirt *hissing* like a snake, her eyes blazing, red lips curled back from white teeth.

Now Rusty caught the twin tails of the rawhide quirt. With a quick jerk he pulled her off balance, out of the saddle. Then he held her in his arms, arms that had the grip of steel bands. Mona was fighting like a tigress, but she was no match for this red-haired cowboy who was made of rawhide and barb wire.

Through a smear of trickling blood that came from the slashes of Mona Quillan's quirt, Rusty grinned at the infuriated girl. Gradually her struggles lessened. Suddenly Rusty kissed her on the mouth, then let her go.

"That," he told her, wiping the blood from his face, "pays for the quirtin'."

Rusty's blood was on the girl's lips. She stood there, swaying a little, panting like a spent runner, staring at the man's lacerated face. The anger was gone from her eyes as she stared, fascinated, at the bloody face of the grinning cowboy.

Then the grin on Rusty's bloody mouth became rigid. His nostrils had caught the odor of smoke. Cigarette smoke. Mexican cigarette smoke. He whirled, gun in hand, ready for fight.

On the other side of the little creek stood a tall, dark man in garb that was a bit fancy for the common cowboy—a white

Stetson, gray flannel shirt, leather jumper, California pants tucked into fancy boots, silver spurs, and a sagging cartridge belt that was weighted down by an ivory-handled gun. The man was handsome, with a slim black mustache and black hair. His eyes were black, unfathomable. A Mexican cigarette of the finest brand hung from his well-shaped mouth. This was Poe Parsons, chief of the lawless men who rode the rim of Apache Basin, the most dangerous man of them all. As Rusty's gun swung to cover him, Poe Parsons raised his hands in the air. White teeth flashed in what might have been a smile.

"Put up your gun, my red-headed friend. You and I have no quarrel."

Rusty shoved his gun back in its holster. Poe Parsons lifted his white hat in salute to the girl.

"For once, Mona," he said, "you met a man who gave you spade for spade, no?" He stepped back in the brush, reappearing in a moment on the back of the most perfect mahogany bay horse that Rusty had ever seen. He rode across the creek and dismounted, facing Rusty and the girl.

Mona glared at him from under long black lashes. Rusty dabbed at his ripped face. They were both confused, ill at ease, from the knowledge that Poe Parsons had witnessed their battle.

"I rode here," said Poe Parsons smoothly, "to keep an appointment with a lady. I find her quirting a man, riding him down. Then the tables turn and it is the man's turn. My red-haired friend, it is not easy for a man like me to see the woman I love in the arms of another man. I saw what you call red during those minutes when she fought in your embrace. And when you kissed her, you do not know how near you were to death. Then you let her free and you said what you said to her. And in that moment I knew that you were a man and that the kiss meant nothing. Many men would have exacted a higher price for such a lashing. Had you been such a man, one of us would now be dead, because no man can take what belongs to Poe Parsons and keep on living."

"Since when have I belonged to you?" flared Mona.

"Since the first moment I saw you. When the time comes, I'll take you. But this is not the time or the place for such talk. Just what started this battle?"

"The lady," said Rusty, "was aimin' to herd me over to the Quillan Ranch an' turn me over to Jude Quillan. I don't like the smell of wool, so I argued the question. While I think of it, here's your gun, ma'am, and your quirt."

Mona Quillan smiled suddenly. It was like a glimpse of blue sky through black clouds.

"Thanks for the gun. You can keep the quirt as a souvenir." She held out her hand. "We'll shake and call it square. I'm sorry I spoiled your face."

"Don't let that keep you awake of a night," said Rusty. "There wasn't much there to spoil. Now I'd better be ridin' along my trail. Got some miles to cover before dark."

"Which way are you heading?" asked Poe Parsons. "If that's not too personal a question."

"The Harker place on the Rawhide."

"Would my company be unwelcome?"

"No, sir, I'd be glad to have you along."

"I'll catch up with you in half an hour or so, then."

Rusty mounted his big blue roan and rode on along the trail. His last impression of the girl and man behind him was that they were eyeing one another more like enemies than lovers.

Rusty's face smarted and he wondered just what sort of a cock-and-bull story he could tell the Harkers when they asked him about his disfigured face. The humor of it struck him and he chuckled to himself. He was still grinning when, half an hour later, Poe caught up with him.

"Something amusing, friend?"

"I was just thinkin' how I'd explain away this face of mine. I bet I look like I'd matched a fight with a cougar."

"Which," said Poe without smiling, "you most certainly did." Then he smiled and passed a leather case filled with Mexican cigarettes.

"I'll roll one, thanks. Them gold-tipped smokes are too rich for a common cowhand's blood."

"I would not say, my friend, that you are a common cowhand. It is partly because I know that you are not, that I ride with you. I have a proposition to make you as we ride. That, as I say, is one reason I ride with you. There is a second reason that is, perhaps, more vital to you. I happen to know that should you ride alone toward the Harker Ranch, you would never reach there alive."

Poe Parsons produced a leather-covered flask.

"Few men have ever shared this flask with me. Will you join me in a drink?"

"I will, and with pleasure."

This little act of comradeship accomplished, they rode on for perhaps a mile in silence. It was Poe Parsons who broke the silence.

"I need a man. A man I can put faith in. A man of courage and honor, even though it be the courage of an outlaw and honor between thieves. When you stayed at my camp, I looked you over very carefully. When you left there, you were watched. In the crowd of masked men who paid you a visit that night at Bob Harlan's cabin was one of my spies. He gave me an account of what happened. I know that, in spite of the warning given you, you remained there to aid a friend. Today

Wes Quillan and the paunchy Ed tried to stop you and they came out second best. Wes is rated as a bad man with a gun, a killer. So is Ed. Lastly, there was that little incident at the creek proving that you have a respect for womanhood. A man of such qualities is the man I need badly. There is not one of my men who I can really trust. More than a few of them would, if given the chance, shoot me in the back. If you will join me, I will pay you ten times the money you can make here in the basin. I'm not asking for an answer now. I want you to think it over from every angle. When you arrive at a decision, one way or another, let me know. In either case you may count me your friend because of what happened there at the creek. When Poe Parsons gives his friendship, it stays given. I am not an Indian giver because there is Indian blood in my veins."

He held out his hand, and Rusty gripped it. The red-haired cowboy was greatly impressed by the sincerity of this man. He had never met a man quite like Poe Parsons, a man of education and polish, a killer, a lover of one woman, a self-admitted outlaw and rustler. Rusty could imagine Poe's killing without a qualm of conscience. Yet Bob Harlan had pictured the outlaw's other side, a softer, more human side.

To trail with Poe Parsons meant wealth and adventure, *pasears* into old Mexico on raiding parties, clashes with the law and the lawless, moonlight nights with a swift horse between his legs, the flash of gunfire in the darkness, the rush of wind in a man's face. It meant blood spilled on the moonlit sand, fighting, hiding, returning to balance the accounts, campfires where bearded men sat swapping yarns about strange places and daring deeds. It meant living always in danger, intoxicated, drunk with the thrill of it all, gold in a man's pockets, gold to be thrown away in a single night in some Mexican town where there was music and dancing and the stinging warmth of tequila in a man's belly, living each day as if it were a man's last day on earth, staking his life against odds.

That would be the life a man would like if he rode with Poe Parsons, a short, swift-moving life, a quick end, an unmarked grave. Something like electricity tingled Rusty's nerves, quickening his pulse. Like many another cowboy he felt always that call to break loose from the workaday life, to ride under the rim of the skyline with a good horse under him and a gun in his hand. Not that the cowboy wants to be a criminal. It is the adventure, the excitement, the thrill of it, like a game of win or lose all, the hardships thrown in as a handicap, fighting always against odds, forgetting that death always wins in the end. Well, death comes to every man, be he honest or a thief. Of what value is a prosaic, humdrum life to a man in whose veins runs the blood of the adventurer? Men die of such ailments as smallpox and pneumonia. But an outlaw dies by a bullet or at the end of a rope.

"I'll be a-ponderin' on it plenty," said Rusty after a long silence. "But before I do anything about it, I got a chore to tend to. I came here to kill the skunk that bushwhacked Babe Harker."

VI

"Trail Talk"

Three times on the trail, at points ideal for an ambush, Rusty and Poe Parsons met men, roughly garbed, bearded, armed men whose hands left their gun butts at the recognition of the outlaw chief. While there was no sign of animosity, still Rusty sensed a sullen resentment there as they let the two men ride on. Poe smiled thinly.

"They resent my traveling with a stranger. But there isn't one damn' thing they can do about it. We're as welcome as sand burrs in a man's blankets."

"Who are they?" asked Rusty.

"Jude's imported gunmen. A lousy-looking lot, no? He gathered 'em down along the border towns. Saloon bums, a lot of 'em, gutless in a real fight but dangerous enough when they're well sheltered behind some brush or rocks. He just put them in here last night and they were given orders to stop anybody that traveled along the trail and take them in to his home ranch. I got word that he'd imported some fighting men and that's one reason I came down from the rim. I wanted to see for myself what sort of a gang they were. So far, there's been one in each bunch that knows they can't win anything by trying to stop me. But in case we get halted by some of 'em that don't know me, it will mean a scrap. That's why I've taken the lead and told you to follow me."

"I'd sooner take equal chances, if it's the same to you," said Rusty. "You make me feel kinda harmless."

"You needn't feel that way, Rusty. But if you do, we'll ride side by side through the bad spots. However, I don't look for trouble. They've got their orders regarding me, and a description of me that they can't miss. If any of 'em do open upon us, it will be some personal enemy of mine. It's happened like that before. While I never had proof, still I'd bet all I have that Jude put them in on purpose to get me. Jude is handy at that sort of stuff. He'd give a lot to see me laid out with my hands folded across my chest. In fact, the rustling of the leaves in the trees has told me that he's put a secret price on my head."

"Why?"

"For two reasons, perhaps more. First, as Bob Harlan has

no doubt told you, Jude Quillan wants control of all this country so he can put in sheep. He's afraid of my power up on the rim. Up there, so long as I live, he can never get a toehold. But with me dead, my men would scatter like coyotes and he could move up on some good winter range. That's one reason he'd pay a fancy price to the man who snuffed out my candle."

Poe Parsons lit another Mexican cigarette and smoked half of it before he broke the silence that Rusty knew better than to disturb.

"The second reason is his daughter, Mona. Jude is ambitious and, in his own peculiar way, proud as Lucifer. He does not want his daughter married to an outlaw. He wants her to get a real education and marry some prominent citizen. He gets a case of cramps every time he sees Mona with me. But there isn't one damn' thing he can do about it except kill me off. He don't dare tell me I can't see her. For many reasons he has to swallow that bitter medicine. It gripes him something terrible. . . . I don't exactly know why I'm telling you this, my friend. I've never unloaded it on anyone before. But somehow I trust you and I know that what I'm saying goes no further. I hope you can see your way to join me. I need a man like you mighty bad and I'll pay for your services. It's not your guns so much that I'm needing, but rather the comradeship of a real man. A man I can trust with my secrets. With my money. My life. And with the only woman on earth I ever loved. I'll be waiting impatiently, Rusty, for your decision."

"If I'm lucky enough to locate the dirty snake that killed Babe Harker, and I kill him like I'd kill a rattler, then I'll have to quit the basin, I reckon," Rusty mused aloud. "In which case I'd be plumb glad to throw in with you."

"That's true." Poe Parson's black eyes narrowed ever so slightly. His straight black brows were knitted in a thoughtful scowl. "Yes. If you kill the man that killed Babe Harker, you'll sure have to quit Apache Basin. They'd get you in twelve hours." Poe Parsons also seemed to be musing aloud. He seemed to be thinking out some grave question.

A long silence now held the two men as they rode, side by side, into the heart of a blood-red sunset that bathed the basin and the surrounding hills in a soft glow.

"I'm an old time friend of the Harkers," said Rusty. "I'll be takin' their side in any war that comes up here. I think a heap of the Harkers. I reckon I'd hang and rattle with them, Poe, win, lose, or draw. I'm bound to do that."

"They won't have a chance against Jude Quillan, Rusty, once he opens up in dead earnest. Up till now he's been bluffing, but the man's a little insane on the subject of power. He's going through this valley like a scourge. The Harkers and Ellisons and Bob Harlan won't have a chance against him. You'd be throwing your life away for a lost cause."

"I can't make out to do otherwise, Poe. They're like my own kinfolks to me. And better men than me have died for a lost cause."

"Well spoken, pardner. That rather complicates things for you and me, though."

"Meanin' you're sidin' in with Jude Quillan's outfit?" asked Rusty quickly.

"You haven't joined me yet, Rusty." Poe Parsons smiled. "My plans are mine and mine only. My own men don't know where I stand. No man on earth knows."

"Excuse me." Rusty grinned. "I wasn't aimin' to be pryin'. Just thought we might git the situation cleared up."

Again Poe Parsons smiled, but his eyes were fathomless as ever. Rusty wondered just how deep that smile of Poe's ever went.

"Margaret Harker," said Poe, his smile widening, "is a

mighty fine girl. One of God's finest. I don't blame you, old-timer."

Rusty felt his face grow suddenly hot. Poe laughed. Rusty grinned foolishly and fumbled with paper and tobacco.

"Shucks, Poe, Margaret ain't for me. What has a fool 'puncher like me to offer a woman? She deserves a better life than these ranch women have. Washin' and scrubbin' and cookin' and bein' alone two-thirds of the time. No decent clothes like women want. No fun and all work. It's a hell of a life for a woman. I want her to quit this ranchin' and live in town. She's got a good education. She could marry some man that would give her all the things she deserves. I won't deny I think more of her than anybody in the world. But I think too much of her to imprison her on a two-by-twice ranch with a no-account cowpuncher."

"A man like you would think like that, Rusty. You're a sincere sort of gent. Me, I'm altogether different. If I love a woman and she loves me, we'll share the good and the bad. I'll expect her to go with me to the heights and sometimes into the depths. Take equal chances. Share the champagne of life and the dregs. Mona will do that. She is the only woman I have ever found who could be my mate. You, you're different. Honest-thinking, straightforward, giving all and asking nothing. You think your case is hopeless. I disagree. I am going to do some thinking along those lines, Rusty. I want you to help me. I'll see you don't lose. We'll see what we can see about it."

Again the silence held them as they jogged along a wagon road. Dusk had crept into the basin and the last song of the meadowlark died in the twilight.

"Rusty?"

"Yeah?"

"If you killed a man who murdered Babe Harker, you'd be

forced to join me, for a while, anyhow."

"I reckon so, Poe."

"And perhaps, if you joined me, I could help you work out your problem with Margaret Harker. I think I could. Follow me, Rusty."

"I'm tryin' to, Poe."

"I won't promise anything, Rusty. But it may be that you will learn, by the rustling of the leaves, who killed Babe Harker!"

VII

"Snake Tracks"

When they came to the Harker boundary, Poe Parsons pulled up. In the distance, between the two peaks that notched the starlit sky, showed a pinpoint of light that was the Harker Ranch. For while the Harkers, like all the other ranchers in Apache Basin, lived behind drawn blinds, it was an old custom of Ma Harker's to keep a light burning in a spare room until bedtime, to guide friends to their place. It might be said that this homely gesture rather typified that woman whose life had been spent on cow ranches.

"I'll be leaving you here, Rusty."

"I thought you were coming on to the ranch, Poe?"

"Not tonight. It is necessary that I be in Rawhide before morning. Give my kindest regards to the Harkers. Good luck, Rusty. Think things over. Don't ride alone at night. *Adiós.*"

Poe Parsons rode away into the shadows of the night, and Rusty went on alone. He was within half a mile of the ranch house when a voice challenged him.

"Hold up! Who are you?"

There was a gun in Rusty's hand, hidden by the pommel of his saddle, but he hesitated to use it. It might be a Harker cowboy who was challenging him. On the other hand it might be one of Jude Quillan's killers who was halting him.

"I'm a friend of the Harker family," he gave reply.

"Yeah? Mebbyso. Mebby not. Who's with you?"

"I'm alone."

"Who sent you?"

"Nobody ever sends me anywhere, mister. I'm free, white, and of age. My hair is red and my face is speckled. I come from Montana where the snow stays on the mountain tops and the grass grows belly deep in the coulées. I'm peaceable by nature, but I'm aimin' to visit my friends, the Harkers, and there's a gun in my hand that'll clear my trail. So gimme room!"

He tickled the blue roan with the spurs. Lying flat along the back of his horse, he raced along the road. His gun was ready to belch fire at any man who shot at him. The blue roan, despite the long day's journey, was covering the ground with the speed of a race horse.

But no shots broke the silence of the night. Rusty pulled up at the ranch house and stepped up on the verandah. He rapped at the barred door. A code rap. One, three, one. He heard someone moving inside. Then a man's deep voice.

"Who's there?"

"A red-headed jasper from the Little Rockies. The kid that used to ride the milk-pen calves."

The door swung open. Dad Harker, tall, grizzled, raw-boned, in his shirtsleeves and sock feet, stood there. Then he leaned the shotgun against the wall and gripped Rusty's hand. The old cowman's voice shook as he greeted Rusty. His keen blue eyes were misty.

"Ma! Maggie! C'mere! Look what the houn's fetched in!"

There followed a welcome that brought a lump to the cowboy's throat. Ma Harker wept as she held the husky cowboy in her ample arms. Then Margaret kissed him and hugged him and wept a little. Dad Harker brought out a jug and glasses.

"Let the boy git his breath, dang it," he told the women. "He's redder'n a Sioux blanket. Shucks, a man don't like bein' pawed by a pack of females."

"How about it, Rusty?" Margaret laughed. For the first time she noticed his lacerated face. "Goodness, Rusty, what's happened to you?"

Rusty grinned uneasily. "I reckon I ain't got used to dodgin' these mesquite limbs," he evaded.

Now came a lusty pounding at the door.

"That'll be Frank," said Dad Harker. "How'd you ever git past him without bein' stopped, Rusty?"

Frank Harker came in, a tall, rangy, long-muscled cowboy with the blue eyes of his father and rugged features. With a wild yelp he rushed at Rusty and for minutes the two wrestled and pummeled one another, till finally Rusty pinioned Frank's arms and sat on his heaving chest.

"Got enough?" he panted. "Holler Injun, you son-of-a-gun!"

Rusty let Frank get up, and they joined the others.

"He like to rode me down, Dad." Frank grinned, as the three glasses were filled. "He shore was hell-bent to git here."

"Welcome home, son." Dad Harker lifted his glass. They drank in silence.

Ma Harker got busy getting supper for the red-haired cowboy. Margaret was setting the table. The three men talked, after Frank and Rusty had put up their horses. The door was barred, the blinds drawn low.

Underneath their bantering talk, their exchange of news,

ran that undercurrent of lurking danger. Against the walls
leaned rifles and shotguns. None of the three men had
removed their guns. The two women moved about the house
with a sort of cautious tread and seemed always to be listening for some outside sound.

Now and then Rusty's glance fastened on the tinted pho-
tograph of Babe Harker in its gilt frame above the old oak
sideboard. Babe, youngest of the Harkers. Babe, who had
loved life so well. There, in its black case, was Babe's fiddle.
He'd loved music and dancing and laughter. He was always
laughing or cracking jokes or singing songs or playing his
beloved fiddle. Now Babe was dead. Murdered. And while no
one of them mentioned him that evening, still they all felt the
emptiness that his death had left.

Once Rusty saw Margaret wiping away the tears from her
eyes. After the women had retired, the three men drew their
chairs closer about the stove. Dad Harker filled their glasses,
and in low tones they talked of those things which were not
for the ears of Ma Harker and Margaret.

"I reckon," said Rusty, "that I'm on the track of the snake
that got Babe."

"When you git his name, Rusty," said Frank grimly, and
his blue eyes were like old ice, "pass it on to me. It's my job."

Rusty shook his head. "I rode down here from Montana to
handle the job, Frank."

There was a certain finality to Rusty's tone that silenced
Frank and his father. They knew how Babe had always been
closer to Rusty than to his own brother, how, from childhood,
he had worshipped Rusty, how he had tried to walk and talk
like the red-haired cowboy. Rusty had been Babe's idol, his
great hero, and Rusty had loved the curly-haired youngster
like a brother. Yes, it was Rusty's job.

The three men drank in silence. Rusty told about staying

with Bob Harlan. He mentioned seeing Poe Parsons, but he made no mention of Poe's proposition to join his outfit up on the rim.

VIII

"King of the Range"

Jude Quillan dreamed of an empire, even as other men, some good, some bad, had dreamed. Ruthless, merciless, sparing no one, he made his plans even as those other men made theirs. Now he sat in his private office at his home ranch, busy with pencil and paper and maps. He knew every section corner, every acre of land, every spring and tank and water hole in the country. To own all of that domain, to put in sheep there, and handle them, as Jude Quillan well knew how to handle them, would make him the sheep king of Arizona. He would build up a vast fortune. He would become a power. He would mix in politics, have the country renamed after him. Quillan County. Quillan County, Arizona. Senator Quillan from Quillan County.

The cabin that was his private office reeked with the odor of strong tobacco. Now and then he took a pull at his jug of corn liquor. No man had ever seen Jude Quillan drunk. Yet he could empty a jug between dawn and bedtime.

In the gun rack beside his desk was an array of weapons that was a small arsenal. There were hidden portholes in the log walls. Under the plank floor was a month's supply of grub. Also there was a well of good water underneath the log building. A man could stand off a regiment of soldiers there, and it would take a month to starve him out. Jude moved slowly, carefully, making his plans foolproof.

99

Now, as he sat in his log cabin dreaming and planning and plotting how he would rid the country of his enemies, he conjured up great scenes. Before him lay but a few puny obstacles that he would brush aside when the time came. On his littered desk was a list of names, names of men who must be either driven out of Apache Basin or killed. To that list he now added a new name—Jim Rust.

A twisted grin on his thin-lipped mouth, he slowly wrote another name—Poe Parsons. For many minutes he studied that name, his convergent eyes glittering wickedly. Then he carefully erased the name. Not that he was eliminating Poe Parsons from the list, but it would never do to let Poe know that there was a price on his head. Cunning as Jude Quillan was, he was not clever enough to guess that Poe knew of that bounty on his handsome head.

A rap came at the heavy door, then Mona's voice.

"How about letting a lady enter the lion's den?"

Jude Quillan's scowl vanished. Above all things on earth, save his dream of power, he loved Mona. She alone, of all the Quillans, was allowed to pass through the door that led to Jude's sanctuary. He slipped the bar on the door and let her in.

Mona blinked a little in the lamplight, for she had come in from the darkness. He barred the door and she dropped into a chair. Booted, she was like some dark, slim, handsome boy. She tossed her Stetson on the desk and lighted a cigarette.

"You hadn't orter be smokin' them things," Jude said with a half-hearted effort at gruffness. "It ain't lady-like."

"I don't want to be lady-like. If I were one of these cake-nibbling, tea-sipping, lisping females, I suppose you'd be proud of me? Is Wes home?"

"Ain't seen him. Him and Ed was supposed to. . . ."

"Supposed to beat up that red-headed cowboy that's been

staying at Bob Harlan's," finished Mona, blowing a smoke ring and poking a slender, tanned finger through it. "But they missed fire."

"How's that, again? Missed fire?"

"The red-headed cowboy took away their guns and sent them on their way. Lucky he didn't kill them both. He had plenty of chances. Wes is too mouthy, for one thing, and, when he's half drunk, which he always is, he can't get to his gun as fast as an eighty-year-old paralytic. And Ed is worse than harmless. They make a great pair. If I had my say, I'd give them each a band of woolies. That's their speed. And another thing, that red-headed cowboy is bad medicine. He does a lot of grinning and joshing, but he's dangerous."

"Where'd he go after he trimmed Wes and Ed?" Jude was scowling blackly now.

"To the Harker Ranch."

Jude grinned crookedly. "Then the other boys along the trail will fetch him in."

"I think not. Poe was riding with him."

Jude was on his feet with a jerk, his fists clenched, his eyes narrowed. "Poe? Poe Parsons?"

"Yep. Poe Parsons. Personal escort for the Rusty cowboy. Try to get a laugh out of that one."

"What business has Poe got, mixin' in thataway? I knowed that red-headed cuss'd be travelin' over to the Harker place. I wanted him stopped. Now that damned dude steps in. He'll move in once too often someday and never live to tell about it. What's his idee, anyhow?"

"Poe didn't say. As you know by now, Poe Parsons is not what you might call gabby. And he doesn't trust me too far, anyhow. He told me so today. Sometimes I could kill that devil!"

"Hmm-mm. Yet you ride twenty miles to meet him. I

don't like the way you go traipsin' all over the country with that danged cow thief. Someday you're gonna be almighty sorry."

"We've talked that out before, Dad. I'll meet Poe when and where I like. I'm as safe up on the rim at his camp as I'd be in church. He's too devilishly proud to take advantage of me until I'm willing to marry him . . . and he knows that, if that time ever comes, I'll let him know. Poe may be a cow thief, but he's never shot a man from the brush and he's never been caught telling a lie to any man, friend or enemy. Poe Parsons has been a gentleman. His early training still keeps him inside his own certain code. I'd trust Poe a heap further than I'd ever trust my own brothers."

"He's a cow thief," growled Jude. "He don't deny it. But he's not a bushwhacker. See what I mean?" Mona's smoky eyes were ablaze. Jude flinched under her steady gaze and sat down heavily. He tilted his jug and let the hot corn whiskey trickle down his leathery throat. "Whatever does he mean, sidin' in with them cow folks? If he's so danged straight an' upright, why's he sneakin' around helpin' that red-headed cowpuncher git to the Harker place?"

"I wouldn't call it sneaking, Dad. Poe does what he wants to do and he does it in the open. He . . . he must have taken a liking to this Rusty fellow. It wouldn't surprise me if Poe wanted Rusty to join his outfit up on the rim."

Jude spat out an oath. "Wouldn't that be sweet! A danged spy up there on the rim!"

"That would be Poe's concern, not ours. You don't own the rim any more than you can own Poe Parsons."

"I'll own it someday." Jude pounded the desk with his hairy fist.

"Not while Poe Parsons is alive, you won't."

"Poe Parsons can't live forever."

"He'll live longer than the men you hire to kill him."

Jude drew back as if struck in the face. "Who told you I hired anybody to kill him?"

Mona Quillan shrugged and smiled, but her eyes did not smile as she stared steadily at her father. "You can be sure that it wasn't Poe who told me, though I'd bet my best horse he knows. The trouble with you, Dad, is you trust the wrong men . . . men who talk a little too loosely when their hide is soaked with corn whiskey. That talk spreads. The leaves rustle. I've known for a long time that there was a ten thousand dollar bounty on the head of Poe Parsons. You can't look at me straight and deny it."

Jude sat slumped in his old armchair. His raw-boned shoulders sagged. He seemed almost old and a little beaten. Mona sat cross-legged, spinning the rowel of one of her spurs with a thumb. The fire died out of her smoky eyes as she studied her father.

"I'd kill the skunk that told you that," he muttered.

"No. No, I don't think you would. But that isn't just what I wanted to tell you, Dad. It's time you and I had a showdown. I've been mighty loyal to you, even when I knew that you were dead wrong. I've defended you a good many times. I've tried to make myself think that you were something big and great and powerful. And God knows it's been hard to convince myself, sometimes, that you weren't what men say you are. I've taken a man's place on this ranch. I've stayed with you when your sons failed you. I've sat, night after night, here in this cabin and listened to you voice your dreams and hopes and plans.

"When men said of you that you were a murderer, not by actual deed but by hiring others to do those murders, I told myself they lied. That they were envious of your power. It was not easy to put aside some of the things that have been said of

103

Jude Quillan. But I remembered the days before we had so much land and so many sheep. When we were poor and I was a kid in pigtails. When you'd take me on long rides across the country and we'd camp out at night under the stars. You never licked me, never scolded me. You were always bringing me home something from town. My first pair of boots. A stamped saddle. A pair of chaps. A spotted pony. And I've gone to sleep many a night when you sat by the campfire and held me in your arms. . . . Those things I can never forget. That's why it is going to be hard to leave you and strike out for myself."

"Leave me?" said Jude huskily. "Leave your ol' daddy, Mona?"

"Yes. Unless you take that bounty off Poe's head, I'm leaving. I'm going to Poe and marry him and follow wherever he goes."

Jude had crumpled like a man shot. His chin sagging on his chest, he sat there in his old armchair. Mona watched him, a stricken, desperate look in her eyes. Defiance and pity mingled there in her glance. She was, perhaps, the only person alive who really loved this grizzled man who dreamed of an empire. Upon her he had spent all his love, if his queer affection could be so called, and now she was deserting him.

It seemed hours before he looked up. His eyes were glazed with pain.

"I had other plans for you, Mona. I wanted to see you take your proper place in Arizona. I'd figgered on you marryin' a real man that could give you a fine home and purty clothes and take you on trips to places I'll never see. More than anything else, I wanted you to be happy and git outta life what belongs to you. If you run off with Poe Parsons, your life would be a coyote life. Runnin' and dodgin'. Fearin' the law, always, till you die. Hidin' like a wild animal bein' hunted by houn's. Gittin' hungry an' cold an' wet an' laig weary. Gawd knows, Mona, that kinda life is tough enough for the toughest kind of a man. For a woman, it's plain hell. You'd hate him in a little while, and he'd hate you because you'd be hinderin' him. You'd be messed up with such skunks as them rustlers that live up on the rim . . . whiskey guzzlin', fightin', cussin'. You're almighty purty to look at and you'd cause trouble aplenty. And some black night they'd kill Poe Parsons and that pack of wolves would have you trapped. Fer your own sake, Mona, don't do nothin' foolish. If ever you went with Poe, it would be like touchin' off the fuse connected with a kaig of powder. Them wolves would have you inside a month."

"Poe can handle a hundred like them. They've never been able to kill him yet, though some of them have tried to collect the bounty on him."

"He's bin plain lucky, that's all. No matter how fast a man is with a gun, there's always another man that's faster. He'll git his."

"You'll take that bounty off Poe?" Mona came back to the subject abruptly.

Jude Quillan's jaws tightened. With Poe Parsons alive, his plans would never be completed. Only with the dangerous Poe dead could he hope to attain his goal, a goal he had fought for all his life, since he was old enough to dream of a future. Now, with that goal in sight, with that empire almost within his grasp, to lose it?

"Poe Parsons has got to go!" His convergent eyes were hard as flint now as he faced his daughter.

Mona Quillan's face was pale under its tan. Her red lips tightened to a thin, straight line. They looked alike now, that father and the daughter who had inherited much of his nature. They stood up and for a long minute they stared into each other's eyes. Then, without a word, without a gesture, Mona turned and unbarred the door. The door closed behind her. Jude Quillan was alone.

He dropped back into his chair, a choking sob breaking from his dry throat. He had lost the only person on earth that he really cared for. Mona had left him. She had deserted him in his hour of need. Grief gave way to a distorted sense of injustice done him. He reached for the jug and drank the hot liquor like it was water.

For the first time in his life, Jude Quillan drank himself senseless. For the first time since he had settled in Apache Basin, he forgot to bar the door of his cabin. . . .

Jude awoke at daylight. His head ached and his hands were shaky. It took almost a quart of whiskey to straighten him up. He soused his head in the water bucket and dried off on an old flannel shirt. Then he took a high-powered rifle from a gun rack and shoved the magazine full of cartridges. Next he buckled on his heavy cartridge belt with its cedar-handled .45. His mouth was a crooked, cruel line under his hawk-like nose.

No need to look in Mona's room. She would be gone. At the stable he saddled his grain-fed horse and shoved the rifle into its worn scabbard.

Wes Quillan and fat Ed, together with some other men, were at the corral catching their horses. Jude passed them by without apparently seeing them. He rode with his hat pulled low across his slitted eyes, out the gate and onto the trail that led out of the basin and up onto the rim where Poe Parsons and his wolves ranged. Jude Quillan was setting out to kill Poe Parsons wherever he found him.

IX

"Gambler's Luck"

The town of Rawhide was a cluster of frame and log build-ings at the foot of the mountains. The cabins were scattered among the pine trees in a careless manner, for those who set-tled there had simply chosen a spot they liked and built a cabin there. The main street, which was the only street in the little town, was composed of three saloons, a general store that was also the post office, a small restaurant operated by the only Chinaman in town, a feed barn, the log cabin that was the sheriff's office, and another cabin that was the stage office which was operated by the justice of the peace. Back on a side road, hidden in the pines, were several small cabins with red curtains and a large frame building that was Raw-hide's honky-tonk and dance hall.

The rocky slopes behind the town were pitted with pros-pect holes and shafts. Three small mines were being oper-ated. Up the creek was a small stamp mill. Ore wagons, drawn by mules, creaked up and down the gulch above the town. During the day the little town was quiet save for the few miners who were off shift and lounging around, perhaps a horse or two tied to one of the hitch racks in front of a saloon, a sheepherder sitting on the edge of the plank sidewalk, his dog between his knees, dozing off a jag. There might be the blatant noise of a scratchy phonograph, the rattle of heavy chinaware in the restaurant. The few respectable women of the town seldom appeared on the main street. They gathered at each other's homes to trade their little gossip and drink tea together. Sometimes they met on Saturdays at the little schoolhouse back in the pines, but they came to the store and returned to their little homes as quickly as possible. For Rawhide was, for its size, a tough little town. Its boothill, quarter of a mile down the gulch, vouched for that fact.

It was at night that Rawhide came to life. There was the banging of tin-pan pianos, the rough voices of men cursing or singing or laughing at some ribald joke. There was the hum of the roulette wheels, the click of poker chips, the pleading voice of some gambling man trying to throw his seven, faro and chuck-a-luck. There were white lights and yellow lights on the main street and, glimmering through the pines, the red lights of the cabins beyond.

It was some time between midnight and dawn when Poe Parsons rode up the main street of Rawhide. Instead of leaving his horse with the other horses at the hitch rack, or stabling the animal, he rode off into a cluster of scrub pines where he dropped the hackamore rope across the limb of a tree. For a long moment he held the soft muzzle of the handsome bay against his cheek.

The horse nibbled softly at his face and Poe talked in a low tone to the gelding, giving him a few lumps of sugar.

"And no matter what horse comes along, Monte, not one nicker out of you, *sabe?* Because it won't do to let 'em know where you are, old son. I'll be needing you before daylight, and I don't want you gone. So long."

Poe Parsons tested the pull of the white-handled gun from its tied holster. It slid free with a swift, smooth, unbroken movement. Then he shoved the gun back in its scabbard and slipped through the pines to the main street.

Probably a dozen horses stood at the hitch racks in front of the three saloons. Poe lit one of his Mexican cigarettes and walked, with just the hint of a swagger, into the saloon above the door of which was a sign labeled **The Maverick**.

Stepping through the swinging half doors, Poe stepped to

the bar. A sleek, red-cheeked, white-jacketed bartender greeted him with a cordial smile.

"Some old medicine, Poe?"

Poe nodded. "Bourbon, Steve. Open a new bottle."

The bartender looked hurt. "Hell, Poe, you know durn' well I wouldn't doctor your booze. Ain't you known me long enough to trust me?"

"You're not the only bartender that works here, Steve. I trust you, sure. But there's two other men besides you that work behind this bar. And there's the swamper. I can't afford to take chances. Open a fresh bottle and put it on the back bar where I can see it all the time. How's business?"

"About the same. Want to check up the jack?"

"Not now. The games making anything?"

The bartender shrugged his thick shoulders. "Everything but the stud game that Lefty Cass is runnin'. Night before last he drops fifteen hundred smackers and last night he goes in the hole another thousand. He's losin' again tonight."

"And Zeb Quillan is doing the winning?" Poe nodded.

"He is," agreed Steve, "but how in hell did you know?"

"The rustling of the leaves, Stephen. I didn't buy this place with the expectation of making a lot of money. If we break even, I'm satisfied. But I don't digest the idea of some tinhorn like Lefty Cass losing the bankroll. Is he drunk?"

"Clear sober, Poe."

"Hopped up?"

"Lefty don't use dope."

"And still he loses to Zeb Quillan. It smells bad, Steve."

"Stinks like a skunk, Poe."

Poe filled a small glass from the newly opened bottle. Steve took a small beer. They drank.

"Steve," said Poe Parsons, "there may be a little ruckus here tonight. Keep your eyes open. Any strangers here?"

"That big guy standin' at the end of the bar."

"The drunken cowboy?"

Steve leaned across the bar and his voice dropped to a whisper. "He ain't half as drunk as he lets on. A school kid could stand up under what booze he's put away. Most of his whiskey goes into the spittoon, get me?"

"I get you. Thanks, Steve, old boy. When the racket starts, take care of the lights."

Steve smiled and nodded. Poe walked down the bar and past the big, red-faced cowpuncher who seemed to be drunk. Poe, with a sidelong glance, saw a pair of keen, greenish eyes follow him as he made his way to the stud table.

Half a dozen men were playing. The dealer was a sallow-faced, pale-eyed, thin-lipped man of slender build. This was Lefty Cass, gambler and gunman. The green eyeshade he wore cast a ghastly hue across the upper part of his face. He looked up at Poe and his lips tightened a little. He nodded, then went back to his business of dealing.

Across from the dealer sat Zeb Quillan. Tall, raw-boned, hawk-nosed, with a heavy jaw that bristled with several days' growth of whiskers, he leered up at Poe.

"H'are ya, Poe?"

"Able to get around, Zeb. Looks like Lady Luck is your sweetheart."

"Don't it, though?"

Poe looked on for several hands. He kept his back to the wall and never for more than an instant did he quit watching the big cowpuncher who was pretending to be drunk.

Zeb Quillan raked in another pot. Poe signaled Lefty to get up from the table.

"I'll take the deal. You can check in with Steve or sit in the game. I'm going to woo Lady Luck away from Zeb's embrace." Poe smiled amiably.

He saw a quick, meaningful glance pass between Lefty and Zeb Quillan. Lefty took a vacant chair at the table and bought a stack of chips. Poe called for a new deck, broke open the seal, and shuffled the pasteboards with deft swiftness.

This was the first time Poe Parsons had ever banked a game in his own place. It was, in fact, the first time that any man there had ever seen the outlaw handle a deck of cards.

Poe's back was against the wall of the building. He faced Zeb and the bar where the pseudo-drunken cowboy leaned. Lefty sat in the chair on Zeb's right. Poe's black eyes swept the crowd beyond. There were two or three Quillan men here. He smiled grimly and began dealing.

"Zeb," he said pleasantly, "I'm betting five hundred dollars, before I look at my hole card, that it's higher than yours."

"Call that." Zeb's face seemed to redden a little. He was not expecting a bet like that but he could not back down.

Card after card, the pot increased in size. Zeb's two queens were high. He bet a hundred dollars. Poe was the only man to call, with an ace in sight. Zeb grinned.

"Beat them two queens, Poe?"

"Two aces usually does it, Zeb. And your hole card?" Poe flipped over his hole card: an ace. Zeb's face grew redder. He had a king in the hole.

Poe raked in the pot. "I'll take that five hundred now, Zeb."

"Ain't my word good?"

"No man's word is good in this place," said Poe. "The green money talks here."

Zeb laughed harshly and counted five hundred dollars from a thick roll of bills.

"Next hand, Zeb, I'll give you a chance to win back. Make it a thousand dollars. Or is that too steep for an Apache

Basin gambling man?"

"You can't bluff me, Poe Parsons. Hell, make 'er two thousand."

"And I'll up you another thousand. Put the money on the table now."

A crowd was gathering. Among the crowd was the big, red-faced cowpuncher. He stood, not so unsteady on his legs now, behind Zeb's chair. Poe and Zeb Quillan counted out their money.

"Supposing," said Poe, "that we leave the others out this time. I'll just deal two cards. High card wins."

Zeb pushed his chair back a little. He shoved his hat back on his head and looked over his left shoulder. His glance met the eyes of the red-faced cowboy. Poe Parsons cast a swift look in the direction of Lefty Cass. Lefty's tongue was wetting a pair of dry lips. Poe had seen Lefty when he was about to jerk a gun. That tongue always flicked out, like the tongue of a snake.

Poe slid two cards from the pack. They lay there, face down, on the green cloth. He sat in his chair, his feet on either side of the front legs of the chair. Now he nodded to Lefty Cass.

"Turn both cards over, Lefty."

The gambler turned over Zeb's card first. The king of spades. Zeb grinned widely. Now Lefty flipped over Poe's card. The ace of spades.

"Damn you, Poe, this is crooked!" snarled Zeb. "You ain't gettin' away with. . . ."

Poe's left hand grabbed the money and over went the table. The gun in the hand of the red-faced cowpuncher roared, but its slug went wild. His big frame slumped across the litter of chairs and spilled chips. There was a round, black hole between his eyes and a larger one at the back of his skull

Join the Western Book Club and GET 4 FREE* BOOKS NOW!
A $19.96 VALUE!

Yes! I want to subscribe to the Western Book Club.

Please send me my **4 FREE* BOOKS**. I have enclosed $2.00 for shipping/handling. Each month I'll receive the four newest Leisure Western selections to preview for 10 days. If I decide to keep them, I will pay the Special Members Only discounted price of just $3.36 each, a total of $13.44, plus $2.00 shipping/handling ($19.50 US in Canada). This is a **SAVINGS OF AT LEAST $6.00** off the bookstore price. There is no minimum number of books I must buy, and I may cancel the program at any time. In any case, the **4 FREE* BOOKS** are mine to keep.

*In Canada, add $5.00 shipping/handling per order for the first shipment. For all future shipments to Canada, the cost of membership is $16.25 US, which includes shipping and handling. (All payments must be made in US dollars.)

NAME: _____

ADDRESS: _____

CITY: _____ STATE: _____

COUNTRY: _____ ZIP: _____

TELEPHONE: _____

E-MAIL: _____

SIGNATURE: _____

where Poe's soft-nosed .45 slug had torn its way through.

Lefty Cass crouched back in his chair, his left hand a bloody, broken mass of flesh and bone. Poe's gun now covered Zeb Quillan.

"Unless you want breakfast in hell, Zeb, keep away from your gun. And stand with your hands up while I tell you what kind of a skunk you are. You framed it with Lefty Cass to make some big wins at my place. You saw to it that news of Lefty's losings reached me up on the rim. You knew I'd come here to see what was going on. And you had that big, red-muzzled hunk of beef here to kill me. But it didn't work, did it, Zeb? It takes a man with brains to cook up a deal like that and brains is something that you sorely lack. I took back my money. I got your lousy gunman. I've spoiled Lefty Cass from ever dealing another crooked card. Lady Luck left you, Zeb Quillan. Go back to your sheep. Go back and tell Jude what you've done. He'll be proud of you, his oldest son. Now you, and every man that's with you, line up against that wall. Don't any man leave this place for fifteen minutes unless he wants a ticket to hell."

Poe, his gun covering the crowd, backed toward a side door. His left hand found the knob and the door opened.

"Let 'er go, Steve!"

There was the thudding, crashing roar of a repeating shotgun, the sound of smashed glass, the room in thick, smoke-filled darkness.

Poe Parsons ran for the thicket where he had left his horse. A few minutes later he was riding at a run down the street and out onto the open trail. Now he slowed to a long, tireless lope. He lit a cigarette and filled his lungs with the smoke of the heavy Mexican tobacco. Instead of taking the trail that led to the rim, Poe Parsons rode along the wagon road that would take him to the Harker Ranch.

X

"The Wolf Pack"

So it was that Jude Quillan, pushing his horse hard, failed to find Poe Parsons at the horse camp on the rim. Nor was Mona anywhere to be found.

"Where's Poe Parsons?" he spat at the men gathered around the campfire where fresh meat and beans and hot bread and coffee were cooking.

"Dunno, Jude. He pulled out night afore last and he ain't showed up since. 'Light and set, Jude."

"If I thought you was a-lyin'," rasped Jude, "I'd kill you."

"We got no call to lie to you, Jude. Why should we be a-lyin'?"

"Seen anything of that gal of mine? Mona?"

"Nary sign. She ain't bin up here on the rim fer two, three weeks. Not since she roped that big spotted steer an' tied him down by herse'f."

Jude stepped down off his horse. He reached for the whiskey jug and drank like the stuff was water. He wolfed some food, then rode away. The eyes of the renegades followed him.

They all hated Jude Quillan, hated him because he treated them like they were yellow mongrel dogs, hated him because he ran sheep in Apache Basin.

"Sheep-stinkin' ol' scoundrel!"

"Ornery ol' buzzard."

"Looks like he's a-gunnin' fer Poe, personal."

"Shore does. An' the Mona gal is missin' at home. What do you make of that?"

"Same as you do. Poe and her has run off. We lose our

chief, Jude Quillan loses his gal. And the ol' son-of-a-bitch is on their trail. He's gonna kill Poe an' save payin' out that bounty he's put up. Pass that jug."

"Poe bein' gone," said a wide-mouthed, snub-nosed, tow-headed cowpuncher with a drooping, corn-colored mustache, "we better be electin' a new chief. I hereby nominates myself, Tom Macey, for the job. Has any of you gents got objections?"

He had gotten to his feet and stood on widespread legs, thumbs hooked in his sagging cartridge belt, a wide grin on his face. Tom Macey was a swaggering, burly, rough-and-tumble bully.

"It takes brains," drawled a swarthy Texan who squatted on his boot heels, "to ramrod a spread like this 'un. I'm wonderin', Macey, where you're gonna borrow the brains you'll need."

"All the brains I need," said the tow-headed bully, still grinning, "I pack around in this gun."

The two shots blended as one. The Texan was on his hands and knees now, blood spilling from his mouth. Tom Macey stood there, swaying on his feet, a crimson blotch on his shirt. The Texan fired again. Still Tom Macey kept his feet, although he was mortally hit. He thumbed back the hammer of his gun. Slowly. His grin was now a grisly grimace. He took steady aim. His gun roared.

The Texan slid forward on his face, shot through the head. Tom Macey stood there, his smoking gun slipping from his numbing fingers. Then his knees buckled and he collapsed, his gray flannel shirt soggy with blood.

"So long, boys," he muttered. He was dead when some one of the gang sought to give him a last drink from the jug.

The double killing had its effect on the others. Tom Macey and the Texan were rated as the two toughest men of the renegade gang. The bodies were carried off to one side and covered with the same tarp. The jug went the rounds as the gang discussed the double killing.

"Somebody had ought to kinda jigger the spread," said a weazened, leathery-faced man with bowed legs and bald head. "We'd better take a vote on it."

"Why don't you take the job, Baldy? You're the oldest hand amongst us?"

"Baldy suits me," agreed another.

"Them in favor of Baldy raise their hand."

The vote seemed to be unanimous. Baldy, the undersized, bowlegged veteran of the dim trails, was proclaimed leader of the pack. Again and again the jug went the rounds, and of them all Baldy was the only one who did not fully satisfy his thirst for the corn liquor. Baldy pretended to drink but only a small quantity of the whiskey went down his throat, this in spite of the fact that Baldy was as fond of a jug as a bride-groom is fond of his bride. Baldy had ridden too many crooked trails in the company of tough men to get drunk now. Whiskey had dethroned too many bandit leaders. He knew that, among the tough crew who toasted his leadership, there were a few who desired that job. So he sat with his back against a big pine tree and drank only enough to keep his innards warm.

Not only did he watch the crew of drunken renegades. His keen eyes, puckered at the corners, watched the shadows beyond because this weazened little old outlaw did not believe that Poe Parsons had deserted them. He reckoned that Poe would return to camp, maybe fetching Mona with him, this time for keeps. Baldy knew what that meant. Bad enough when the gal came up for a day. He'd seen the effect of her presence on this gang of tough cow thieves. How they all tried to show off when she was here. How they looked at her like they wanted to own her. Poe was a fool ever to let the gal come up here to camp. She just naturally raised hell with every man's nature, and, if she showed up now, hell would pop for sure.

Baldy liked Mona Quillan. Mona had always treated Baldy well. Once, when he'd been crippled up by a horse turning over with him, she'd fetched up liniment from the ranch, and she'd always talked to him when she came up. She'd never poked fun at his bald head or his bowlegs. Last Christmas she had given him half a dozen heavy wool shirts and six suits of thick underwear. God knows he needed 'em, too.

Baldy hated Poe for bringin' Mona Quillan up here among such a tough gang, but he'd stand by Poe and help him fight them off when that time came. Most of the gang were sleeping off their booze. Only one or two staggered around. Baldy, failing to rouse the cook, set about getting breakfast. He was making biscuits when, from somewhere in the distance, there came the sound of a shot. Two shots. Then silence. Baldy wiped the dough from his hands, got his carbine, and, saddling his picketed horse, rode away from camp without a word to the two drunken outlaws who were shooting craps on a blanket.

The puckered eyes of the weazened little old outlaw were glittering dangerously as he rode with his carbine across his lap. He kept off the main trail and followed a twisted course through the pines. Just what he expected to find, he did not know, but he was ready for anything.

XI

"The Prisoner"

The evening of the day that Rusty had started for the Harker Ranch, it was Pete Ellison who brought word to Bob Harlan that Jude Quillan had every trail in Apache Basin guarded, that his tough gunmen had orders to bring in every man who rode those trails. There were to be no killings unless it was absolutely necessary, but, if it came to a showdown, to shoot.

"Then Rusty ain't got a rabbit's chance, Pete," said Bob Harlan, taking his Winchester from its rack. "They'll git him."

Bob put on his hat.

"Where you goin', Bob?"

"I'm goin' to find out what they done to that red-headed pardner of mine. He stuck by me, Pete. I'll do the same by him."

"You'll git what he got, bonehead. What chance have you got to do him any good?"

"I dunno, Pete. All I know is that, if I didn't make a try, I'd feel lower than a snake's belly."

"Let's grab a bite to eat before we go, then."

"This ain't one of them we jobs, Pete," explained Bob Harlan. "I'm goin' alone. Two men together is a heap more dangerous than if I ride alone. I'll keep off the main trails and Injun 'em. Just do a little scoutin'. There's a lot of tricks I learned up home from the Injuns that will help me slip past their guards. If they got Rusty at the Quillan Ranch, I'll spring him loose, if I have to fill Jude and his three sons full of lead. Pete, you take another route back to your place. Git

118

Frank Harker an' Dad Harker an' all the men you kin gather. Jude is fixin' to su'prise us an' we better beat him to the draw if we don't want to be massacred. I'll join you as soon as I kin."

It was dusk when Bob Harlan set out. He rode a gaunt-flanked, hammer-headed, rat-tailed, line-backed dun horse that could cover more ground on slim rations than any horse in the country. A vicious-tempered, tough, game-hearted horse that no man but Bob could approach without being met by flinty hoofs and snapping teeth. Even Bob had always to be on guard when he came near the big dun horse.

"Strychnine," said Bob grimly, as he stepped up in the saddle, "you and me travels long and hard tonight."

Strychnine, when Bob's weight was in the saddle, suddenly broke in two, pitching and bawling, while Bob sat his saddle with a wide grin. Strychnine never failed to buck every time he was saddled. Then the ugly hammer head came up, the white eyes rolled back, and the big horse hit a long, rough trot that ate up the miles.

Avoiding the main trails, keeping always off the main-traveled roads, Bob Harlan had skirted Jude Quillan's outposts. He kept the big dun horse at the same long-gaited pace. He rode with his gun near his hand, his eyes peering into the night. He reckoned it must be near midnight.

Suddenly he pulled up with a jerk. From out of the night ahead there came the sound of shots. Hoarse shouts. The scream of a woman. A woman calling for help.

Jerking his gun, Bob Harlan spurred the big dun horse to a run. Through some brush and trees he caught the yellow glow of a campfire. He heard a man laugh loudly, a woman's voice, husky with anger, rather than fear. Now Bob's better judgment made him slack his swift gait. He slowed to a trot, then a walk. Then he slid from the dun's back, his carbine ready.

That big yellow horse, for all his ornery ways, would stand there in the shadow of the brush all night without being tied.

Now Bob went on foot, crouching low, his chaps and spurs left back on his saddle. He made no sound as he approached the campfire. He was within forty feet of the fire where four men, bearded, heavily armed, vicious-looking, squatted around the fire. On the ground near them, bound hand and foot, lay a man.

Bob crept closer, his carbine ready. He gave a slight start. That bound figure was not a man. He had caught a glimpse of the face. It was Mona Quillan.

Something inside Bob Harlan's body gripped his heart like an icy hand. He had never known Mona Quillan, but he had seen her a thousand times, usually in the company of Poe Parsons at the dances and rodeos. Bob caught himself trembling as if with a chill. There were beads of cold sweat on his forehead. The palms of his hands were moist and clammy. He crouched there, motionless, fighting for his self-control. He could see the girl's face, tanned, unafraid, and there was a gag made of her own gay-colored neck scarf tied across her mouth.

The four men were looking at her with leering grins on their faces. They had evidently been hitting the jug that stood near the fire, as unsavory and vicious-looking a quartet as a man would care to avoid on a dark night.

"She says she's the boss's daughter," chuckled one of the men. "Kin you beat that? Well, she might be, but she's a long ways from home tonight. I ain't kissed a gal in a coon's age."

"And you ain't a-kissin' this 'un, Heavy, till we lets the dice decide it."

"Jude put me in charge here," growled the big, black-bearded one they called Heavy, "and what I say goes."

"Like hell it does," snarled another one of the four. "Not

in a case like this. This is outside of the regular business hours, see? The dice decides it."

"You bet," put in the third member, reaching for the jug. "The winner gits the gal. And from the way she fought, he ain't gittin' no easy bargain, neither. Drag out the bones, Blackie."

The dice game now commenced. All four were absorbed in the game when a harsh, menacing voice ripped out of the shadows.

"Reach for the stars, you skunks!"

Instead of complying, all four men jerked their guns. Now those guns were spewing flame.

"Roll into the brush, Mona!" yelled Bob Harlan, and punctuated the command with a shot that sent the big black-bearded man to his knees, writhing in pain. Bob's carbine was cracking like a machine-gun. He kept shifting his position.

Another man was down now, and a third was shot in the shoulder. The fourth man, crouched in the brush, was giving Bob a heated battle. The other three, wounded, started to crawl into the brush.

"Stay where you lay, you skunks," barked Bob, "or I'll kill you now!"

The fourth man had evidently changed his mind about fighting it out. Bob's bullets were clipping the twigs too close to his head. The swift pounding of hoofs told of that fighting man's precipitate departure. Bob called to the three wounded men.

"Stay in the firelight. Move and I'll plug you. Mebbyso I will, anyhow."

He slipped noiselessly through the brush. A few moments later his knife had freed Mona from the ropes that bound her. He helped her to her feet and together they slipped away into the darkness. The girl seemed weak and Bob had to help her mount her horse.

"Hurt, Mona?" he whispered.

"Not much. Never mind it. Let's get out of here."

They made their way to where Bob had left his horse. He mounted, and they rode on. Bob kept watching her. Mona was swaying a little in her saddle. When they were far enough away from the camp of the hired gunmen of Jude Quillan, Bob reined up. They were on the bank of a small creek.

"Now," he said, trying to keep his voice steady, "let's see how badly you're hurt."

As he lifted her from the saddle, she went limp in his arms. Making a pillow of his jumper, Bob laid her unconscious form on the grassy bank of the creek. He filled his hat with water and bathed her face. Her eyes opened, their smoky gray depths seared with pain.

"I owe you more than I can ever pay back, Bob Harlan," she said, trying to sit up.

Bob pushed her back gently. "Never mind that. You're hurt. Just lay quiet while we take a look at this shoulder. It's goin' to hurt some."

"I can stand that, Bob."

Harlan felt his blood pulse harder. Mona Quillan, who had never spoken to him before, had called him by his first name. Gosh, that was something to remember. Bob found a flask of whiskey in his chaps pocket and made her swallow some of the fiery stuff. Then, with his pocket knife, he cut away her flannel shirt from the collar to the elbow. In the uncertain light of the moon, for he dared not kindle a fire, Bob's fingers gently, skillfully examined the bullet hole in the girl's shoulder. Luckily it had been a steel-jacket bullet and had gone through above her armpit without hitting the bone. He poured raw whiskey in the wound and used his undershirt to bandage it.

"It's a clean undershirt. Just put 'er on this evenin'. Better take another nip of this likker, Mona."

"I hate the stuff," she told him. "This is the first time I ever tasted it. The men of my family do enough drinking for all of us. I'm feeling better now."

"You stood it mighty game," said Bob. "I've seen enough tough men whimper when whiskey was poured into a bullet hole. It shore stings. I know from experience."

"Yes. When you were shot by one of the Quillan tribe," said Mona, a little bitterly. "It's mighty white of you to do all this for Jude Quillan's daughter. Not many men would do what you did for the daughter of a man who wants you killed or run out of the country. But I always knew you were a white man . . . even if you have always treated me like I was covered with sheep ticks."

"Shucks. . . . Gosh, Mona, I never meant it like that. I always figgered you hated cow folks!"

"I hate sheep as bad as you do. I hate it all. Why shouldn't I hate it? Do you think I enjoy going to dances where Poe Parsons and a few of the men in town are the only ones that ever ask me to dance? Do you think it is easy being the daughter of Jude Quillan here in Apache Basin? Where I'm hated and snubbed and laughed at? Where they say all sorts of things about me? They say I'm wild and bad and that I'm Poe Parson's woman. They say worse than that. They hate me, and I hate them back. Do you know where I was going when those men stopped me?"

"No, I don't reckon I do, Mona."

"I was going up on the rim to give myself to Poe Parsons. To marry him and follow him to hell." Her smoky eyes were resentful now, and her red mouth twitched at the corners.

"I reckon Poe thinks you're the only woman on earth," said Bob. "Some ways, Poe's one of the finest men I ever met, for all he's a rustler. There's a heap to Poe Parsons. I don't blame you for lovin' him."

"But supposin' I don't love him?"

"Then why would you be ridin' off up there to marry him?"

Mona laughed a little. A broken, queer little laugh that was more like a sob. There were tears in her eyes. The first tears that any man had ever seen there. "I think, Bob Harlan," she said in a husky voice, "I'd better be riding on. On up to the horse camp on the rim."

"Yeah? Ride thirty miles over that rough trail with a bullet hole in you and mebbyso more of them skunks to stop you again? I reckon not. I'm takin' you to your home ranch."

Mona shook her head. "I'm not going back to the ranch. Not tonight. Not ever. My father and I quit last evening. Never mind why. But I never want to see that ranch again."

"How about your mother?"

"She's not my mother. She hates me. Zeb and Luke and Wes are her sons. My mother was a dance-hall girl in Juárez. When she died, she made Jude Quillan take me because I was his daughter. Jude's wife hates me. The boys are jealous of me. Jude Quillan was the only one who ever treated me decently. And now he and I have quit. There's nothing left, you see, but for me to go to Poe Parsons. Poe loves me. He's never been unkind to me. He'd die for me. So you see, Bob Harlan, you'd better let me go on along my own trail. On up to the rim. Life with Poe will be exciting, anyhow, and I'll be among my own kind . . . beyond the boundary lines of society where I don't belong. Now, will you let me go, Bob?"

"No." Bob's drawling voice was firm, uncompromising. "You'd never make it, Mona. You won't go home. We can't git through to the Harker Ranch or the Ellison place. So I reckon our one best bet is for us to go back to my place. I'll send somebody for the doctor. Then, when you're able to travel, I'll ride with you up to the rim and turn you over to Poe for better or worse. Let's git goin'."

"To your place, Bob?"

"It's the only place left, seems like."

Mona got to her feet slowly. Bob made her take another swallow of whiskey, and so they rode through the starlit night and into a red dawn. The last ten miles of the trail Bob Harlan carried Mona Quillan, weak and half conscious, in his arms, while her horse trailed behind.

At his cabin, Bob put her on his bunk. He made a fire in the stove and heated water. Then he forced some more whiskey down the girl's throat and set about his task of playing doctor and nurse. Once, while Mona laid there, her eyes closed, her white face pillowed against the jet, black curls, Bob bent over her and kissed her. Her closed eyelids with their thick black fringe of lashes quivered a little, and the cowpuncher drew back guiltily, his face crimson. His hands shook as he cut away the blood-soaked bandage and bathed the ivory white shoulder with its ugly wound with warm water that had a few drops of carbolic acid in it. Bob was thankful that the doctor, when he had come up to patch up his leg, had left a good supply of bandages and dressings.

Mona's eyes opened after a while. She smiled a little when she found Bob's hand holding one of hers. When he would have let it go, she tightened her clasp. Then her eyes closed again, and Bob sat there for a long time, holding her hand in his. He had given her one of the little pills the doctor had left him to ease the pain. After a time, when her deep breathing told Bob that she was asleep, he left his seat beside the bunk and went about his usual chores outside.

He kept watching for some chance rider who he might hail, but nobody showed up. At noon, Mona was awake, but

Bob knew that she had a fever, for her face was flushed and her hands were hot and dry.

"I got some hot tea for you, and some chicken soup that come in a can. That dude huntin' party that was through here last fall left me a lot of that fancy canned stuff. And here's a nightshirt. I'll go on out to the barn while you git fixed. I got your boots off." He flushed crimson and Mona laughed at his embarrassment.

While he was at the barn, Bob sighted a man on horseback. He saddled a horse and rode to intercept the rider, who proved to be a cowboy on his way to Rawhide.

"Tell the doctor to git to my place quick as he kin make it. He's needed bad. But don't say anything to anybody else and tell Doc to keep his mouth shut. A . . . friend of mine has bin shot. And you better take the outside trail to town, feller, because Jude Quillan has the other trails guarded. If you want to see Rawhide, rim out of the basin and foller the trail under the rim to the Ellison place, past Harkers', and on up the Rawhide to town. Because Jude's set to make war."

The cowpuncher thanked Bob and agreed to get the doctor down from town if he had to rope and drag him.

Bob went back to the cabin. He kept thinking of Rusty. Finding Mona Quillan wounded had halted his plan to locate the red-haired cowboy.

Mona's clothes were hung on a nail behind a blanket curtain in the corner. She was propped up against the pillows, reading a book that Margaret Harker had loaned him. Margaret's name was on the flyleaf.

"You look worried, Bob," she told him. "I'm sorry I'm such a pest."

"It's my pardner, Rusty, that's frettin' me. He set out for the Harker place."

126

"And he no doubt got there," said Mona. "Poe went with him." She told Bob part, but not quite all, of the story of her meeting Rusty.

Bob grinned his appreciation. "He's one in a thousand, that boy. Old friend of the Harker family. So Poe took him there? That won't be good news for Jude."

"No." Mona looked at the book and smiled. "Or for Bob Harlan."

"Meanin' what, Mona?"

"Your pardner may beat your time with a certain young lady. He's come clear from Montana to see her." With a sudden gesture, Mona tossed the book onto the table near the bunk. "Loan me the makin's, cowboy."

Bob handed her tobacco and papers. "I'd be right proud to see Rusty and Margaret git married," he said quietly. "I'd shore like to dance at their weddin'."

XII

"Gunmen Gather"

Poe Parsons and Rusty rode away together from the Harker Ranch. Poe had visited the Harkers a few times before and had found a welcome there. An admitted cattle rustler and gunfighter, still he had, several times in the past, done them favors that they could not ignore. Now he had come, with the dawn, to their ranch, had talked for perhaps half an hour with Rusty, and as a result of this conversation between them Rusty had bade the Harkers a brief and somewhat mysterious farewell. But Frank Harker and his father both knew, without being told, that Rusty had ridden away with Poe to find and kill the man who had murdered Babe Harker.

Poe had talked briefly with the two Harkers.

"Take your women," Poe had told them, "and go to the Ellison Ranch. Get every cowpuncher you can find. Jude means war and he's going to strike without giving warning. Probably tonight."

So Poe Parsons and Rusty left the Harker Ranch and took the trail that led up to the rim. By some odd kink of fate, they missed Jude Quillan who had quit the rim and come back into the basin.

Jude, like a man tortured, could not summon the patience to wait up on the rim. His brain seemed on fire. He was like a man gone mad. His one aim was to kill, to find Poe Parsons and Mona and shoot Poe down where he found him. Then he intended to gather his gunmen and sweep Apache Basin from one end to the other, killing any man who would not run, driving every man in the basin out of the range he coveted. The pockets of his chaps bulged with yellow banknotes. He would buy them out at his own price. If they refused to sell, he would kill them. The only law he knew was Jude Quillan's law. Made reckless by Mona's desertion, he was now determined to force the issue—today, tonight—and God have mercy on the man who tried to halt him.

As he left the horse camp after failing to find Poe there, he met a horseman. It was one of the quartet that had captured Mona and had been put to flight by the unseen gun wielder who had rescued her. The man had ridden to the rim to join Poe's outfit. He and Jude met face to face.

"What the hell you doin' up here?" snarled Jude.

For reply, the fellow went for his gun. Jude's six-shooter spewed fire. Once. Twice. The tough gunman pitched sideways from his saddle. Jude rode on without even glancing at the bloody, huddled body that lay alongside the trail.

Shoving fresh cartridges in his gun, Jude rode on, his bloodshot eyes staring ahead, down into Apache Basin. He met his son Luke.

"Gather your men, Luke. Meet me at the ranch. Seen Poe Parsons?"

"No. Zeb ribbed a game that he figured would ketch Poe in town. If the trick worked, Poe Parsons is plenty dead by now."

Luke explained Zeb's trick. Jude's eyes glittered.

"If Zeb pulled 'er off," he growled, "I'll make him a present of ten thousand dollars. Seen ary sign of Mona?"

"Nary sign. I just come down from the sheep camps. We'll meet at the ranch?"

"At sundown. Have every man you got there. See you later."

Jude rode on at a long trot, gathering in his men. He found Wes Quillan and, much to the relief of young Wes, did not cuss him out for letting Rusty get the better of him.

"Git your men and meet at the ranch at sundown. Seen Mona?"

"Not since she left the ranch. Where'd she go? Don't you know?"

"How in hell would I know?"

Jude rode on once more. At the ranch he found Zeb and some of the Quillan riders.

"Did you git Poe Parsons?" was Jude's first question.

"No . . . he got away. Killed that big feller that claimed he was fast with a gun. I tell you, that Poe Parsons is. . . ."

"Git outta my sight, you whinin' whelp! I got no time fer to listen to excuses. Git your men ready to pull out at dark. Come near my cabin before then and I'll fill your belly full of buckshot."

Jude turned his horse over to the stable man, gave orders to have a fresh horse grained and saddled by sundown, then stalked over to his private cabin.

Behind the barred door, he drank heavily from his jug, then dropped into his chair. And there he sat, drinking and muttering and cursing, until darkness approached. Then he quit his cabin and went to the bunkhouse.

"Zeb, take your men and head for the Ellison place. If they won't sign this bill of sale, run 'em off or kill 'em."

He handed Zeb a package of banknotes.

"Luke, you draw the Harker place. Here's their bill of sale and the money to buy 'em. Try not to kill or hurt the wimmen. Killin' wimmen sets bad in court. Your orders are the same as Zeb's." He turned now to Wes, the youngest and most dangerous of the three sons. "You ride with your men to Bob Harlan's. You don't need no money. He's done too much a'ready ag'in' us. Kill him an' burn the place down. Take three men with you. That'll be aplenty."

Jude stood there in the lantern light, a terrible figure of a man, a killer, if ever one stalked the night. The stable man brought up a fresh horse. For a moment he regarded it uncertainly, then mounted abruptly.

"Where are you goin', Paw?" asked Zeb.

"I'm a-goin' after Poe Parsons."

XIII

"The War Is On"

"And the name of the skunk that killed Babe Harker?" asked Rusty, as he and Poe climbed the steep trail to the rim.

"When the sign is right, Rusty, I'll tell you. But not now. Because I don't want you to make any foolish move that will mean a bullet in your brisket. You're too impulsive, pardner, and you'd be apt to go at it all wrong. You'll know your man when the time is ripe, but not until then. In case anything should happen to me, his name is on a slip of paper in my shirt pocket. Now let's go up to camp and see how my wolves are faring. I have a hunch, Rusty, that all is not so good up there. So keep your gun handy. They're a pack of jackals."

They rode on up the trail.

"We'll need 'em tonight, though, Rusty. Jude has a lot of men."

It was high noon when they rode into the camp. Poe, riding in the lead, pulled up with a quick oath.

The camp on the rim was deserted. On all sides was strewn evidence of a hasty and untidy departure—empty jugs, cold ashes of last night's campfire, an empty corral. Poe Parson's gang had quit camp.

Poe lit one of his Mexican cigarettes and smiled twistedly. "They must have smelled a hard fight coming. Hmm-mm."

He swung off his horse and lifted an edge of the blood-stained tarp that covered the stiff bodies of the Texan and Tom Macey. His smile became a little more crooked.

Now a man stepped from the brush. It was little old Baldy. As Poe's gun covered him, Baldy cackled like a setting hen.

"They didn't take the time to plant 'em, Poe. Doubt if they was a man of 'em sober enough to dig a grave, anyhow."

"Where'd they go, Baldy?"

"Town. I let 'em go. I was kinda juggerin' the spread, so I told 'em to hit fer town. You see, Poe, I figgered you'd be fetchin' the Mona gal up an' they was drunk an' primed fer raisin' hell. So I got shut of 'em. Did you meet up with Jude Quillan?"

"No. Why?"

"He's a-gunnin' for you. Gonna kill you on sight. He thinks the Mona gal has run off with you. Ain't she with you?"

"No." Poe's lips tightened. "You sure you're right about this, Baldy?"

"Plumb. Mona run off from home. Four of Quillan's men ketched her but some gent shot hell out of 'em and stole her away. I got it from one of 'em that Jude gunned over yonder a ways. He talked afore he cashed in his chips. I figgered it was you as rescued her."

Poe shook his head. "Got a horse saddled, Baldy?"

"I have."

"Then get aboard. We've got a hard night ahead of us. I figured on my men being here so I could take 'em down into Apache Basin. Jude is planning on wiping it out tonight. Instead of twenty of us, there's three. You don't need to come unless you're willing, Baldy."

"The bigger the odds, the sweeter the fight, Poe. And I'm right worried about the Mona gal."

The three men rode down into Apache Basin. They headed for the Ellison place. Mile after mile they rode in silence. Sunset, dusk, then night came with a white moon climbing the sky.

Baldy gave a sharp exclamation. "Lookee yonder. Ain't that a fire?"

"It shore is," said Rusty.

"They've fired the Harker Ranch," said Poe grimly. "The ball is rolling, boys. Hell's popping tonight."

Standing in their stirrups, they rode at a long trot. No need for words. Rusty whistled tunelessly through set teeth. Now, from a distance, they could hear the sound of gunfire. Half an hour and Poe gave the signal to pull up. They were within five hundred yards of the Ellison Ranch. The night was filled with the rattle of gunfire. The ranch buildings were in darkness, save for the intermittent flashes of rifles poked through the improvised portholes between log walls.

"We can do more from here than if we tried to make the house. We'll split up. Each man for himself. Injun warfare, boys. Rusty, here is that slip of paper. Good luck, pardner. Good luck, Baldy. When daylight comes, we'll have to pull out, unless we're lucky enough to lick Jude's army. Baldy, you work in around toward the barn. I'll take the front of the house, while Rusty does his work around the back."

As Baldy moved away, Poe spoke to Rusty in a low tone.

"I'm afraid, Rusty, that our plans won't work out so bright as I thought. Not for me, anyhow. You'll understand what I mean when you see the name on that slip of paper. My men have quit me, as I knew they'd quit me someday. I'm a lone wolf now. But I've got a good stake saved, and, when this war is over, I'm pulling out for the Argentine. I'm going alone, most likely. I'll see you before I quit the country, though. But in case I don't, I left a letter for you with Margaret Harker. Open it when I'm gone."

He held out his hand. Rusty gripped it. Then they each faded into the night.

Rusty wormed his way on foot toward the rear of the ranch house. A dark form loomed up in front of him. The two almost collided. Rusty's carbine *thudded* against the man's head and the fellow dropped like a shot beef. The red-haired cowpuncher took the man's neckerchief and tied his hands behind his back. He ripped off a leg of the man's overalls and bound the unconscious man's ankles tightly. Then he stuffed part of the man's shirt in his mouth for a gag.

Number one, he told himself grimly.

He crept on, crouching low, his carbine ready. He halted. Voices ahead, there in the shadow of some brush. Rusty crouched low, listening. He recognized the voice of the man who had been drunk the night they had raided Bob's cabin and found him there.

133

". . . I tell you, Zeb, it's too raw fer me. I don't like it. Fightin' like we're doin' is not so bad, but, hell, the feller is knocked out. Stickin' a knife in him, layin' here like he is, knowin' nothin' about what's goin' on, that's too damned cold-blooded for me. What if he is Frank Harker? I ain't your man fer the job."

"Then gimme the knife, you lousy coward. I'll show you how to finish off a Harker like he. . . ."

"Yeah?"

Rusty leaped like a cougar as Zeb Quillan, a long-bladed hunting knife in his hand, bent over the unconscious form of a man lying on the ground. Rusty had dropped his carbine and was swinging a .45. The barrel of the heavy six-shooter caught Zeb's wrist with a force that smashed the bone, sending the knife spinning. Now the two were locked in a tight death grip. The gun in Zeb's other hand spat fire. Rusty's six-shooter crashed against the other's skull. Zeb went limp. Zeb's companion was shooting. Rusty's gun belched red flame and the man buckled up in a heap, his right shoulder smashed and a bullet in his leg.

Rusty picked up the unconscious Frank Harker and pulled him into the black shadows. Other men were coming that way now. Rusty sent them back to cover with a fusillade of shots. When his gun was empty, he began using Frank's six-shooter. Frank groaned and sat up dizzily. Rusty whispered hoarsely.

"Easy, Frank, old boy. Take 'er easy. Hurt bad?"

"That you, Rusty?"

"Nobody else but, old hoss thief. Load my gun while I scare off these sheepherders. Work fast, boy, we're in a tight."

Now they came at Rusty, five or six shadowy forms. Frank and the red-headed cowboy pumped lead at them. Three men went down, cursing and calling for help.

"Time we got outta this," gritted Rusty. "Rent's due. Time to move. Let's go."

Dodging, twisting through the brush, fighting, retreating, returning, Frank Harker and Rusty went side by side. Frank had a cut scalp that smeared his face with blood. Rusty's left ear had been nicked by a bullet. But wherever they went, Quillan's gunmen had a taste of their hot lead.

From all indications, Poe Parsons and the weazened Baldy were doing their share. Now, in the darkness out there, news was spreading through the ranks of the Quillan men. Word passed from mouth to mouth that Poe Parsons had brought down his wolves and those wolves were silently, efficiently slaughtering the sheepman's army. Poe Parsons, only a blacker shadow in the shadow of the brush, heard the rumor spread like a prairie fire down the ranks of Quillan's men. They were getting uneasy, on the verge of panic. Now Poe made his way around to where he hoped to find Rusty. He had no trouble locating the red-haired cowboy and Frank Harker. They had taken shelter behind a pile of cordwood and were doing effective gun work.

"Hi, Rusty!" he called softly, when there was a lull in the firing. "Hold your fire a minute."

"Come on, Poe."

Now Poe was with them. "We've got 'em scared spooky. Let's get our horses. Charge 'em. They'll scatter like sheep."

They gathered in Baldy, who had run out of cartridges and was attempting to stalk one of the enemy, rap him over the head, and replenish his supply of ammunition.

"Last 'un I knocked over was shootin' a danged .Thirty-Thirty. Mine's a .Thirty-Forty."

They went back to where they had left their horses. Frank managed to steal a Quillan horse. With a wild yell, they charged blindly, each from a different direction.

The trick worked. The Quillan men, badly demoralized, not knowing how many men were attacking, fled as fast as their horses would carry them. But two men stood their ground. Standing erect, ignoring the advantage of the brushy shadows, stood Jude Quillan, jerking the lever of his Winchester. He had come from a fruitless search for Poe Parsons up on the rim. Alone, deserted by his men, even by his son Luke, who had fled only to drop under Rusty's quick aim, Jude Quillan stood his ground. Fighting alone, snarling his hatred for his enemies, he stood on his long, widespread legs, throwing lead at the men who came toward him.

Poe and Baldy were riding together now. Poe recognized the lanky sheepman and gave a curt order to his companion.

"Git away, Baldy. *Pronto.* He's my man."

Poe leaped from his horse. His white-handled gun was in his hand. He walked slowly toward Jude Quillan, who had dropped his rifle and drawn his old .45. Poe kept coming on, slowly, there under the white moon, until but a scant thirty feet separated the two men. Neither man had raised his gun. Poe halted now.

"Ready, Jude?"

"I'm ready, you scoundrel!"

"Count to ten, Jude. At ten we open up."

Jude counted, slowly, in a rasping voice that was harsh with hatred for the man he faced.

". . . eight . . . nine . . . ten!"

Their guns roared. Both men were on their feet, thumbing the hammers of their six-shooters. Jude went down. He lay motionless. Poe Parsons, his smoking gun in his hand, walked steadily across the intervening space, to stand over Jude's dead body. Parsons shoved the white-handled gun into his holster. With steady hands he lit one of his gold-tipped Mexican cigarettes. As he cupped the match flame in his

hands, Rusty rode up. Poe, his face a little white and drawn-
looking, looked up at the red-haired cowboy.

"You can tear up that slip of paper now, Rusty. Here lays
your man. Better, much better, that I did the job, no . . . ? The
king is . . . dead."

"Gosh, Poe, you're hit. Your shirt is all blood! Man,
you're hurt bad."

Rusty was off his horse, but Poe Parsons motioned him
back.

"Couple of ribs nicked, perhaps. Nothing to get excited
about. I gave him his chance, but he must have been too
drunk to shoot straight. We'll go into the house and I'll get
taped up. Have a ride to make. Get somebody to carry
Jude inside. After all, the old hellion had guts, Rusty.
More guts than the rest of his pack combined. He deserves
a decent laying out."

Poe walked on to the house, Rusty at his side. Lights were
now being lit, although the shades were pulled down. Dad
Harker let them in. With a broken sob, Margaret was in
Rusty's arms. Ma Harker and one of the Ellison boys took
Poe under their care. Poe, by some miracle, had escaped
serious injury. But before Poe let them attend to him, he
helped two cowboys put Jude's dead body in a back room.
For perhaps five minutes Poe Parsons was alone with the
dead body of the man who had always hated him. Swiftly Poe
searched the dead man's pockets. Afterward, the thick roll of
yellow-backed bills that had been in Jude's chaps bulged in
Poe's pocket.

Back in the front room, Parsons told Rusty to bring in Zeb
and Luke Quillan, who were among the prisoners that the
cowboys had herded into the bunkhouse. Zeb and Luke, each
with a lump on his head made by Rusty's gun, were brought
in. Poe opened the door that led into the back room where lay

the dead Jude. Neither of the sons showed any visible signs of grief. Jude had been a hard father.

"The king is dead," Poe told the two brothers. "He was the only real man that wore the Quillan name. He won't be here to back your plays any more. And without him, your scurvy lives aren't worth a plugged dime. Apache Basin, in fact the Territory of Arizona, is too small to hold the three sons of Jude Quillan. You're selling out. Here's the money that buys all the Quillan holdings. You have one week in which to move out every sheep you own. Any wooly left in the basin after one week from today will be shot. The same medicine goes for the Quillan men. Dad Harker, you and Frank Ellison will draw up the bill of sale for the Quillans to sign." Poe turned to Ma Quillan with a quick smile. "Now, if you'll just stake me to a roll of tape and some bandages, I'll patch up those nicked ribs. Then I'll be on my way."

The Quillan brothers were glad enough to sell at any price. They knew full well that with their father dead their lives were in grave danger in Apache Basin. They feared the power of Poe Parsons.

Rusty helped bandage Poe's ribs. "Where you ridin', Poe?"

Poe Parsons smiled thinly. "Come with me and see, Rusty."

Something in Poe's tone and the expression on his face told the red-haired cowboy that Poe's ride was something of great importance.

"I'll be with you, Poe," he said quietly.

XIV

"The Last Ride"

The rustling of the leaves, men called it, that word of mouth passing of news. It had told Poe Parsons that Mona Quillan was at the cabin of Bob Harlan. That bit of news, carried by a Quillan spy, had been meant for the ears of Jude Quillan only. But Poe had intercepted the man there in the dark, had choked that bit of news out of him, then sent him, badly scared, with instructions to ride and keep riding till the Apache Basin was far behind him.

As Poe and Rusty rode toward Bob Harlan's place, Poe was wrapped in a black, brooding silence, a silence that Rusty had not the temerity to break. Poe also knew what Rusty did not guess, that Wes Quillan had been sent, with three men, to kill Bob Harlan.

It was mid-afternoon when they neared Bob Harlan's little ranch. Poe pulled up and Rusty followed suit. Poe spoke for the first time since they had left the Ellison Ranch. His face was drawn, grim-lipped, tight-jawed. His black eyes looked red in the sunlight. When he spoke, his voice was brittle, rasping.

"I go on alone from here. You stay here where you are."

There was no sign of life at the Harlan place. No smoke came from the chimney. No sound broke the stillness. The place seemed deserted. Something in Poe's manner chilled the blood of the red-headed cowboy. He nodded, without speaking. Poe's manner forbade questioning. He let Poe ride alone across the clearing to the closed door of Bob Harlan's cabin.

Now, even as Poe was swinging out of the saddle, there

sounded the *crack* of a rifle, then a puff of thin, white smoke from a patch of brush. The figure of a man crouched there. Rusty's carbine cracked, and the crouching man sprawled forward on his face. Rusty saw Poe cling for a moment to the horn of his saddle. Poe looked back across his shoulder and Rusty saw his white teeth bared in what might have been a smile.

Now the cabin door swung open and Poe walked inside. The door closed again. Rusty frowned, trying to puzzle out the situation. He quit his horse and made his way on foot to where the man he had shot lay motionless. His aim had been accurate. Wes Quillan lay on his side, shot through the heart.

No sound came from the cabin, and again that tomb-like stillness. Rusty, puzzled, uneasy, waited impatiently, watching the cabin.

Inside the cabin Poe Parsons faced Bob Harlan and Mona Quillan. Mona, fully clothed, was sitting on the edge of Bob's bunk. Bob Harlan had an ugly wound across his cheek, his eyes were bloodshot and hard, and his mouth a lipless slit. The floor of the cabin was littered with empty shells.

Poe ignored Bob. He stood there, his back against the door. There was a bullet hole in his white Stetson and from under the sweatband a trickle of blood was staining his cheek.

"The war in Apache Basin," he said in a toneless voice, "is over. Jude Quillan is dead. The bushwhacking Wes just departed from this life. Zeb and Luke have sold out and are quitting the country, and they will take their mother along with 'em."

Poe lit one of his gold-tipped Mexican cigarettes. His hands shook a little as he cupped the match aflame.

"You always cared a lot for Bob Harlan, Mona. But I never believed that you would come to him like this."

"Look here, Parsons," said Bob. "She. . . ."

"I'll talk to you later, Harlan. Right now, I'm talking to Mona. I'd prefer to be alone with her."

Bob looked at the girl. Mona nodded. Bob stepped outside and closed the door upon Poe and the woman he loved.

"You used to tell me that you cared for Bob Harlan, Mona. But I always thought you were just trying to make me jealous. I heard you were at his cabin. I came here to kill him."

"I knew you'd come," Mona said quietly. "I told Bob that you'd come. He's not afraid of you, Poe. If he had been afraid, he'd have killed you when you rode up. Bob Harlan is a man. A real man."

"He aims to marry you?"

"He asked me to marry him, yes."

"You'd be happy living on a ranch, cooking and washing and slaving?"

"I'd be happy anywhere, doing anything, with the man I loved."

Poe nodded. "When I heard you were here at Bob Harlan's cabin, I rode here to kill him. You are the only woman on earth, Mona, that I ever wanted. My love for you has been the one decent thing in my life. I'm leaving Apache Basin for good. I'm going to the Argentine where I already own a ranch. I'm camping on the rim tonight for the last time. Then I ride on, alone, to a new life in a new country. This is good bye for you and for me, Mona."

Poe walked over to where she sat. He was smiling a little.

"I told you, Mona, that Jude Quillan was dead. I killed him in a fair fight."

Mona nodded, dry-eyed, her face white, drawn with pain. "Yes. I knew that someday you would kill him unless he killed you."

She got to her feet.

They stood there, facing one another. Then, without a word, Poe Parsons turned quickly and walked to the door. He opened the door, passed outside, and closed the door behind him. Mona Quillan, trembling, swaying dizzily, caught the edge of the bunk for support. Now she was kneeling beside the bunk, her bloodless lips moving in prayer. It was a prayer of her own making, a prayer that came from the innermost heart of this girl whose whole world had been ripped into bloody shreds. As she prayed, she waited for the crash of shots that would mean another tragedy in her life that had been so drained of happiness.

Her seconds seemed eternity, but still there was no sound of gunfire. Now the door opened softly and Bob Harlan came into the cabin. As his hand touched her bowed head, Mona gave a stifled little cry.

"Bob," she cried in a husky whisper. "Oh, God! Where . . . where is Poe?"

"Poe has gone, Mona. Gone for keeps. I expected a gun-fight, but, instead, he shook hands and wished us happiness. He stopped for a few minutes to talk to Rusty, then he rode away. Rusty is at the barn."

"Poe shook hands with you, Bob?"

"And wished us happiness and good luck, honey."

With a broken sob, Mona crumpled in a pitiful little heap. She pushed Bob away and he knew that she wished to be alone. So he left her there in the cabin and joined Rusty at the stable.

There, squatted on their heels, the two cowpunchers talked.

"I'm gittin' married, Bob, soon as we kin locate a parson. Me and Margaret ain't gonna wait."

"We'll make 'er a double 'un, Rusty, if Mona is willin'. I'll put it up to her after we git Wes and them other skunks planted and things straightened out. I aimed to take Mona over to the Harker place where there's other wimmenfolks. She'll be needin' a woman's company."

"You sure you love her, Bob? Plumb sure?"

Bob Harlan whittled thoughtfully on a stick. "She's plumb alone, Rusty. She ain't got a soul in the world to turn to. I'll always be good to her an' give her all I kin to make her happy. I don't reckon it's in me to go plumb foolish over any woman. I'll be as happy with Mona as I'd be with any girl I know. But I can't make love like Poe Parsons or certain kind of red-headed gents that talks in their sleep about brown eyes and such. . . . Ouch, you sorrel-headed sheep thief! I'll shut up. But you shore oughta break yourse'f of that sleep talkin'."

"If we're goin' to git these dead 'uns planted, we better hop to it, Bob. I'll git the shovel."

"You're a-stayin' over tonight, Rusty."

"Yeah. Me 'n' you kin bed down in the barn. Come mornin', we'll take Mona to the Ellison ranch. The Harker place is burned down."

"Did you know who rode in for the doctor the time Wes shot me?"

"Mona?"

"Yep. Gosh, there's a shore game girl. She'll make a man a wife he kin be plenty proud of." Bob pulled a jug from some hay in the manger of an empty stall.

"Here's to the double weddin', Rusty."

"To the double weddin', Bob."

XV

"Nothing but Death . . ."

A round white moon rode the sky above the rim. By a small campfire, Poe Parsons sat, his head bandaged, a cold cigarette between his lips. His eyes, no longer hard, stared into the flickering blaze of the lonely campfire that was to be his last here on the rim. The hard, bitter lines were gone from his face. He was thinking of the girl he had left behind, the girl that he had given into the keeping of another man. That had taken more courage than Poe had known he possessed.

Now his quick, trained senses told him that someone was coming. He heard the *crunch* of rocks under shod hoofs. Poe's first instinct was to quit the firelight and hide in the shadows. Then he smiled crookedly and remained as he was. What difference did it make now, if some enemy took a pot shot at him? What had he left to fight for? He lit a fresh cigarette and did not even look up when the rider pulled up just beyond the rim of the firelight and dismounted. Now the rider was approaching on foot, but still Poe stared into the fire. He heard the *tinkle* of spurs.

"Poe!"

Poe Parsons was on his feet in an instant. There, across the campfire, smiling a little, stood Mona Quillan.

"Mona!" he cried huskily. "Why are you here?"

"I told you long ago, Poe, that if ever I made up my mind that I loved you, I would come up to the rim to you. I'm here, Poe. I'm going with you, wherever you go. Nothing but death will ever again separate us."

"But how about Bob Harlan?"

Mona smiled. "I didn't know my own mind, Poe, until I

144

knew that you had ridden out of my life forever. Then I knew that there could never be any other man but you in my life. I told Bob. He understands. Poe Parsons, are you going to stand there like a statue of dumbness?"

Poe leaped over the campfire. His arms were around the girl he loved. His lips found hers, and, although they were both tired and both suffering from bullet wounds, they sat, there by the fire, until dawn streaked the sky. They had a breakfast of bacon and biscuits and black coffee. Then they rode away from the rim, their stirrups touching, into a new dawn, into a new life that lay on the other side of the skyline.

Border Wolves

In 1909–1910 Walt Coburn attended Manzanita Hall Preparatory School in Palo Alto, California. His father believed a college education vital if Coburn was to be a successful cattleman. Coburn planned to attend Stanford, but his application was rejected. The reason, as Coburn would later recall, was that he "had lost the battle to John Barleycorn." It was not to be the last time he lost that battle. The Coburns at the time lived in San Diego while still operating the Circle C Ranch in Montana. Robert Coburn used to commute between Montana and California by train and he would take his youngest son Walt with him to Montana. When Walt got drunk one night, he had an argument with his father that led to his leaving the family. In the course of his wanderings he entered Mexico and for a brief period actually became an enlisted man in the so-called "Gringo Battalion" of Pancho Villa's army. Coburn's experiences in Mexico later served as background for a number of stories, including "Border Wolves" that first appeared in *Action Stories* (12/30). It was later reprinted as "Canyon of the Damned" in *Action Stories* (2/41).

I

"Hired to Kill"

The cattle, tallied by the two men who sat their horses on either side of the narrow cañon, numbered 517 head. They were stolen cattle that were being delivered by Add Ferguson to Mose Clark, who owned the Two Circle iron. Add and Mose were the two who now tallied these cattle, which had come out of old Mexico. When the last drags of the gaunt long-horned cows and steers had been hazed on by the unshaven, dust-powdered cowhands that drew top wages from Add Ferguson, Mose rode down to meet Add.

"Five seventeen, Add."

"That's right, Mose. Pay me ten thousand, three hundred and forty bucks."

"Some of that stuff ain't worth it, Add."

A hard glint crept into the puckered gray eyes of Add Ferguson. "Pay off for that many cattle at twenty dollars a head, Mose. You're gettin a bargain and you know it. It took us five weeks to make this gather. I lost two good men down yonder. I cut out the culls and I've givin' you a good herd. Stout cows and three-year-old steers. You'll keep your bargain with me, Mose."

"Of course, of course I will, Add." Mose Clark smiled uneasily under the cold scrutiny of the rustler's eyes. "I'm a-payin' the same as I always pay."

"And you bellyache the same as you always bellyache. Me and my boys take all the risk, we work twenty hours a day, and live on beans and jerky and black coffee. We eat dust and git shot at. And we turn over these cattle for a lousy twenty dollars a head. You'll double your money in six months. But you just can't help hollerin'. Pay off, Mose. We gotta be gittin' back. Got a deal on with a white man."

Mose Clark smiled knowingly. His eyes, pale blue, crafty, shifted cunningly, avoiding Add's gaze. Mose was rated as the smoothest dealer in stolen Mexican cattle that ever worked along the border. A short, thick-set man of perhaps fifty, smooth-shaven, bald, inoffensive-looking. He sat a horse awkwardly, for he feared horses and never felt at ease in a saddle. But he had foreseen a fortune in the handling of Mexican cattle and had, therefore, some fifteen years ago, sold out a fairly lucrative clothing establishment in Phoenix to go into the cattle business.

By untiring study and shrewd observing, he had gained a remarkable knowledge of the cattle business. He bought, fed, and sold cattle. He had pasture land in half a dozen states, did his own feeding, and marketed in Kansas City and San Francisco. No man knew the extent of his holdings or the amount of money he had made in his crooked dealings. He paid cash for the cattle he bought and was in the habit of traveling about the country with huge sums of money on his person. Usually he carried with him a bodyguard, but when he received cattle from Add Ferguson, he invariably came alone from his San Fernando ranch on the border. Mose, for some reason known only to him, liked to meet Add alone.

"So you got a deal on with a white man, Add." He chuckled softly. "Ain't I white?"

"I seen a guy with a funny red cap peddlin' rugs once in El Paso, Mose. He looked a lot like you. He was a foreigner of some kind."

Mose Clark smiled and took a thick roll of bills from his pocket. "Armenian, eh? But that ain't me, Add. Just like some think I'm a Jew. Let 'em think what they please, Add. I been called a lot of names, but callin' names buys nobody nothing. Some that has called me names has had bad luck, Add. Very bad luck. It is always bad luck for any man to call Mose Clark hard names. Count off the money, my friend, and you will find in that package of banknotes exactly ten thousand, three hundred and forty dollars. I had a man count them cattle early this morning and I had the money ready. They got to rise up early in the morning, Add, to get the best of Mose. And so you got a good deal on with a white man, Add? I'll beat his price."

Add Ferguson grinned thinly. "I seen that gent on a pinnacle when we trailed the cattle through the Sanchez cañon. He was gittin' a count on the cattle for you, was he? You shore enjoy your little jokes, don't you, Mose? Well, that's all right with me. You'll beat the price on the deal I'm makin' with my white man, will you?" Add Ferguson shoved the money in his overalls pocket and rolled a cigarette. His cold, gray eyes held a peculiar glint. "Sure about that, Mose?"

"Absolute, Add. I'll beat it ten percent."

"That ain't enough, Mose."

"Twenty-five percent, Add."

"Cash?"

"Always cash, Add. You know me."

Add Ferguson pulled a match head across the leg of his Levi's and lit his cigarette. Through the white smoke he grinned twistedly at Mose Clark.

"First, Mose, I'll tell you a little yarn. Night before last, when we held our herd in the dry wash near the Yaqui River, some gents tried to stampede the cattle. They had a little hard luck and one of them gents got captured. After I'd told him how I was goin' to take him out on the desert, gouge out his eyes, and leave him, he talked. He told me who hired him to stampede the cattle. Does that begin to make sense, Mose?"

Mose Clark shrugged his soft shoulders and smiled a little.

He was trying to hide the fact that he was badly frightened. "Go on, Add," he said, licking his dry lips with a thick, red tongue.

"Take your pencil and book and figure this out, Mose. Five hundred and seventeen head of cattle at ten dollars a head. That makes fifty-one hundred and seventy dollars, doesn't it?"

"What you drivin' at, Add?"

"Then add twenty-five percent to that and you've done made the deal. And you know damn' well what I'm drivin' at, too. You thought, by stampedin' and scatterin' them cattle night before last, I'd lose my herd and your own cowboys'd gather 'em. But I'd kinda expected somethin' of the sort. We plugged a couple of your boys and held the cattle. Yesterday I made a dicker with a man to sell him this bunch of cattle after I steal 'em back from you. You've got no bill of sale for these cattle, Mose. I got your money, though. And until the cattle are put into the Two Circle iron, you'd have a hot time provin' ownership. You kin take your choice of losin' the cattle or buyin' 'em again. Which way are you goin' to jump?"

"I'm payin' up, Add." Mose Clark's smile was a sickly grimace and his pale eyes, looking craftily from under colorless brows, showed the hatred and fear he had for Add Ferguson. "I ain't got the money on me. I'll make you out a check."

"And stop payment on the check. Think again, Mose. It looks like you're goin' to lose them cattle, shore."

"I swear I ain't got the money on me, Add. I brung only what I needed today, the same as always. But I'll meet you somewhere tomorrow night and have the cash. I swear it, Add."

"Figure out how much it amounts to, Mose. Be in the Cantina Madrid at midnight tomorrow with the money in a leather sack. Somebody will come to your table and say to you that the orchestra is going to play 'La Paloma' for you. You will hand over the money to whoever tells you that. And if I was you, Mose, I wouldn't try any double-crossin' game. You'll be covered."

"The Cantina Madrid at Los Gatos, at midnight tomorrow. I'll be there, Add."

"Fetch along that new bodyguard of yours if it'll make you feel safer. But no funny work, mind."

Without a word of farewell Add Ferguson turned and rode up on a high point. He waved his hat and in a few minutes he was joined by his men. They rode away together, headed south toward the border town of Los Gatos.

Mose Clark watched them ride away. He cursed them under his breath for some time, then a sly smile turned down one side of his thin-lipped mouth.

"The Cantina Madrid is it, Add? OK." He was chuckling. "Only I bet a ten spot you don't know Mose Clark is the feller that owns that joint. Mebby it will be that you won't win so much, after all."

He was still muttering and nodding his wide head when a tall man with dark, hawk-like features rode up. White teeth gleamed under a slim black mustache. His clothes were rather fancy for a common hand, and his outfit was silver-trimmed and with beautifully carved leather. This was Jim Teal, bodyguard and gunman for the owner of the Two Circle. Teal had come from down in Mexico with a letter to Mose Clark. His origin was shrouded in mystery. Until he had put in an appearance at Los Gatos in the employ of Mose Clark, no man had seen him before. But later it somehow leaked out that down in Mexico Jim Teal had the reputation of being a killer and a man of cold nerve. He had been mixed up in two or three revolutions, had been engaged in gun running and smuggling, and had been captured at Mazatlán and sentenced to be shot, but at the last minute his execution had been stayed and he was allowed to leave the country.

There were stories told that Jim Teal had, with his own gun, executed many Mexicans and some few Americans, that he had fought a dozen gun and knife duels, that he was a dead shot and handy with knife, and that he made love to every woman he met who happened to please his fancy. Now he smiled at Mose Clark, his opaque black eyes dancing.

"You look annoyed, chief. Did Add Ferguson give you a trimming on the cattle?"

"He did. Teal, we're goin' to be at the Cantina Madrid tomorrow night. Add Ferguson will be there. I want you to kill him."

Jim Teal pulled at his mustache and smiled. "The Cantina Madrid is in Los Gatos, on the Mexican side of town. And Mexico is a bad place for any man to kill another man. However, I'll do my best to please."

II

"Pueblo of Sudden Trouble"

Add Ferguson, about dusk of the evening that he was to keep his appointment with Mose Clark, rode alone down the main street of the little border town of Los Gatos. Across the street, dividing Mexico from the United States, was a high wire fence guarded, at the big gate for vehicles and the smaller gate for pedestrians, by Mexican and United States officers of the Customs and Immigration departments of both countries.

Add Ferguson was duly halted and passed through to the Mexican side of town. If they recognized him or suspected him of handling stolen cattle, they gave no sign. He rode boldly down the street. Near the edge of town he halted at an adobe dwelling that boasted a stable in the rear. He put his horse in the barn, unsaddling and feeding the animal cracked barley and hay. Then, unbuckling his chaps and removing his spurs, he went into the adobe house by way of the back door.

There were the sounds of a heavy bolt sliding and Add Ferguson's voice, talking to someone. He was talking in Spanish. Now another voice replied in a low tone, from the front part of the house. Then silence.

After some minutes, a match flared in Add's hand, and he lit a kerosene lamp that stood on the table in the kitchen. As if the lighting of the lamp were a signal, a tall, white-haired, white-mustached Mexican in brush-scarred jacket and trousers of leather, booted and spurred and belted, appeared in the doorway that led from the kitchen into the front part of the house.

"You are followed, *señor?*" asked the straight-backed, bold-featured old Mexican.

Add Ferguson grinned and replied in English. "As far as the gate at the border, anyhow, *Don* Miguel. Mose wants to make sure I'll keep a date I made with him for tonight at the Cantina Madrid." He took a money belt from around his waist where it had been buckled under his shirt.

"There it is, *Don* Miguel. Twenty dollars a head for your cattle. It's all there, to the last dollar."

"But *Señor* Add," said the older man gravely, "you should have taken out your commission."

The grin on Add Ferguson's bronzed face widened. "I'm collectin' mine tonight from Mose Clark. I'll tell you about it while I shave off this brush on my face and wash off a few pounds of dust. I'm playin' a little joke on Mose. You'll shore appreciate it. And don't look so danged solemn, my friend.

Ain't it better to bleed money from the dirty little crook than it is to shoot him?"

"You do not understand, *señor,* what is here." *Don* Miguel touched his left breast above his heart. "Someday I shall. . . ."

"Someday, shore thing. But not yet. We have to sell him some more cattle before you slip him his ticket to hell. Anybody bin snoopin' around?"

"Nobody that one could suspect. But one never knows what beggar on the street, what goat herder, what wood hauler may be watching. One cannot ever be free from danger. It is not for myself that I fear, but for María. Always, when she leaves here to go to the *cantina,* I fear for her. María is too beautiful to be working there at the Cantina Madrid. *¡Válgame Dios!* . . . working for that toad! Sometimes it is more than I can bear without going loco. María, my own María, working for Mose Clark! That toad of a man whose fat hands are fouled with the filth of this border traffic in whiskey and drugs and Chinese and white slaves. To know that María, whose blood is of the finest in all of Mexico, is playing her guitar and singing her songs to the drunken *gringos* who think evil of a girl in her position."

"You are not the only one, *Don* Miguel, that hates to see María working there in the Cantina Madrid, even if she is always under the guard of our friends. She's safe enough, so far as that goes. And Mose learned at the start that he was to keep his hands off her. There's never a minute when one of my men is not there to watch out for her. She's plumb safe. It ain't that part of it that makes me want to take her out of there. It's havin' those soused tourists lookin' at her like they do. Well, it won't be much longer. Where is Panchito?"

"He went with María to the *cantina.* He will be back soon."

"I'll need a fresh horse. Tell him to bring in that big line-backed dun called 'Dobe. And there is a note he's to take to the waiter they call Pelón. Here it is. And in my saddle pocket is a little present for Panchito. It's some silk shirts. The pinkest silk shirts I could buy in Tucson. Now I'll take a bath and shave, and, when you've sent Panchito on his errands, I'll tell you the joke on Mose Clark. Keep your eyes peeled for any visitors, though I reckon the boys at the line will hold up that cuss that followed me. They're always watching for that."

Add Ferguson left the kitchen. There was the sound of a shower running and Add's voice humming as he scrubbed under the hot water. He had finished shaving and was dressed in clean clothes when *Don* Miguel came into the bedroom to tell him that his son, Panchito, had gone to bring in the dun horse and deliver the note to the waiter known at the Cantina Madrid as Pelón.

Bathed shaved, dressed in a gray flannel suit and white shirt, a well-chosen necktie, a pair of polished boots of soft tan kangaroo, Add Ferguson bore little resemblance to the bearded, overalled, dust-caked cowpuncher who had delivered the bunch of cattle to Mose Clark. He rolled a cigarette and briefly related his argument with Mose.

"He'll most likely fetch along this gunman of his, this Jim Teal. But I don't look for Teal to start anything. Pelón gets the sack of money. I'll be nearby. At the table next to the one where Mose and Teal will sit, there'll be some of my men. And they'll make it known to Mister Teal that he'd better keep his gun in the scabbard. Nothin' at all rough, *sabe?* All very quiet and polite."

"The toad will have his men there, also," said *Don* Miguel, shaking his head. "Those men who run his gambling tables, his waiters, his bartenders. Your plan is a dangerous one, my friend. I fear for its success."

"With a gun covering him, Mose will be mighty slow to give any fancy orders. He's all *coyote*, that gent."

"But, all the same, it will be dangerous!"

Add Ferguson shoved a heavy automatic in the holster under his left armpit. Then he slid a single-action .45 into the waistband of his well-tailored gray trousers. He buttoned his coat and picked up a white Stetson from the bed.

"I reckon I'm all set for a pleasant evenin' in town. It'll be good to hear María sing again. I'll be meetin' you, *Don* Miguel, at the Rancho de Mañana three nights from tonight and we'll throw a *fiesta*. Good luck to you."

"And luck to you, my good friend. I shall be relieved to see you safe at the rancho. *Adiós*."

III

"Juggled Guns"

The soft strumming of a guitar. A smoke-filled *cantina*. The babble of voices, subdued, then fading into silence as the voice of María Teresa Dominguez began to sing.

Mose Clark and Teal, the latter with his back to the wall always, sat with their drinks on the table before them. At the next table sat three cowpunchers who seemed to be having a good time without being noisy while, at another nearby table there sat several Mexicans who wore the uniform of the border patrol service. Under the searching gaze of the Mexicans, Teal felt uncomfortable, and, whenever he looked at the three cowpunchers, he found them looking at him. It was fifteen minutes until midnight.

"I don't see any sign of Add Ferguson," said Teal. "He's got a case of cold feet, maybe."

Mose Clark mopped a moist forehead with a purple handkerchief. His shirt collar was wilted and his suit of white linen was wrinkled. "It ain't likely Add Ferguson has cold feet, Teal. He's got nerve and he goes anywhere he wants to go. Hah! Look, there by the bar. Talking to that Mexican cop. The tall feller in the gray suit. That's him, all dressed up like he does when he's in town. Get ready for him, Teal. He's comin' this way. Get ready, Teal. For God's sake, don't miss."

"Don't be a fool, Mose. I can't kill him like that. Not with the Mexican patrol men and those three cowpunchers watching me so close. This smells to me like a grand set-up."

"Ya ain't gettin' scared, Teal?"

"Scared?" Teal's lips parted in a snarl. "Scared, did you say, Clark?" Then he sat back, smiling a little, while the anger that had found voice a moment ago still glittered in his black eyes. "No, Mose, I'm not scared. Neither am I so damned foolish as to shoot Add Ferguson here and now. I'll take my own time and pick my own place. If he comes over here to the table asking for a fight, you may be sure he'll get it without having to wait long. But anybody can see the folly of killing Add Ferguson in cold blood. Let me handle my job, Mose."

"Here he comes," whispered Mose Clark, gulping his drink of whiskey and pouring out another.

Add Ferguson was taking his time. He seemed to be listening to the singing of María, whose dark eyes followed his tall, broad-shouldered figure. Now Add paused at the table where the Mexican patrol officers sat. He shook hands with them and talked to them in their own tongue. Then he nodded and moved away from their table and toward an empty chair at Mose's table.

As he walked toward the empty chair, there came one of those incidents that can be both annoying and amusing in a

Mexican town on the border. An American tourist, tall, tanned, blond-haired, with an infectious grin, dressed in white flannels that showed the stamp of the finest tailoring, staggered drunkenly between Add Ferguson and the empty chair. With a wobbly salute, he dropped into the chair.

"I'm sorry, gentlemen," he said with intoxicated gravity to Mose and the scowling Teal, "but I jus' cou'n' walk 'nother dam' step. Been shakin' the ol' dogs, trippin' the light fantastic, doin' all the steps from tap dancin' an' dreamy waltz to the *fandango* an' the Highland fling. An' when I get through buyin' an' drinkin' 'nother drink, jus' to show you gentlemen I'm no ord'nary dancer, I'll do a sailor's hornpipe, an Irish jig, or a hula dance. Take your choice. I'm buyin' a bo'l'. Bo'l' of champagne. Waiter's somewhere behin' me with the wine. Wine's paid for. He'll have plenty glasses. Good ol' bo'l' in bucket of ice. And I'll jus' buy you gentlemen a wee drink. I'm on a champagne diet. Doctor's orders."

He grinned and offered cigarettes from a case of hammered silver. Now came a waiter with the wine. The man in white flannels made a gesture that included Mose and Teal. They looked annoyed.

"Do your act, waiter. Three glasses of wine for three gentlemen." He leaned across the table confidentially. "Recall the li'l' ruckus we had, jus' a few years ago, with Germany? Well, I came back from the li'l' argument with an appetite for good wine an' one lung. Damn' fool doctor tells me I got six months to live, but I gotta live 'n Arizona. And now here's the sad part of it. Ol' Uncle Tobias up an' dies, leavin' me more jack than ten men could spend. So here I am. The six months is gone and forgotten. On this day an' date, 'cordin' to the calendar I keep, markin' off the days, I'm three years, two months, five days an' . . ."—he consulted a wrist watch—"ten and one half hours overdue in the handiest cemetery. Joke on the doc. Pardon. My name is O'Brine. Patrick O'Brine. Call me Pat. Rank sergeant, machine-gun company. Ninety-First Division. And if this wasn't a public place an' if my modesty didn't forbid, I'd show you gentlemen the marks of exactly thirteen scars. A heine machine-gun nest an' we're . . . but hell, the war's over. No sense in boring folks. I butted in here an' I owe you men an apology. If I get on your nerves, gimme the good ol' gate." He lifted his filled glass. Mose and Teal did likewise.

Behind the genial drunk in the white flannels stood Add Ferguson. Add's eyes never left the group.

The waiter, a bald-headed Mexican in waiter's tuxedo, was at Mose Clark's elbow. "The orchestra," he said in a low, clear-toned voice, "is to play 'La Paloma' for you, *Señor* Clark."

Mose gave a nervous jerk that spilled wine across his shirt front. Teal's right hand was under the table. Add Ferguson gripped the automatic under his left armpit. The tanned, lean-featured face of the drunken Pat O'Brine seemed to have lost its drunken mask. His eyes, blue under quirked brows, mocked Teal. His lips hardly moved when he spoke and his voice had lost its thickness.

"You will notice, gentlemen, that my right hand is on the table under the napkin. In that hand is a gat that I packed through some hot spots durin' the war. It is coverin' the dark-complexioned gentleman who sits next to me. Teal, I believe, is the name. You will be so kind as to put both hands on the table, Brother Teal. And the gentleman who just spilled his wine will be so good as to compose himself and give the waiter a sack made of glove leather. . . . Thank you, gentlemen."

Teal's hands were now on the table. Mose, his face a putty color, handed the bald-headed waiter the bulging sack.

159

"I'll take the sack, Pelón," said the man in white flannels, and under the napkin something moved. The waiter handed over the sack.

"Now," said O'Brine, "you two gentlemen may be excused. Use the front door when you go out. Teal, unless you want to be laid out with a lily in your hand, don't make any gun play. You and your fat friend get across the border as quick as you can. And keep your traps shut. I'm tipping you off for your own good. Gentlemen, you're free to depart."

Grudgingly Teal and Mose Clark left the table and walked out of the *cantina*. Add Ferguson took the chair that Teal had vacated.

O'Brine flipped away the napkin. His hand held no weapon. His forefinger pointed at Add Ferguson; he grinned waggishly. Cocking his thumb, he lowered it quickly, pistol fashion.

"Bang!" He grinned. "You're dead. If Pelón will bring a glass for you, we'll try out this wine, buddy."

"Would you mind tellin' a man who you are and how you got in on this game?" asked Add Ferguson, staring at O'Brine in a puzzled manner.

"Not at all," said the man in flannels, as Pelón filled a glass for Add Ferguson. "My name is Boris Zarnowski. I'm a Russian prince and served in the French Foreign Legion. I lost an eye at Ypres and my nose was partly taken away at Soissons. Only that there are ladies in the joint, I'd show you the marks of exactly fifteen scars made by exploding shrapnel. Call me Borrie. Rank buck private in the rear rank, French Foreign Legion. Let's drink this up, then I'll go into my dance or a song or tell a Scotch story in Yiddish dialect. *¡Salud!*"

"You talk like a man with the d. t. s," said Add Ferguson, and his smile was a little grim, "but you act plenty smart. I hate to remind you about it, but you're nursin' a leather sack that belongs to me."

The blond man in flannels grinned widely. "For a second, I was afraid the Teal gent might pull the trigger on me. And me without so much as a squirt gun. Speaking of artillery, I'd be awfully obliged for the loan of a gun right now, if you happen to be heeled with any odd weapons. There's several guys in this place that would love to mow me down and I'd like to go out with something besides a glass of bum wine in my hand. As for this sack full of *dinero*, I'd like to put the bee on you for whatever the amount is that said sack holds. My remittance is overdue and I'm strapped. I'll pay the debt in three days."

Add Ferguson looked at the man with narrowed eyes. "You ain't full of some kind of hop, are you, mister?"

"Snowed to the roots of my hair, buddy," said the fellow wisely. "I use cocaine, morphine, opium, and on Sundays and holidays I go after hashheesh and marijuana. I'm the greatest dope along the border."

"You're a damned liar," said Add calmly. "You never used dope in your life."

"Wrong, buddy. I take an aspirin tablet every morning for an eye-opener. I formed that bad habit in Hong Kong."

"Supposin' we talk sense for a minute?"

"Check."

"Teal was about to put a bullet in my belly. You pulled as slick a bluff as ever I saw worked. I'm obliged."

"One of Mose Clark's men had come up behind you. He had a gun in his hand. See that mirror on the wall? Well, I was watching the game in the mirror. They had you in a hot spot, buddy, and I don't mean maybe. That's why I had to throw a monkey wrench into the works."

"But how come you bought chips in the game?"

For the fraction of a second the blue eyes of the man were

cold as old ice. Then he smiled. "Just a little secret, Ferguson. A personal matter. You don't mind my being secretive, I hope?" He tossed the leather sack across the table. "There's your money, old man. All I ask of you is the loan of a gun. Glad to have met you and I wish you luck."

"Hold on a minute, pardner," said Add Ferguson. "No need to get huffy. If you need money, I'll do the best I can. And I'll stake you to a gun if you want one. You did me a favor. I'll do you one."

"I'll be frank with you, Ferguson. I was after that sack of money. Just now I need five thousand dollars about as bad as ever a man needed six-bits. So I figured I'd highjack it from Mose Clark or from you. I'd overheard a conversation between Mose Clark and his man, Teal. And I happened to get hold of a note you wrote Pelón. Simple enough, when the cards are turned face up. But instead of getting the jack before Mose and his gunman get in the place, which I might easily have done, I let my sense of the dramatic get the better of my cupidity, as it were. I wanted to stage a little act. Well, so I did. And I lose the money. If I had been heeled, the story might have had another ending. But the only gun I own is in hock. The bartender has it. The money I got for it bought this bottle of wine, which is too warm and of new vintage. Ferguson, I'm not a beggar. I . . . . hell, let's not get maudlin. If you think I've done you a favor, I'd have the crust to borrow a gun. Beyond that, I won't impose upon the good nature of a stranger."

The man's grin was gone. In the blue eyes that suddenly seemed to grow old, there was written tragedy and grief. The lean brown hand that held the glass of wine now tightened, snapping the slender glass stem. The glass cut the man's hand and he smiled crookedly at the thread of blood that was paled by the spilled wine.

"Quit that!" Add's voice was a quick growl. "Damn you, snap out of that!"

"Pardon, Ferguson." Now the man forced a smile.

Add shoved the bag of money back across the table. What he had read in the eyes of the blue-eyed stranger had made the border cowboy know that he sat with a man who was in desperate straits.

"We'll leave here together," Add told him in a low tone. "The money is yours if you want it. How long have you bin drunk?"

"Since the day the Armistice was signed. Three years, roughly speaking." He reached for the bottle of whiskey Mose and Teal had left. Add let him fill a wine glass and drain it of the raw whiskey. "Sorry, Ferguson. I'm . . . just a bit shaky. Be all right in a minute when this hooch hits my toes. Damned stupid of me to make a mess of everything, but that's a habit of mine."

"Shut up," snapped Add. "I don't know what's on your mind and I don't give a damn. Ever ride a horse?"

"Rather."

"Well, you'll be ridin' one tonight. You're goin' with me on a long ride. For some fool reason, I like you. I'm takin' you along with me. And nobody is goin' to bother us when we leave here. In case they do, here's a Forty-Five that'll shoot whenever you pull the trigger. Shove it under your coat. Now let's go."

"Ferguson, that's decent of you."

"Shut up!"

"Thanks. But before we shove off, call Pelón. I want him to give this money to somebody reliable who will see that it gets into the hands of Mose Clark!"

IV

"Where Powder Trails Split"

A white moon hung over the Mexican hills. Add Ferguson and his odd companion, both in overalls and flannel shirts and chaps, rode along a twisting trail that would eventually take them to the Rancho de Mañana. Now and then Add watched the other man from the corner of his eye. It was not the nature of Add Ferguson to ask questions. He had not even showed surprise when the man said he wanted that money to go back to Mose Clark. Nor had he, by so much as a flicker of an eyelid, betrayed surprise when the man gave Pelón certain instructions regarding the five thousand dollars that were to be paid to Mose.

"Get that amount into the hands of Mose Clark," the man had told Pelón in perfect Spanish. "Five thousand dollars. Take the balance of the money and buy for yourself a haircut or a new knife. Then, when you have gone from Los Gatos, that remains no longer a healthy climate for you, due to certain loyalty you have shown a friend, proceed to San Diego, California. Wait there until money comes into a bank we both know. Reimburse the *Señor* Addison Ferguson, by a cashier's check, for the exact amount in this sack that holds a certain amount of money. You will do that for me, Pelón. And you will stand ready to be again called upon. And should anything happen to me, there is a paper in the San Diego bank that will take care of everything. *Adiós,* my friend."

Then he had turned to Add Ferguson with a twisted grin on his lips. "I am now ready for the horseback ride you promised. And as I view the situation, I don't think we'll be bothered on our way out. The men that were waiting to kill me

164

have gone. Let's go, buddy."

"Now," said Add, when they had gone some ten miles in silence, "if it ain't goin' to draw too hard on your powers of imagination, how do you and me figure?"

"That's a fair question, Ferguson, and deserves a fair answer. But I'm sorry to say that I can't, at this moment, offer the sort of reply that would materially aid either of us. I can't, without lying, tell you who I am or why I'm in Mexico with a hide full of assorted likker. What's the use in lying when you wouldn't believe me, anyhow? Just call me Abdul Labullbull Labeer. I'm a colonel in the Turkish army taking a rest after the battle of Constantinople and am here getting one of these snappy divorces. A blanket divorce covering all the dames in my harem. I lost both ears at the Dardanelles and all my teeth were blown out when I bit into a dynamite cap some Russian slipped in my coffee." He grinned and pulled a bottle. "Drink?"

"I reckon not. I never punish it much."

"I'll take one for each of us, then. Would you mind my asking where we're bound for and the nature of the business. I'm with you in almost any kind of a racket, but if you'll give me some sort of a rough idea of the number of men to be killed and beautiful ladies to be kidnapped and how many American millionaires to be held for ransom, I'd rather be prepared, as it were. And how am I to tell friend from enemy when the shooting starts?"

Add Ferguson grinned. "We're headed for the Rancho de Mañana to pick up a bunch of cattle. We cross those cattle into the United States without botherin' to pay any duty. We sell those cattle to Mose Clark or some other cowman at a mighty low figure."

"Wet cattle, Ferguson?"

"Wet cattle, mister. Just that. Or so they're called along

the Río Grande. Here, where we cross our stuff, it's mountains and desert instead of a river to cross."

"We'll be stealing these cattle, Ferguson?"

"Some folks would call it stealin', I reckon."

"Ever have much trouble crossing the border?"

Add Ferguson gave his interrogator a swift, sidelong glance. "Sometimes, yes. Mostly we slip across without bein' seen."

"It must be a rough country where you can cross a bunch of cattle without being seen."

"Plenty rough."

"Must be a good spot for smugglers to slip back and forth."

"Plenty good. Any more questions you'd like to ask, mister?"

"Pardon, Ferguson. I didn't mean to be putting you on the witness stand. Whiskey loosens my tongue."

"Yeah?"

They rode on in silence for quite a distance. Add Ferguson was beginning to distrust his odd companion. The man asked too many questions and answered no questions at all. Plainly the man was drunk; yet he kept his every faculty. His brain was clear as a bell; he moved with the easy co-ordination of muscles that belongs to a trained athlete. Yet he was drunk and had probably been drunk for a long time. While Add Ferguson did not trust the man, he could not help liking him. He kept wondering why the man had told Pelón to give the five thousand dollars to Mose Clark.

"You've acted mighty queer, mister, plumb from the start," said Add, pulling his horse to a halt. "Before we go any farther, I'll have to know more about you. Otherwise, our trails split right here an' now."

"I understand, Ferguson. No hard feelings, either. You

think I might be almost anything from an international spy to a cheap crook. I put the bee on you for a nice pile of jack. I act like I was playing hooky from a padded cell. And then I ask a lot of questions. And the hell of it is, buddy, I can't give you the kind of an answer you want. I've got a reason for being down here. To tell that reason to any man might mean failure for me. It might mean. . . . Look out, Ferguson!"

The automatic that had somehow appeared in the man's hand rattled a staccato bark. Somewhere behind Add Ferguson a man's startled yelp ended in a death rattle. Now Add and the man with him were off their horses, shooting at other men that seemed to surround them. Add's companion was whistling tunelessly through his teeth as he continued firing.

Add Ferguson was making every shot count. When the flash of a gun betrayed the location of an enemy, Add sent several shots into that region, then shifted his own position, dodging, crawling, shooting.

Then a lull came. A man's voice challenged Add.

"The gent with you kin go, Ferguson. It's you we want. Tell the man with you to drag it fer the border and ride like he was doin' a Paul Revere."

"The man with Add Ferguson," called the drawling voice of that odd gentleman of parts, "needs no interpreter! Whoever you are, get this. I'm with Add Ferguson. When you get him, you get us both. And while you short sports are getting a meal, Add and I will be grabbing off a mouthful here and there. What kind of a lousy rat do you think I am, neighbor?"

The automatic in his lean brown hands *cracked* twice. There was a groan from the brush patch where their challenger had laid hidden.

"I bet he's got a bellyache, pardner," gritted Add. "That was nice shootin'."

"More fun than I've had since the Argonne push. How's

the chances to borrow some more cartridges, buddy? Do you know the name of the party who stopped my last effort in the way of lead throwing?"

"Name is Dunlap. Hop smuggler and gunrunner."

"So I thought. I'd heard his voice before." He crawled closer to Add Ferguson. "Be back shortly. Lost my bottle back there when we quit our horses."

Add Ferguson nodded. "I reckon you know what you're doin'." He saw the man wriggle away, not in the direction of the trail, but toward where the wounded Dunlap lay moaning in the brush.

A minute or two, perhaps five minutes, passed. Add Ferguson kept shifting his position. Now, from the brush, a startled cry suddenly choked into silence.

It must have been fifteen minutes later when Add's queer partner rejoined him.

"Dunlap is dead," he whispered to Add. "He deserved hanging or a slow death, that baby. I got his cartridges and an extra six-shooter off him, anyhow. And almost a full quart of rye. Drink?"

"Don't mind if I do. How come you didn't take the gent's boots or maybe his Levi's?"

The man chuckled softly. "Didn't happen to need 'em. I got a swell pair of cavalry boots once, on the Belgian front. German aviator. Drink hearty, buddy."

"Looks to me like they're sneakin' off on us."

"Dunlap's finish took the scrap out of 'em. We can go almost any time now. This is where our trails split, I believe."

"Not unless you want it thataway," said Add. "You kin trail with me and you kin ask all the fool questions you like. You had a chance to pull out and quit me, but you stuck. You're a mighty regular gent."

"Thanks, Ferguson. But figure this out. Dunlap wanted

me just as badly as he wanted you, or more so. If I'd stepped into the saddle, I'd have been shot out of it damn' quick. No, I'm not so much of a steadfast buddy as you think. I had a selfish motive."

"Maybe so, but I reckon you'd've stuck, just the same. The bet is still open. Want to come with me?"

"More than you know, Ferguson. Yonder ride the brave bushwhackers. They're calling it a day."

Some minutes later Add Ferguson and his companion were again in the saddle.

"What does a man call you when he needs a handle for you?" asked Add.

"A long time ago the kids at home called me Skeeter."

"Skeeter it is, then." Add grinned and reached for his tobacco and papers. "You wouldn't think I was bustin' any rules of polite manners, would you, Skeeter, if I was to tell you that you got a hole in your off arm? It's kinda bleedin'."

Skeeter grinned twistedly. "Dunlap had a knife on him. I used his neck scarf to make a tourniquet. It'll stop bleeding soon."

"Sure you got it tied tight?"

"Positive, Add. I studied for three and a half years at Johns Hopkins. Later at McGill in Canada. A year in a base hospital in France. Yes, I think I have the scratch well tied up. Drink?"

V

"Land of Song and Clashing Steel"

Dust. The bawling of cattle. Mexican *vaqueros* riding silver-mounted saddles and handling fifty-foot rawhide reatas. A branding fire. The pungent odor of burning hair. Leather and steel and silver and silk of gay color. A brassy sun in a cloudless sky of turquoise. A song that sometimes broke through the bawling of the cattle being held on a bald mesa. Dust and sweat and the heat of the fire that heated a dozen branding irons. Now and then the careless swearing of a cowboy from north of the border. Add Ferguson and *Don* Miguel doing the roping, heeling calves with a deft ease that might easily trick a tenderfoot into thinking that calf heeling is not an art.

Teams of flankers, Mexican and American, sweaty and grimed with the dust, stretching out the calves. A Mexican *vaquero* with a blood-spattered knife doing the earmarking. A short, bowlegged Arizona cowboy handling the branding irons, stamping the Mexican brand of *Don* Miguel on each calf. An old Mexican in scarred leather and a huge felt sombrero keeping tally.

"Hot iron here, Skeeter!" barked the Arizona cowboy. "Rattle your dew claws. *Don* Mike is three calves ahead of Add."

"Add wasted three loops a-tryin' to snare the hind laigs of that big 'un."

"*Don* Mike's gonna lose afore the last calf gits looped," prophesied a lanky cowboy whose sweat-streaked shirt hung over his waistband. "Got a ten spot that says Add ketches more calves than *Don* Mike."

"An I call thees bet, Sleem!" said one of *Don* Miguel's flankers.

"Hot iron, Skeeter!" bawled the cowboy who was stamping a brand on a spotted calf.

Skeeter, soaked with sweat that stung his eyes and streaked lines through the yellow dust that powdered his face, came trotting with a branding iron that was cherry red. He was utterly tired, terribly thirsty, his heels were blistered, his muscles aching. But he grinned gamely as he took the cooling iron from the brander and shoved the handle of the fresh iron into the hands of the bowlegged cowboy.

Skeeter put fresh sticks on the fire. A thermometer would have told him that it was over a hundred in the shade, had there been any shade. He was tending fire and handing the hot branding irons to the bowlegged cowboy. His stomach felt like a bowknot, tied hard and fast. His tongue was thick and dry. His eyes were bloodshot from the heat and dust. But through the grime of his face there showed that infectious grin that no amount of punishment could erase.

He had come to the Rancho de Mañana with Add Ferguson. Add had told him that there were some cattle to be gathered down there. Stolen cattle, so Skeeter had surmised. Instead, they were branding calves belonging to cows that wore the iron of *Don* Miguel.

"Hot iron, Skeeter!"

So they labored, through a dusty day, changing horses, gulping tortillas and beans and *carne* spiced with chili peppers. When, at sundown, the white-haired, white-bearded old Mexican who kept the tally book added up his figures, Add Ferguson had beaten *Don* Miguel by ten calves.

"Ten years ago," said Add, "it would've bin a shore different story. *Don* Miguel is old enough to be my father. He is the best roper I've ever seen, bar none."

Dusty, tired, hungry, thirsty, they rode together back to the Rancho de Mañana. The cattle had been turned loose. The rodeo was over.

At the rancho there waited a bath and a razor and clean clothes. Music and wine. The moonlight would shed its mellow glow on a patio with walls of washed blue. There would be the call of a parrot, the barking of a dog, giving challenge to the coyote that sang its song to the stars that would spot the night sky. There would be dancing, there on the tiles of the patio, tiles worn into hollows by the feet of countless men and women. Sandals, bare feet, high-heeled boots of the finest leather, slippers from Spain. *Padres,* Indians, *vaqueros,* the most beautiful women had come there and gone. Those walls of that ancient patio had heard the echo of songs and sobbing, of laughter and the moaning of a man in his last moment on earth. The strumming of guitars. The rattle of rifle bolts as men stood with proudly held heads and a straight back against adobe walls to face the rifles of a firing squad.

Lovers had sat on those benches under the olive trees. The bloodstained steel of *caballeros* had caught the white light of the moon that would, tonight, light that patio. Brown-robed Franciscans had tolled their beads within those four walls. What could a *gringo* know of the suffering, the laughter, the songs and the shedding of blood of Mexico? What could Skeeter know of these people who, when he rode to the great gate of that walled patio, bade him get off his horse and come in.

"Enter your house, *señor*," *Don* Miguel had told him in that soft, deep, grief-mellowed voice that one finds only down there in the Mexico that has been pillaged and robbed and ravaged. *Don* Miguel had swept off his dusty sombrero in a gesture that no man can find north of that country of laughter and music and bloodshed and sorrow.

That night there was a barbecue. Afterward, the music and the dancing. The *fiesta* would last for another day and night. Tomorrow there would be roping and riding and horse racing and other sports. Then Add Ferguson and his men would begin their long drive with the cattle that they had gathered. Cattle already under loose herd of the *vaqueros* hired by *Don* Miguel. Stolen cattle? *¿Quién sabe?* Who but *Don* Miguel and Add Ferguson could know?

Skeeter shared the room occupied by Add Ferguson. Much to the surprise of the former, there was laid out on his bed his own clothes that he had left at the hotel in Los Gatos. Add grinned at him.

"Thought you might be needin' clean clothes, so I had one of the boys put your bags in the buckboard that was comin' down. You take the first bath. Man, I bet you sweat a gallon of booze out of your hide today there at the brandin'. Feel sick at all?"

Skeeter looked at his reflection in the mirror. With a three days' stubble of beard, dust-caked, sweat-streaked, in a cotton shirt and denim jumper and overalls, he looked like a scarecrow. His hands were blistered and grimy.

"My own mother would disown me if she saw. . . ." Suddenly the man broke off his words and turned abruptly away from the mirror. Again Add Ferguson saw that tragic, haunted, hopeless light in the blue eyes of the man who asked to be called Skeeter. Some bitter, terrible memory had hit Skeeter between the eyes. Add pretended not to notice.

"There's Scotch and ice, Skeeter. You haven't had a drink for more than six hours. Take a hooker of that whiskey. You need it."

"Think I do, Add?"

"You're shakin' like a leaf in the wind. You can't cut 'er off too sudden. Have at it, pardner, and I'll join you."

"Look here, Add, you and these Mexican people have treated me like I was a real guy. It's damned decent of. . . ."

"Take a drink, bonehead, and then step into that box stall there beyond the serape. A *mozo* is waiting with some buckets of water that he'll stand off and throw on you while you get busy with the soap and the scrubbin' brush. Not exactly the Waldorf for bath fixtures, but it gets the dirt off. Here's lookin' at you, Skeeter." He slapped Skeeter between the shoulders, pretended not to notice the man's shaky hand or the eager gulping of the raw whiskey.

Now, as Add began undressing, he sang a Mexican song that had a gay, swashbuckling lilt to it. Skeeter listened, puzzled. Add's soft baritone voice had depth and tone.

The grimness had slipped away from the cowpuncher and he was like a boy let out of school as he pulled off shirt and undershirt. It was hard to believe that this easy, grinning cowpuncher was known as the toughest, hardest-riding, fastest-fighting rustler on the Mexican border. Add Ferguson, handler of wet cattle, yet he was welcome here among the Mexican people. It didn't make sense.

Skeeter stepped through the doorway into the improvised shower. An Indian *mozo* threw buckets of cold water on him. Soap. A rough scrubbing brush. Bucket after bucket of water sloshed on his tingling body. Then a quick rub-down, a shave, and clean clothes.

Next Add Ferguson was getting his shower. Add talked with the *mozo*, asking about his squaw and his many children, naming them in the order of their ages. Add had brought gifts, nonsensical trinkets for each of them. The Indian was trying to thank him. Now there came a noise of confusion from the shower room and a moment later the *mozo*, deluged, trying to pry a goat-hide bucket from his head, staggered into the room.

Behind him came Add, laughing heartily. He pulled the goat-hide bucket off the Indian's head and eyed the fellow sternly.

"The next time you try to thank me for something, I will tie on that bucket for keeps. Skeeter, this man comes from a mighty old race of people. He and I have explored some mighty odd places. And once, when I was stripped and staked out on an ant hill, this man risked his life to save mine. The four men that staked me out are buried not far from that ant hill. And he tries to thank me for a few cheap toys! Someday, my Juan, I'll get rough. And when you're done sputtering, my Juan, and, when the water is out of your eyes, there's a package there on the chair for you and the missus. For her, some bolts of cloth she likes. For you, my *amigo,* a gold watch and chain that the man at the store says will keep time in any kind of weather. And if you open that mouth to thank me, I'll cut out your tongue."

Add Ferguson finished his rub-down and nodded his approval of Skeeter. "I bet there'll be more than one *señorita* makin' eyes at you, feller, before the evenin' is over. There's a big *baile* . . . a dance, tonight." He knotted a red tie. "I heard you talk to Pelón in good Spanish, so I reckon you'll git along. Ever bin among these people much?"

"Only in a couple of border towns and one trip to Mexico City. But I get you, Add. I'm a guest here. And outside of that, old man, I like to believe that I know how to act like a gentleman."

"So I figured, Skeeter, or I'd never've brought you to the home of *Don* Miguel. And, anyhow, the *Señorita* María Teresa Dominguez has already told me that you are a real gentleman. María plays the guitar and sings at the Cantina Madrid. A few evenings ago, so she tells me, you gave a drunken *gringo* tourist a sweet licking when he got fresh. For which I'm obliged, pardner.

"Someday, when things come around right, and the *Señor Dios* is willing, María and I will be married here in this old *hacienda* that has stood for two hundred years. *Don* Miguel is to me like my own father."

Skeeter held out a lean, tanned hand. "May I offer congratulations, Add?"

"Thanks, pardner. María is here tonight. It's no longer

175

safe for her to stay in Los Gatos. She worked there in the Cantina Madrid for a certain purpose. Mose Clark didn't know who she was or why she was there. Until the night you and I met there. Some stool pigeon had told him."

Skeeter lit a cigarette. "Add, you're making it hard for me to keep some secrets. It was I who told Pelón to get word to the lady that Mose Clark knew she was the daughter of *Don* Miguel Dominguez."

"So I figured." Add Ferguson looked squarely into the eyes of the other man. "That's another reason you're welcome here, Skeeter."

"Mind if I take another drink, Add?"

"Have at it, Skeeter. It's the only medicine that'll help you."

"That second night out of Los Gatos, Add, I went to pieces. I had a great case of d.t.s. You took care of me. Perhaps I talked. I'm rather a damned fool, I suppose, in your estimation. I can't recall what I said or what I did. But I remember giving you a letter that I took away from Dunlap. The man was only slightly wounded, Add. Dunlap needed killing and I killed him with my bare hands. He had a letter that I wanted. The letter that I gave to you when I thought I was dying."

Add Ferguson reached into an empty boot. "Here you are, Skeeter. I kept the letter in my boot."

Skeeter took the sealed letter in his hands. There was a queer look in his eyes when he looked at the unbroken seal of a letter that bore no name or address.

"You didn't open it, Add."

"The letter wasn't mine to open, if you get what I mean."

"Here it is. Open it. Then you'll know the sort of a lousy rat I am. You'll know. . . ."

Add Ferguson tossed the letter back onto the table.

"You're talkin' like a fool, Skeeter. I don't want to look at the letter. And hang onto your bushy tail, Skeeter. You're all right, but you don't know it. And we'll cut down on the drinks for a few hours. There's a barbecue beef in the pit. Music and grub and real folks to talk to. Take that letter an' burn it or swaller it whole. Skeeter, you got a lot to learn, down here in Mexico."

VI

"Shades of Pancho Villa"

It was the second evening of the *fiesta*. A starlit sky and the music of a Mexican orchestra. Black velvet, scarlet silk, silver. The yapping of coyotes. The distant bawling of cattle. Music and laughter and goblets filled with red wine. Inside the adobe walls of the old *hacienda,* there were the muttered gossiping of the *mozos* who brought food and wine and whose hearts were softened by the small comfort they gleaned from the gay pleasures of the *don* they served.

Out beyond the *hacienda* men rode with carbines across their saddles. Beyond the whitewashed adobe walls of the Rancho de Mañana lay danger, perhaps death. Perhaps, before dawn, one of those serapes that now covered the shoulders of a *vaquero* against the chill of the night, would be stained with blood. *¿Quién sabe?* Who knows?

Don Miguel, a glass of cold wine in his hand, spoke, and his words spelled out the songs and the sobs of Mexico. "And so it is, my children, that perhaps we drink tonight, and tomorrow we fill the grave, no?"

Even as he spoke, there came a low, muttering, rumbling sound, the pounding of hoofs that, to the men who handle cattle, spells a dread word: Stampede! *¡Válgame Dios!* God help the men who are caught in that whirlpool of tossing horns. May the *Señor Dios* ride with the luckless *vaquero!* May fate find mercy for the cowboy whose horse steps into a hole! May the god that cares for the cowpuncher give him luck tonight. Because the cattle of Mexico are wild, their horns are sharp, their flinty, cloven hoofs like the rip of a dull knife. The man or horse that is caught there is doomed. Stampede.

Guitars wailed a discord. There was the hoarse, fear-riven cry of a man, a woman's stifled scream, and then sounds of men rushing toward the stables. Some of those men would never come back. Some of those horses would never again see sunrise on a green pasture.

Add Ferguson was the first man to swing a leg across a saddle.

"Let's go. Hell's a-poppin'! Come on!"

Fifty men were in the saddle in five minutes, serapes and slickers swinging to slap back the steers, guns to spew flame into the fear-crazed eyes of a stampeding herd of outlaw steers, horses and men thrown into a conflict that is between cowboy and steer. On the fringes of that wild stampede were men who held guns loaded to kill, bushwhackers, outlaws, ripping the night apart with gunfire.

The thunder of pounding hoofs. The crack of pistol shots. Songs blotted into silence when death rides down the singer, because it is the song of a cowboy that wipes out the fear in the heart of a stampede. A song, the slap of a slicker, the crack of a gun. But the song must wait. There is the other work to be done. The leaders of that herd have to be swung back. May God ride behind the saddle of a man that rides in the night to swing back the leaders of a stampede!

The long horns crashed like thunder as the steers raced on. The ground underneath was quivering as if in the throes of an earthquake. There was the slanting light of a moon that threw the scene into an unearthly light. Steers from behind were running down one another in mad fright, steers that had been brought from the far spots of a wild range, steers that had never known the feel of a rope since the day, some years back, when a man burned a brand on their hides when they followed their mammy.

There came the heart-splitting squeal of a gored horse, the gritted prayer or curse of a cowboy going to his death under that smothering, tromping, lancing blanket of hoofs. Shredded slickers were slapping into the red-shot eyes of fear-crazed steers. Pistol shots. Hoarse voices yelling. A milling, deafening chaos. The thread of a song. Death riding behind the drags. Tomorrow's sunset would bless the graves of the men fated to go down.

The moon that shines over the cow country had shed its white light on the broken, blood-spattered body of many a man and many a horse that had a stout heart. For neither man nor horse who follows the longhorn through drought and northers and fear-drenched nights knows how to quit the game without courage. Singing, cursing, perhaps praying. Who knows what thoughts grip the heart and brain of a man who dies?

Now they rode, those men from the Rancho de Mañana, swinging the leaders of that stampeding herd of long-horned cattle. Some rode to death, others into the dawn of another day on this earth. Slowly, slowly, the leaders swung back. Stubborn, with an insane stubbornness born of fear, the cattle gave away to the riders. It would be hours until they slowed to a milling, bawling, sullen herd.

Add Ferguson, riding a played-out horse, looked at the dawn through eyes that were bloodshot, dust-reddened slits. His mouth was dry, but he sang his song to the milling cattle.

Ti yippy yi yay, git along little dogies. . . .

Out of the gray dawn rode a man. Add grinned crookedly.

"Howdy, cowboy," he croaked hoarsely. "Good work."

"Thanks, Add. Did my best," replied Skeeter. "Got any more shells that will fit my gat?"

"Two, three. I said, howdy, *cowboy*. Get me?"

"I hope, buddy, that you're not flattering me."

"Here's your shells, pardner. You made a good hand. I watched you once or twice. This ain't your first stampede. You'd better pull out for the ranch now. These cattle need some singin' to and there's no need of all the men stayin' out here. I'm sendin' back every second man. Half of us stay here. The other half kin relieve us about seven o'clock this mornin'."

"Add, somebody stampeded the cattle on purpose."

"Dunlap's men, or Mose Clark's outfit. We lost three or four men, all told. I found three of their renegades. Skeeter, you stayed with us in good shape. You look plumb tuckered out, so you better go on back to the ranch. *Don* Miguel is there by now. He'll take care of you right."

"I'll be seeing you later, then, Add."

Neither man had made mention of the blood stains on Skeeter's cream-colored silk shirt, where the tight bandage had slipped from the wounded arm. Neither man spoke of the huddled form of a dead man within a stone's throw of where the two men sat their horses. Skeeter rode away, headed for the rancho.

Add Ferguson waited until the man had gone, then he rode to where the dead man lay, and dismounted. He searched the dead man's pockets thoroughly.

"Somebody," he mused in a muttered tone, "has beat me to it. The same as every other dead man that went West last night. And unless I'm plumb stupid, the man that done the searchin' was none other than the Skeeter gent. Now what in hell is his game, anyhow? Who is he and why is he here? And why does he stay drunk? And where did he learn to punch cows? And where did he ever meet Pelón so that Pelón quits me to carry out his orders? Yeah, and a dozen more questions along the same line. That gent is not so dumb, no, sir. And the game he's playin' is about as safe as slappin' a mountain lion in the face. But whatever else he is, he's a game gent."

Add hailed a cowpuncher who came riding around the milling cattle. "Get some of the boys and plant this dead feller, before the buzzards get here. Come on an' take a look at him."

The cowpuncher swung out of his saddle. He looked at Add with a queer sort of smile.

"It's one of Mose Clark's men. A gent called Hurley. Red Hurley. Used to tend bar in Juárez, when Dunlap worked there. They was *muy amigos*. Hurley had a rep as a dope peddler."

Add Ferguson nodded. "I think the Skeeter feller killed him. And then he frisks Hurley's pockets. This Skeeter proposition may be a souse, but he's as wise as a fox. Pass that along to the boys and tell 'em to keep their traps shut. We don't know this Skeeter and we ain't in any shape to make a mistake. I'm driftin' back to the border today. Nobody but you boys and *Don* Miguel will know where I'm goin'. I want this Skeeter gent kept down here, even if you have to hog-tie 'im."

Add licked the brown paper that was rolled around some natural leaf tobacco. "Nothin' rough, *sabe?* This Skeeter is a great guy and he's bin right with me. But he ain't here for his health and he ain't here for pleasure. He's tangled up with Mose Clark an' Teal and before I'm many days older I aim to find out the connection between 'em. I want Skeeter kept here."

"It ain't any of my put-in, Add," said the cowboy, "but if you're goin' into a tight spot with Teal, I'd be proud to go along. I knowed that jasper in Montana."

"Say that over, cowboy. Montana?"

"Up in the Musselshell country when he was stealin' horses with Long Henry."

"Teal? Hell, man, he's a Mexico product."

"So he claims. Add, that hawk-beaked cuss was never any fu'ther in Mexico than mebbyso Cananea. He never saw fu'ther into Sonora or Chihuahua than a man kin see with a good pair of field glasses."

"What do you mean, Joe?"

"I mean that Teal comes from the old Cherokee Strip country. He's a Cherokee quarter-breed that was run out of the Nations by his own people fer bein' mixed up in the killin' of men that trusted him up there. He shot his daddy-in-law and even his kinfolks is ag'in' him. He's a yaller-backed coyote. He'll shoot a man in the back, but never in a fair fight. His name ain't Teal. He stole that name from a man that was killed at Torreón. Add, this killer Mose Clark has hired at top wages is. . . ."

Skeeter suddenly appeared out of the brush. He had a bottle in his hand and he was smiling broadly. On foot, he came up to Add Ferguson and the cowboy.

"Drink?" He held up the bottle. "Sorry to startle you boys, but my horse got away from me when I stepped off to shoot a rattlesnake. I came back here on foot and. . . ."

"And listened in on what we was talkin' about," finished Add Ferguson. "I hope you got an earful."

"I don't think," said Skeeter, his voice brittle now, "that I'd say that if I were you. Hell, man, if I had wanted to listen,

I'd have stayed quiet. I came back to get the horse that belongs to this dead man. I was left afoot and couldn't quite see myself hiking the miles between here and *Don* Miguel's ranch. If I overheard any of your conversation, then I am sorry. Drink?"

"No. And keep to the brush. These damn' cattle are snuffy and will start another run if they see a man afoot. There's the dead gent's horse. Fork it and head for the ranch."

Skeeter mounted the horse and rode away. Add Ferguson scowled after him.

"He heard what we was sayin', Add. He must've bin hid there in the brush."

"He turned his horse loose and crawled back through them catclaw thickets." Add nodded. "He listened to what we had to say. I dunno if it got him anywheres, though. We didn't say anything much. You was tellin' me about Teal."

"Yeah. Yeah, I was tellin' you about Teal, Add. About Jim Teal. Teal was with Pancho Villa when I was a machine-gunner for Villa. The real Jim Teal was killed at Torreón."

"Yeah?"

"Yeah."

Add Ferguson grinned crookedly. "What was your name when you was a machine-gunner for Pancho Villa?"

The cowboy shifted his weight to one stirrup. There was a dangerous look in his bloodshot eyes.

"Add, you got no right to ask me that question. I ain't givin' you any answer. Does a man have to show his damn' birth certificate to work wet cattle in this man's country?"

"You told me your name was Tom Dunn," said Add, "when you hired out to me at Nogales. Personally I don't give a hoot what your name is, providin' you ever had one. But when a man works for me, I want to know which way he's goin' to jump."

"I bin with you three years, Add. Ever see any snake tracks where I've made trail?"

"No," admitted Add thoughtfully. "No. Can't say as I have, Tom. But I. . . . Never mind. Let 'er go as she lays. Take care of this dead man."

Add Ferguson rode on, leaving the cowpuncher there.

Tom Dunn stared after Add, a worried look in his eyes. He saw Add spur his horse to a lope, and watched the horse and rider out of sight. Then he rode into a narrow barranca. There Skeeter squatted beside his horse, an unlighted cigarette between his fingers.

"Long time no see you, pard'."

"A long time, Tom Dunn. Step off and have a drink. Add has pulled out for the ranch?"

"He started for there, but that don't mean much. Add Ferguson has a habit of changin' his mind. He never lets any man know what his plans are, for certain. Gosh, you've changed, Captain."

Skeeter nodded. "Yes. Ten years since we met, Dunn, and ten years puts age on a man. Been with Add Ferguson long?"

"Three years, Captain."

"Never mind that captain stuff. I'm called Skeeter down here. Three years with Add, eh? Then you might be able to tell me how he happens to be in with old *Don* Miguel?"

"I might be able to tell you a lot about Add Ferguson if I was that kind of a skunk. I work fer Add and draw good pay. I ain't squealin' on any man that I work for."

"You always had plenty of guts, Dunn. I recall the jail at Nacozari when we were to be shot at sunrise. I knocked the sentry on the skull and got us both out. I saved your life, didn't I, Dunn?"

"And so you think that's why I should double-cross Add?

What kind of a bum do you think I am? And if you're layin' me out that kind of a proposition, then I'll say you've changed. Changed to beat hell!"

"Supposin' this gat I have in my hand should go off. It would hit you square in the belly."

"Then why don't you pull the trigger?" sneered Tom Dunn.

"I always figured a man could trust you, Tom." Skeeter holstered his gun with a grin. "I just wanted to make sure you hadn't changed these ten years. I'm not asking you to squeal on Add Ferguson, any more than I want Add to know who and what I was ten years ago. I wanted to make sure you hadn't told Add who I was."

"I didn't tell him. I don't aim to tell him. But if you and him lock horns, it'll put me in a tight spot. I'm obliged to you both."

"I hope nothing like that happens, Tom. I like the man a lot."

"He's shore a prince. He's got a heart as big as a Mexican hat, but I'd hate to have him hatin' me. Add Ferguson is one fightin' son-of-a-gun and I don't mean perhaps. I'd shore hate to see you and him do battle."

"I hope we never do," said Skeeter earnestly, "but a man can never tell what tomorrow or tonight may bring, down in this country, playing the racket Add is playing."

"And the racket that you play ain't any safer than his."

"Right you are, Dunn. Drink?"

Tom Dunn reached for the bottle. As he did so, Skeeter brought the bottle down across the cowpuncher's head. Then he caught the man's limp form in his arms and laid it on the ground. Swiftly Skeeter went through the pockets of the unconscious man. He paid particular attention to some dates and figures in a tally book, jotted down the same dates and figures in his own tally book, then smiled grimly into the stunned man's face.

"Sorry, Dunn, old comrade, but it just had to be done. I heard Add Ferguson tell you to hog-tie me and keep me at the ranch. You'll wake up with a headache, but it's all in a day's work. Until our trails cross once more, my comrade, *adiós*." Skeeter stepped into his saddle. He eyed the bottle he had proffered as a libation, then used as a club. The bottle was cracked.

"Losing my technique, I am," he muttered. "I damn' near broke this crock. And it's as good likker as one finds in Mexico. Pony, you and I have an appointment to keep in Los Gatos. Let's hit a trot."

VII

"Split Loot"

"Teal," Mose Clark told his gunman, "why don't you trade that fancy gun off for somethin' you can get some use out of?"

"That'll be about all from you," snarled Teal. "How was I to know that the fellow was playing drunk? What could I do with him coverin' us with that gun he had hid under the napkin? It was Add Ferguson I was watching. I paid no attention to the drunk till he made that smooth play. Don't make the mistake, Mose, of trying to rub it in. I'm in a bad mood."

Mose Clark spread his thick hands in an expressive gesture. "And what kind of a temper do you think I'm in, Teal? Look what it cost me in good money! You, it ain't cost you a dime. It's Mose Clark that paid the check."

"Well, you can afford to lose six-bits once in a while. You

make plenty. I saw you collect five thousand cash off that Mexican cop. What kind of a gag was that, anyhow?"

"Some of my personal business, Teal. But somewhere there was a fast deal put across. If you are as smart as you claim to be, you find out how that cop got the money I give him a receipt for. Because, listen. That money I had for Add Ferguson was marked, understand. I marked it careful so that only with a magnifying glass could anybody, even with the eye of an iggle, see it."

"The eye of a what?" Teal smiled thinly.

"The eye of an iggle. The American iggle."

"Eagle." Teal grinned. "Yes, yes, go on, Mose. You've got me all excited."

"Listen, Teal, do I pay you to make bum jokes, or do I pay you to carry around a fancy gun you never use except to catch with it the eye of the dames? There is times, Teal, when you give me pains in the stomach."

"That's a mutual ailment, Mose. What about this marked money you had in the sack?"

"Five thousand smackers of it comes back to me on a little deal where this Mexican cop is the go-between. Now how does this cop get that money that I was robbed of in my own joint when a guy I pay a fancy salary to is sitting there like a dummy? I ask you?"

"It's worth good money just to put up with your squawk, Mose. Someday I'll lose my temper and poke holes in your fat paunch. Who was paying you this five thousand, and why? You want me to work out crossword puzzles, but you don't give me anything to work with. Who was paying you this protection money? The cop was just a contact man for somebody. What was the deal?"

"You like to know a lot, Teal. It was a business deal."

"Then I'll tell you what you won't tell me, Mose," said

Teal easily. "The five thousand was the price paid to you for a woman. You had a very quiet little auction the other night in the back room of the Cantina Madrid. A select little party you were giving for a very select number of guests. There was a girl they call María who plays the guitar and sings. She's a beauty and an accomplished musician. She'd make money for any of the select guests who run dives in various border towns. I was told to stand outside the door and not let anybody in to your so-called banquet. The reason you wanted to sell this girl was that you had found out she was the daughter of a *Don* Miguel Dominguez, who is an enemy of yours. She was working for you in order to find out things that might be valuable to her father. It was your idea of a sweet revenge to sell her to the highest bidder among the men who make a business of dealing in beautiful women. You have your own way of delivering a girl to the man who buys. And she was sold for five thousand dollars to a pockmarked bird who was acting for some Mexicali or Tía Juana joint. He agreed to pay you the money the night we met Add Ferguson at the *cantina*. He told you that he'd handle the business of kidnapping her while she and her younger brother were on the way home from the *cantina* after work. But here is something you can't figure out. Where did your pockmarked purchaser pull off his kidnapping? The girl has gone. The buyer has gone. The cops have no news of any kidnapping. You get paid off by a cop and give him a paper in your own handwriting describing this dame like you'd describe some horse. A bill of sale. And you're fool enough to give it to the cop. And he pays you in marked money that was stolen from you by the Add Ferguson outfit. Is that it?"

"You are a smarter fellow than I thought, Teal. That was the transaction. Now gimme the answer about how did that Mexican cop get money that was took off me in my own joint by them burglars, and I'll make it right by you, Teal."

"The answer to that will cost you some real change, Mose. No lousy chicken feed, but real yellow money."

"A hundred smackers, Teal." Mose beamed. "A hundred simoleons, no less. I'm a good sport, always, a piker never."

"It'll cost you five grand and you're getting off cheap at that."

"Five grand? Five thousand dollars? Now I know the kind of a bum you are. You draw big wages and to date you ain't ever dirtied that fancy gun. Five grand? There is something wrong with your head, Teal."

"How would you like to do a twenty-year stretch in the big house, Mose? How much would it be worth to you to save taking that rap?"

"What do you mean, Teal?"

"I mean that, if you were smart, you'd try to get along with me. You've made a sucker out of yourself, that's all. When you gave that bill of sale to that cop, you just simply wrote out your own ticket to the pen. They can hook you in Mexico or across the border. Mose, whoever told you that you were smart?"

Mose Clark's face had taken on a sort of greenish pallor. If Teal knew about that deal, then how many more knew? Why had he ever been such a fool as to sign that paper, anyhow? The pockmarked man, agent for a man higher up, had the girl and the bill of sale. But what was Teal driving at? That pockmarked man wasn't going to make trouble. It had been a fair deal.

"Teal, don't you be runnin' no bluffs on me," blustered Mose. "I ain't payin' no blackmail to no loafers. I got the notion to fire you."

"Then get that notion out of your head," said Teal grimly. "And no more of your damned back talk, either. Either pay me five thousand cash or else cut me in, fifty-fifty, on your racket. It so happens, Mose, that I have that bill of sale. The pockmarked gent who got it from the cop met with an accident. He was, by the way, figuring on using that paper to take you for a nice pile of jack. I believe the word is blackmail. You played into his hands. But he had an accident. Something in the nature of a blunt instrument rapped him across the head as he was stepping into a dark alley. Incidentally he lost the bill of sale. By the same token, it happened to come into my possession. Yes, Mose, I think we can work now on a basis of understanding."

Teal and Mose Clark were in a back room of the Cantina Madrid. As Teal finished speaking, Mose sat limply in his chair, his flabby face a mottled, putty mask of despair. Teal's white teeth were bared in a nasty smile and his black eyes mocked the other man. Mose Clark was badly frightened. He poured himself a stiff drink and downed it.

"I've always wanted to get into some good-paying business, Mose," Teal taunted him, "like this business of yours. I always hated the cattle business except that it gave me opportunities to steal a little. But there is no money in cattle stealing and the risk is great. Now, the way you play your game, you are safe, unless you make a mistake like you did when you wrote out that bill of sale for the beautiful young lady. That's why you need somebody smart as a partner. I can handle the cattle we get from Add Ferguson. I can be there in the hills when your men run their hop and booze across. I'll oversee the job of smuggling your Chinamen over. That leaves you free to sit back and enjoy life. I'll run the risks, do the active overseeing, and take my fifty percent of the net proceeds. I make us both some real money and you have time to live the life of a real gent. What could be fairer?"

"You got me into a tight spot, Teal. I'll have to stand it.

Partners it is, then." Mose forced a weak smile and held out a flabby hand. "Gimme the paper, Teal."

"When the contract of partnership is drawn up, Mose, then you get the bill of sale for the lady. Go get an attorney to draw up the contract. I'll wait here while you bring him."

"Damn you, Teal!" Mose was on his feet, his heavy body shaking with desperate fury. "You robber, you thief, you low-life blackmailer! Damn you!"

Teal slid to his feet with an easy movement. His hands, lean and powerful, gripped Mose by the throat. When he had Mose choked down to his knees, gasping, pale eyes protruding, terror twisting his mottled face, a brisk rap came at the door.

Teal flung Mose into a chair and shoved a glass of whiskey into the flabby hand. Then, his black eyes glinting, he unlocked the door and opened it. A Mexican waiter with a tray, glasses, and a shaker full of cocktails stood there.

"Your drinks, *señores*."

"We ordered no drinks," snapped Teal, his eyes alight with sudden suspicion.

"At six o'clock every evening the *Señor* Clark has cocktails," said the waiter, a tall Mexican with a ragged scar across one cheek. "It is now that hour, *Señor* Teal."

"Who told you my name? Damned if I remember ever seeing you before."

"Perhaps not, *señor*, but everyone knows the bodyguard of *Señor* Clark. I am taking the place of my cousin who is sick tonight."

Mose Clark had swallowed his whiskey and was gingerly fingering his bruised throat. Now he got to his feet and brushed past Teal.

"We'll drink at the bar. Take the cocktails out there."

The waiter smiled. "*Si, señor.*" He stood back from the

door to let Teal pass, but Teal, scowling blackly, motioned curtly.

"I'll follow you. Get going."

Teal, scowling at the tall, wide-shouldered, slim-waisted waiter, was wondering where he had seen that scarred face before, and he was wondering how much the fellow had overheard. How long had he been standing outside the locked door, listening?

VIII

"Mose Clark Pays Off"

In the barroom Mose leaned gratefully against the bar and glared with injured, defiant, frightened yet desperate eyes at Teal, who was now in an ugly humor. That damned waiter worried Teal. As his narrowed black eyes searched the room, he saw men there that he knew worked for Mose Clark below the border. They were at the bar, dusty and smelling of horse sweat. One of them had his arm bandaged and in a sling, while another limped painfully.

A broad, red-whiskered cowpuncher now edged to Mose Clark's side. Mose looked at him inquiringly.

"Bad luck, Mose," said the whiskered cowpuncher in a low tone. "Dunlap got his. We lost three more men last night when we stampeded the Dominguez herd. Ferguson's men and them *vaqueros* of *Don* Miguel's was too many for us. They was havin' a *fiesta* at the ranch and there must've bin a hundred of 'em. We never had a chance."

"You say Dunlap is croaked?" muttered Mose.

"He got his when we jumped Add Ferguson an' another gent. Only for this man, we'd've got Add all right. The boys has got a bellyful of Mexico. They won't go down there no more, Mose. And we need some cash. We're thirsty and hungry and two boys need a doctor. They shot hell out of us."

"What did you do to them?" asked Teal, a thin sneer on his tight-lipped mouth.

The red-whiskered man started, scowling hard at Teal. "Who in hell are you and where do you get the call to sneak up and listen when I'm talkin' to my boss?"

Teal's sneer became a twisted line of contempt.

"Teal's my new partner," said Mose.

"That bein' the case," said the red-whiskered man, his hand on his gun, "make my time out in full, Mose. I'm kinda fussy about who I work for. Your name is Teal, is it? Well, it wasn't Teal the last time I saw you. You sure it's Teal now?"

"Pay him off, Mose," said Teal. "We don't need him any more. When he's sober, I'll take care of him."

"So his name is Teal now, is it, Mose? Is he any kin to Jim Teal?" asked the red-whiskered cowpuncher, speaking to Mose, but never taking his eyes off the hawk-featured gunman.

"He is Jim Teal, Red."

"He is," said Red, laughing coarsely, "like hell! If he was Jim Teal, he wouldn't be standin' there without some kind of a gun in his hand. I knowed Jim Teal before he was killed at Torreón. This new partner you drawed, Mose, is a damned liar."

Red's voice, raised in a rough, uneven growl, had stilled the voices around him. Men looked curiously at them.

Now Teal, lurching into Mose, using Mose's heavy body as a shield, jerked his silver-mounted gun. A roar. Crimson flame belching. Red's heavy form pitched drunkenly against the bar. Teal's second shot ripped into the big cowpuncher. Red went down in a huddled lump, his gun in his hand.

Half a dozen Mexican police and border patrol officers took a hand. The dusty, half-drunken cowpunchers who had been with Red were under the cover of Mexican guns. Teal, with a twisted sneer, offered his smoking weapon to a Mexican officer.

"My partner, Mose Clark, will tell you that I shot in self-defense. The man was drunk and forced me into shooting him. The bartender will tell you the same thing. This red-complexioned fool would have killed Mose Clark and myself. Is that right, Mose?"

"Yes." Mose licked his dry lips. "Yes. Teal is right. Red was makin' fight talk and was goin' to kill Teal. Teal is . . . is my fifty-fifty partner in the business. I'll stand good for him."

"We take him to the jail just the same, *Señor* Clark. He has killed a man and there must be the proper things done in the way of the arrest. It is the law."

Teal shrugged. "Get busy, Mose. I'm not sleeping in any jail. Get busy and spring me."

Under Teal's narrowed stare, Mose nodded. Teal had him where he wanted him. Too bad Red had not killed Teal. What was it Red had been saying about . . . ?

"Get busy, Mose," gritted Teal. He lifted his drink and smiled crookedly at the Mexican officers who were around him.

"*¡Salud!*" He smiled, and drank. "And now we march to the jail."

When Teal had been led away, when the dead body of Red had been removed, Mose took three big drinks to steady his shaking nerves. He had been mighty near death a few minutes ago. Now the other cowpunchers, talking in low tones, approached Mose, who stood between two big, rather stupid-looking Mexican policemen.

"Pay us off, Mose," said one of the cowpunchers, acting as

the spokesman for the rest. "Us boys know when we got aplenty."

Mose nodded. His pudgy hands shook as he counted their wages over from a thick roll of bills, after consulting his note-book that kept the time of his men. He was just finishing the payoff when Add Ferguson came into the Casino Madrid.

IX

"Sprung Trap"

Add Ferguson walked up to Mose Clark and, ignoring the scowling cowpunchers, spoke directly to Mose. "Get rid of these men, Mose. I want to have a medicine talk with you. You kin bring Teal along if you're scared."

"Ain't you heard Teal is in jail?" asked Mose. "I'm just payin' off these cowboys."

Add's eyes looked over the renegade crowd that was quit-ting Mose. It was a shifty-eyed, ugly-looking lot. Add smiled contemptuously at them.

"You boys had bad luck lately, no? Well, try again, when-ever you feel lucky. Or are you leaving Mose for keeps?"

"They're leavin' me, I'll say," said Mose grimly. He paid off the last man. "And I don't want it that they be stickin' around this place of mine no longer. Already that Red feller got killed. Such stuff gives the joint a bad name. Them cops is watchin' you fellers, so you better move along."

"You and Teal murdered Red," growled one of them. "It was murder and all framed. Lemme tell you somethin', Mose, you won't pick up another bunch of cowboys like us."

"I hope not," snapped Mose testily. "Not once did you give me nothin' but the wrong end of the stick. Always excuses. You ain't made me a dime. Now move along or I call over them cops that sits there drinkin' beer that the house buys. What with taxes and free drinks and now a killing in here that has got to be squared up, where can I make money off a joint like this? Get out."

Sullenly the cowboys left. Add grinned at Mose, who was still shaking with fright from his recent narrow escape.

"Have a drink with me, Add. I tell you, but it was a close call I had and I don't want no more such narrow ones. What'll it be, Add?"

"Beer. Have the drinks sent into a back room. What I got to say to you I don't want the whole cock-eyed world to know."

"Back rooms is bad luck, Add, but I'll risk it. You ain't goin' to hurt an old man that ain't no fist fighter nor either a gun shooter?"

"I ain't hurtin' you, Mose."

Gratitude showed in the pale eyes of the older man. "I'd buy wine, Add. The best in the house ain't none too good. We've had our little arguments, Add, but you're not like that Teal. You ain't pushin' holes in my belly with no gun and you ain't chokin' a man old enough to be perhaps your papa." He turned to the bartender. "Wine in my back room."

"No. If I was goin' to kill you, Mose, I'd stake you out on the edge of a slue and let the young ducks and fish nibble you to death."

Mose forced a shaky laugh, then followed Add along the narrow hall to the back room. The same tall Mexican waiter served them, the waiter with the scarred face whose timely appearance had saved Mose from a bad choking at the hands of Teal. Already the nimble brain of Mose Clark was working.

"Before we get down to our talk, Add, I want to send out a note by this waiter."

"Go to it, Mose. But I'm tellin' you now that if you're tryin' to pull a trick, you'll be the first one to get hurt."

"No tricks, Add. I swear it on anything includin' the Bible and maybe the Koran, if you could get hold of one. Nope, this note is just concernin' a business deal with Teal."

He sat at a desk in a corner of the room and wrote rapidly. Then he carefully read what he had written.

Frisk Teal for papers. Whatever you find, bring to me, personal. Yours truly. Mose Clark.

Mose blotted the note carefully, put it in an envelope, and sealed it.

"Give this to my friend Jose Picó of the police department. Nobody else. Send word in to Teal that I am working hard to spring him out of the hoosegow. Now beat it, and don't stop no place to kid with no dame or lose your money gambling on rooster fights."

When the tall waiter had gone, Add stepped to the door. He opened it with a jerk. Nobody was in the hallway.

"What I got to say, Mose, ain't goin' to take long. First, I'm askin' you a question and I want the right answer to it. Who was the drunken gent that lifted the money off you in the *cantina* the night you and Teal let him bluff you into thinkin' he had a gun under the napkin? Who is he and what is he?"

"You asking me that? I should be askin' you. All I know is that he hung around here, two weeks or perhaps three weeks. He was a good spender and always, until he makes that play, he acts like a gentleman. He sits by himself with his bottle of whiskey, drinking alone. Listening to the music and especially to the girl called María. Like he is stuck on her, maybe, though he don't never make no bum play for her. Just listens to her music and pays even as much as a hundred smackers for her to sing songs that he likes. Sad songs, always. When the jazz music commences, he takes his bottle and goes out.

Nobody but that Pelón can serve him. Nobody but that María can play his kind of music. And one night, when a big tourist gets gay with her, this feller knocks him down with one poke and it is an hour before the guy wakes up. For a feller that is drunk, that gent hits like the kick from a mule. Figure that one out, too. And when he says there is a gun under the napkin, Teal ain't got no desire to make him prove it, and me, neither. And all the time this feller . . . who says he is Pat O'Brine and the bartender tells me that he is a Swedish aviator and another bartender tells me this feller claims to be a captain in the Swiss navy . . . all the time this feller is in with that Pelón and you to get that money off me. Hijacks. And now you ask me who is he? You should be asking a sucker like me such a question, Add."

"We'll let 'er go at that." Add grinned. "I got the answer I wanted anyhow."

"And some good money to boot, Add. What a poke in the snoot that deal was."

"I've got one more bunch of cattle for you, Mose," said Add. "Five hundred head. I'll deliver them cattle five days from now, at your Two Circle Ranch. Twenty dollars a round. And you pay me ten thousand cash money."

"Cash on delivery"—nodded Mose—"the same as always."

"Not this time, Mose. It is seven o'clock now. I want ten thousand cash at daylight, in the morning. Bring the money to me at the pass where your smugglers use that goat trail to cross their hop."

"What kind of a game are you putting over, Add? Always I have paid cash on delivery."

"And always, Mose, up till now, I was purty certain you'd be there to meet me on the date of delivery. Now it happens that I ain't so sure. The cattle will be delivered, Mose, but you might not be there."

"What are you drivin' at, Add?" Mose gulped his glass of wine and lit a cigar. "You talk like you was tryin' to scare me."

"Scare you, Mose? Not me. But I was put to a lot of hard work and expense a-gatherin' these cattle and I want my money. You bin playin' a strong game, Mose. You handle anything from an ounce of cocaine to women an' wet cattle in big bunches. You bin makin' money faster than ten men kin count it. You got a bunch of hop, twenty head of Chinamen, and a mule train loaded with case whiskey crossin' the line tonight. You've bought off the patrol men. The hop alone is worth ten thousand bucks. The Chinamen will fetch you five hundred apiece. That Scotch whiskey, which has bin cut here at your plant, will net you thirty dollars a case. The Mexican patrol is watchin' for cattle to be crossed at what we call The Notch In The Mountain. The U.S. patrol has likewise bin tipped off that there is some stolen cattle comin' across, because, Mose, you knew that I was holdin' a second herd that is booked for delivery across the line at some time between midnight an' daylight. You knew I was crossin' them cattle tonight. Teal got that information from a drunken cowpuncher. You thought you had a trap all set to ketch Add Ferguson an' his cowboys. There'll be enough border patrol men there waitin' fer that herd to eat the cattle, which means that the two, three men guardin' the smuggler pass can't any more stop that gang of hop runners an' Chinamen smugglers an' whiskey peddlers than a man kin use a cork to plug a bullet hole in his belly. You're a slick customer, Mose. You shore make 'er hard on the pore cowboy that's tryin' to make a few dollars handlin' Mexican cattle. It ain't the first time a herd of mine has bin stopped there at The Notch. But it'll be the last 'un. That herd is goin' on into The Notch, Mose, tonight. But when it goes, I'll have ten thousand cash in my

Levi's. Otherwise, I tip off the border riders that you're shovin' some hop an' Chinamen an' booze over. I'll deliver your cattle in five days. But you're payin' me half tonight."

"You win, Add. Don't tip off them border men. Let that herd start across through The Notch. I'll pay tonight."

"I reckoned you would, Mose. Thought you'd see my angle of it. Them cattle will be delivered at the Two Circle Ranch in good shape. I hope you're there to look 'em over."

"I'll be there, Add. Why shouldn't I be there?"

Add Ferguson lifted his glass of wine. He sipped it, then put down the glass.

"A man can't never tell, in our game, when they're liable to ketch up with him. Take a tip from me, as one cow thief to another, keep your man Teal in jail unless you want him to get hurt. His name is Teal, ain't it?"

A knock at the door made Mose jump. Add Ferguson eyed the door with a speculative air, then grinned.

"I reckon that's your waiter, Mose."

It was. The tall Mexican with the scarred face stood there in the doorway when Add unlocked and opened the door.

"Well?" questioned Mose curtly.

"I deliver the letter, *Señor* Clark, to Jose Picó, of the police. He regret to say there was no paper on thees *Señor* Teal. And *Señor* Teal ees now release."

"Teal turned loose?" croaked Mose. "Who got him out?"

"*¿Quién sabe?* Only I find out thees moch. A gentleman call' at the *cuartel* where they put the *Señor* Teal een the prison. The *soldado* on guard tell me thees *americano* ees quite dronk. He tell the *soldado* een Spanish that he ees the Preence of Wales an' has personal business weeth the *commandante*. He ees out een the bar room now, thees *Señor* Teal."

X

"Lone Hand"

Teal leaned against the bar, a black scowl on his face, as Add Ferguson and Mose walked into the *cantina* from the back room. At sight of Add Ferguson, Teal's scowl was yellowed by a look of fear. Then he smiled coldly and drank the liquor he held in his glass.

"How are you, Ferguson?"

"Me? I'm in good shape, Teal. See you later."

Add stalked out, mounted his horse outside, and rode down the street to the adobe house where he made his headquarters. Entering the house, he walked straight to the room where he had once taken Skeeter, the night he had given that mysterious gentleman some overalls and boots and chaps to make the ride to the Rancho de Mañana.

Add looked around the room, then gave a slight grunt of satisfaction when he found a folded envelope shoved into the silver frame that held a portrait of María Teresa Dominguez. Ripping open the envelope that bore no name or address, he beheld two papers. One of these was the bill of sale given by Mose Clark to the supposed purchaser of María. The other was a note addressed to Add.

When you read this, burn it. Sorry I had to leave down below, but I had an appointment here in Los Gatos. The enclosed document explains itself. It came into my hands in a certain way that would take too long in the telling. I got Teal out of the *cuartel*, never mind how. Give him and Mose Clark plenty of rope tonight, and they'll hang themselves. Take your cattle on

201

through The Notch. I am after Teal and Mose Clark. I
ask you to trust me tonight, Add.

Tomorrow, if the gods are kind tonight, I will meet
you at the Cantina Madrid. Should anything prevent
my being there, get in touch with the tall waiter who has
a scar across his face. More than this much I cannot tell
you now. Tom Dunn did his best to detain me, but I
out-foxed him. Dunn is all right.

In case I stop the bullet with my name on it tonight,
Tom will tell you some things. Pelón will supply more
details. But we'll hope for the best and for our meeting
tomorrow. Until then I remain your friend, Hashimura
Toto, Japanese envoy and general on the staff of The
Mikado.

P.S. Take your cattle through The Notch.

P.P.S. Let me take care of Mose Clark and Teal.

P.P.P.S. Thanks for the bottle of Haig & Haig I'm
borrowing.

P.P.P.P.S. And some more cartridges.

Signed, etc. , your friend, Lord Fauntleroy. *Adiós*.

"Drunk," muttered Add Ferguson. "The man's drunk as a
fool. And if he thinks I'm lettin' him play a lone hand, he's
likewise loco."

Add shoved his belt loops full of cartridges.

There was a noise at the rear door. Add put out the light
and waited. Somebody was trying to get in the door. A crash.
That was a window smashed. There were the growl of voices
and the tromp of feet.

Add's six-shooter roared, emptying six chambers into the
blackness. Somewhere a man groaned. Then Add slipped out
a side door and was gone in the night. His horse was hidden in
some brush. His threw his leg across the saddle. Bullets

snarled around his head as he raced for the open country. He caught the echo of Teal's voice shouting profane orders.

Then the night hid Add Ferguson and he was riding hard for the rough hills through which twisted what was known as the goat trail. Only once did Add Ferguson quit his course. That was when he rode nearly ten miles off the course to give orders to some cowpunchers who were driving a bunch of cattle.

"Keep them dogies a-movin', boys. Right on through The Notch. I can't go along with you. Hell's gonna pop tonight over on the goat trail and I got a pardner over there that's gonna need help. If the border boys stop you, grin an' take it. Tell 'em Add Ferguson will pay the bill, same as always."

"What's the row, Add?"

"A damn' fool friend of mine thinks he kin do me some favors and me not lend him a hand, that's all. He's drunker than a hoot owl and he thinks he kin whip the world, includin' the toughest bunch of renegade smugglers that ever staked a man to an ant hill. What in hell does he take me for, anyhow? He kin be the Tsar of Russia and the King of Turkey an' the Commodore of the Swiss navy, but he can't play solitaire in this game. He's the drinkin'est, lyin'est, gamest damn' fool I ever met."

"Want any of the boys, Add?"

"I reckon not. Not on the goat trail. You know what that is. The less the better. Two good men with plenty of cartridges is an army. Me and Skeeter will hold 'em."

"Skeeter?"

"Amongst other names, Skeeter. The gent that was at the barbecue and *fiesta*. He's drunk as a fiddler's pup and he's tryin' to hijack the stuff that Mose Clark is puttin' across the border tonight."

"How many men has he got fer an army, Add?"

"Men? He's got nobody."

"Look out!" shouted one of the cowpunchers. "Here's a rider a-comin'."

The rider was Tom Dunn. He had a lump over one ear and a grim smile on his mouth.

"Where's Teal?" gritted Dunn.

"With Mose Clark, I reckon," said Add. "What the . . . ?"

"I don't mean that hawk-beaked son-of-a-bitch. I'm talkin' about the real Jim Teal. The gent that bent a bottle acrost my head. The toughest, gamest, slickest *hombre* that ever bucked any man's game. He might be callin' hisse'f the Duke of Poland er somethin'. Add, I gotta find him. Even if I gotta quit you here an' now. Whenever that boy starts a ruckus, I just gotta be with him. He ain't after you, Add. Wet cattle don't bother him. He's after big game an'. . . ."

"You mean Skeeter?"

"That's your huckleberry. Where is he? Seen him, Add?"

"Tuck in your shirt tail, Dunn. You mean this Skeeter is Jim Teal?"

"That's Jim Teal. The fastest, gamest, damnedest fool that ever busted up a smugglin' racket. That's the boy. Him and me was together in some hot spots in Mexico. He come outta the big war with Germany with about all the medals a man kin pack, and he ranks plenty big at Washington. He's a warthawg."

"Jim Teal was killed in Torreón."

"Guess again, Add. Git me?"

"I get you. Swap that played out horse for the horse this cowboy is forkin'. Your friend Teal is in a tight and we're about to lessen the pressure on him. Let's go!"

"Let's go!" echoed Tom Dunn from a fresh horse, "and go hard!"

XI

"Blood Sign"

The goat trail was the passageway used by the smugglers of illicit drugs, liquor, and Chinese illegal aliens. It was a twisted, climbing trail that writhed through boulder-stewn cañons and clung perilously to the rocky cliffs. Only the surest-footed mules could hold safe footing on the goat trail, called by the Mexicans *el paso del cabrón*.

Now and then one of the men would dismount and lead his mule across some particularly treacherous spot along the trail. The pack mules were so divided that each man had the care of two mules. Not a cigarette glowed in the moonlight. No man spoke.

Herded along with the pack mules were twenty badly frightened Chinamen, sweating and puffing. For them there were no mules to ride because, as Mose Clark had once explained to his men, a good mule costs money and a Chinaman can't ride. Two or three mules had gone over the cliff because a Chinaman had tried in vain to rein the animal and a man would be losing money if his mules kept getting killed, to say nothing of the head price on the Chinaman, although you could get plenty more Chinamen. It was losing the mule that was so bad for the business.

Mose Clark's smuggling crew were hand-picked. The toughest men he could find. These men knew every foot of the goat trail, even on nights when the moon was not full. They were heavily armed. Their instructions were to kill any man they found blocking the trail, no matter if the man were some innocent Mexican or Indian.

The trail, sometimes for several breathtaking miles where

205

it was but a thin ledge along the sheer wall of a granite cliff, was a one-way passage, impossible for two mules to pass abreast. It was told that the narrow cañon floor under the high cliffs held the bones of many a man and mule that had the misfortune to meet Mose Clark's smugglers on the narrow trail. As the tales of dead men grew in number, while the list of missing men increased in length, it was almost impossible to hire a man to cross the goat trail, even in broad daylight.

The missing men were not all Mexicans or Indians. Numbered among the missing were prospectors from north of the border, following the gold lure across the pass, a few cowboys who had started across but had never reached the other end of the goat trail, and there were three men of the border patrol who had never been heard from after they had left their camp to watch for smuggling along the trail.

With the rising of the full moon, Mose Clark gave orders to the waiting men. Before they had got started several of Mose's spies had come in with the definite news that every border patrol man available was stationed at The Notch to grab Add Ferguson and his herd of Mexican cattle. There was but one more messenger to report. He would be coming down the goat trail from the opposite direction and was already an hour overdue. But the hours between moonrise were all too brief for these men who played such a dangerous game.

"We ain't waitin' no longer for him. Maybe his mule went lame or somethin'. Anyhow, it's a clear trail we got."

"If we meet this guy coming, Mose," asked one of the men, "what then?"

Mose smiled wickedly. "Teal, my new fifty-fifty pardner, will be riding in the lead. Teal will handle the situation."

Teal scowled darkly. He had not intended riding in the

lead. But a score of slitted, challenging eyes were fixed on him, waiting to see what his reply would be. He dared not refuse, not if he hoped to stay in this racket. The men working under him would hold him in contempt, brand him as yellow, and at the first good opportunity put a knife or bullet in him, if he didn't. The boss of this cut-throat gang must be hard enough to face down the toughest of them. Such a man was the leader whose place Teal would be taking, an undersized, warty, cold-eyed, cold-hearted man with a shapeless nose and one ear pulped, while its mate was shriveled and half gone. This was the notorious and infamous Cocaine Mike, ex-pugilist, barred from the ring for foul tactics, ex-jockey ruled from the tracks for crooked riding, ex-convict paroled from a life sentence by a gullible or dishonest governor. He had always ruled his band of murderers and thieves with vitriolic tongue and a pair of swift hands that could hit, shoot, or swing a knife with incredible speed.

Cocaine Mike, shortened to Coke, now watched Teal with red-shot eyes that glittered from under a pair of battered brows.

"It's a tough spot, Teal," he sneered.

"And I'm the tough egg that can fill it," gritted Teal. "Come on, you sons of sin. I'll lead you over this lousy cow trail. Coke will bring up the drags. And don't hang back, any of you, picking daffodils. Let's go!"

Mose Clark smiled in that crafty, smirking manner he had when he put over a smooth deal. Teal wouldn't last long with these bullies. He was pretty well nerved up tonight on whiskey and perhaps marijuana, but sooner or later he'd be caught in a tight spot and show the rat, the squealing rat, that Mose knew was in the man. He hated Teal. He wondered who had sprung Teal out of jail, who had a drag that could pull a deal like that? Did Teal have a secret partner?

On the other hand, Teal was wondering where that bill of sale had gone. At the jail the Mexican officers had searched him and had put all his personal belongings, including the bill of sale, into a steel box. The box had been sealed. When he had been, by some miracle, set free again, the sealed box was given to Teal who broke the seal and retrieved his belongings, all save that valuable bill of sale which had strangely, mysteriously vanished. He had protested bitterly. The Mexican officers had shrugged. The *americano* was insulting. He had watched them seal the box. The seal had been intact when the box was returned, no? Perhaps, after all, the *americano* was a little loco in the head and it might be the safe thing to put him back into the cell again.

Teal, holding back profane anger, had dropped the matter and gone to the *cantina*. He suspected Mose of the theft of that paper which had cost the pockmarked man a broken head. But the moment he talked to Mose, by indirect questioning, he knew that Mose had not been guilty. Some Mexican official? Who could say? It was gone.

But Mose was still under the impression that Teal had the incriminating document. Teal could still blackmail Mose, and that was all Teal wanted. Tonight's cut alone would be a nice grubstake—providing he ever saw sunrise alive. This was a tough lay-out. Mose had put over a fast one, and no mistake. Teal lit a marijuana cigarette. He heard Mose Clark, who was but a short distance behind, protest at the light.

"If I'm running this outfit, Mose, I'll run it to suit my own fancy. I'll take a smoke when I want one. But that don't mean that the pack rats coming behind me are to get the habit. There'll be a knife in the gizzard of the son-of-a-bitch that tries to light a smoke. Get that, you sons of hell?"

There was a muttered grumbling along the line but no cigarettes were lit. Perhaps, after all, this bragging, fancy-dressed killer was actually a hard egg, especially when he was inhaling the marijuana that makes killers out of men with hearts of coyotes.

An hour. Two hours. Now they were on the narrow ledge of the trail that threaded upwards along the rock wall. From that blackness hundreds of feet below, the roar of a tumbling waterfall echoed up to fill the ears of men along the trail, deafening them a little, with an insidious sensation of dizziness, a feeling of being off balance.

No man spoke. There was that glow of Teal's cigarette in the moonlight that threw their shadows in fantastic outline against the cliff that brushed their stirrups.

Mose took a long pull at his flask of whiskey. While Mose invariably accompanied his smuggling expeditions, he lived in a state bordering on hysteria, dripping with cold sweat every foot of the way. He was there because he dared trust no man when the money was paid over at the other end of the trail.

Once in the safe company of the purchasers of the illicit freight, men who protected Mose because he was the goose that laid the eggs of gold in the shape of smuggled goods sold at an enormous profit, he would pay off his men. He always sent them back by the same route while he went back by way of The Notch, which was safer in many ways.

Mose was worried. The failure of his messenger to put in appearance kept eating into his tortured mind. What had happened to the man? Long ago they should have met the fool, and Teal should have shot the mule from under him, clearing the trail.

Now Teal halted. There, in the trail, was a Mexican sombrero of black felt, decorated with gold braid. Teal called back softly.

"Did your messenger wear a Mexican sombrero of black

felt trimmed with gold braid, Mose?"

"He did. Why?"

"Then we won't be meeting him. He's down yonder. His mule must have lost its footing."

"Or else somebody coming up the trail ahead of us, met him. Any blood or sign of a fight?"

"Just the hat." Teal dismounted carefully and picked up the hat. There was a bullet hole through the curved brim, a bullet hole that told its story. Somebody was ahead of them on the trail.

XII

"Trail to Hell"

That somebody ahead of them on the trail was the man who was called, among other titles, Skeeter. Single-handed, he had planned the capture of the smuggling train that would include in its lawless personnel both Mose Clark and the man who called himself Jim Teal. Alone, gun ready, Skeeter rode a stout, grain-fed mule along the trail. At a certain spot, where the trail rimmed out on a mesa and where the caravan of smuggled stuff always halted for a time to rest the mules and gain a brief half hour of relaxation, Skeeter planned to waylay them.

His trap was set. Every border patrol man would be at The Notch by special arrangement. In a rim rock a hundred feet above the bald mesa, carefully wrapped in oiled silk and canvas, was buried a Lewis machine-gun and cases of ammunition. From this point one man could command a view of the little mesa or park. A machine-gun properly handled could rake them with withering fire.

To run meant the big odds of a misstep—death in the cañon hundreds of feet below, for they must choose either the trail they had just negotiated or the equally dangerous one leading down the divide from the little mesa. But one obstacle barred Skeeter's passage up the trail to that mesa where he planned his bagging of the men and contraband. That was the chance meeting with some man who might be coming along the trail from the opposite direction.

As far as Skeeter had been able to learn, there was one man, a murderous, marijuana-smoking half-breed Mexican who had not yet reported. This Skeeter had learned from one of the men in Mose Clark's band of smugglers, an undercover man who was now tempting death by riding with the renegades, a man who Skeeter was to recognize by a white shirt and a white silk scarf wrapped about his hatless head. When the shooting started, Skeeter would do his best not to hit a man thus garbed.

It was this undercover man who got word to Skeeter that one of Mose Clark's messengers, this half-breed, might be coming down the trail. So, bearing that bit of information in mind, Skeeter rode with a gun in his hand. He was in advance of the smugglers. Up, up along the narrow ledge, nerves tightened to the breaking point, the bottle in his saddle pocket forgotten, Skeeter rode. Presently he did encounter a man on a gray mule, a man wearing a big black sombrero.

"*¿Quién es?*" barked the half-breed.

"Officer of the law, you mongrel!" Skeeter cried. "Surrender!"

The *crack* of a carbine gave defiant challenge to Skeeter's warning. Now the six-shooter in Skeeter's hand spewed flame. The man swayed drunkenly in his saddle, jerking the bridle reins, throwing the gray mule off the narrow ledge. The thin scream of the luckless half-breed mingled with an agonized sound that came from the terrified mule.

Skeeter sat in his saddle, suddenly sick inside. He fought to keep his balance, fought against the nausea that had gripped him. Blindly, desperately, as a drowning man might grope at a life preserver thrown him, Skeeter dragged the bottle from the saddle pocket. His teeth pulled the cork, spat it out. The fiery stuff bit its way down his throat. Then, after a little while, he rode on.

There was a rapidly spreading red smear under his left armpit. By a few inches the slug had missed hitting him in the heart. As it was, it was a painful, nasty, weakening wound. A handicap that, added to his already wounded arm, made him one-handed. Fate had given him now a tremendous handicap. But the man called Skeeter grinned through tightly pulled lips. He'd make the rim rock and get his Lewis gun set up. The whiskey would keep his head steady. Medicine. He'd be needing it.

The damned climb seemed interminable. It seemed years before he rode out on the little mesa. The scramble up the rocks to the rim rock shelf was no man's picnic. He ripped away his shirt and undershirt and fashioned a crude but effective bandage. His brain still heard the scream of that man who had gone to his death in the cañon.

"Got to hold out. Got to get 'em. Got to bottle 'em up here and invite 'em to a cleaning." He took another drink.

The machine-gun was set up. Magazines full of .30 cartridges placed within easy reach. Behind the smugglers there would come the tall Mexican with the scar across his face, the waiter from the *cantina,* game, tough, clever, one of the finest men in the United States Secret Service. To Skeeter he was known only by a number, like Pelón and the pockmarked undercover man.

Skeeter had no way of knowing that Add Ferguson and

Tom Dunn were with the tall Mexican who they had intercepted and joined. He counted only on the fact that the tall Mexican would be holding the trail that led back to Los Gatos. While the man with the white shirt, likewise known by a number, would be guarding the other exit from the little mesa.

The minutes dragged past. Skeeter grinned crookedly. For many long months he had drifted along the border, guzzling whiskey so that he could successfully play the dangerous part allotted him, the part of a rich waster, changing names, or without a name, drinking, spending, playing the clown, making friends where his duty called upon him to make friends, pawning his very life to play the part he was given.

Behind him was a name. His real name—Jim Teal—soldier of fortune, adventurer, explorer, but always an enemy of vice, that brand of vice that has claimed the happiness and health and life of a thousand men and women along the border, vice that bred manifold, countless germs when the United States declared that a man cannot take a drink. From Tía Juana to Juárez, that vice, like a crawling, slimy thing with countless tentacles, reached out its creeping, choking arms to pull into its cesspool the lives of men and women. Jim Teal, soldier of fortune, enemy of that border vice that he had seen suck the life from men who were his comrades, had offered his services to his country. Through certain channels it was arranged to have Jim Teal officially dead in both Mexico and the United States. By a grisly trick of fate, that pseudo death had almost become a truth. Enemies had pulled political strings, and in that firing squad whose rifles had been loaded with blanks there was one gun that held steel-jacket bullets.

When Jim Teal dropped before the firing squad at Torreón—his cigarette, that last, that final gesture of the man who follows the fortunes of war, that cigarette still burning between his lips—there was a bullet hole through his left lung, near the heart. Jim Teal had not been acting when that volley dropped him there by the bullet-scarred wall at Torreón. For many months Jim Teal had lingered between life and death behind locked doors.

He had stood against that wall a tall, wide-shouldered, splendidly framed man. Months later he had crept out of Mexico a living skeleton, his hair thinned and whitened, but his indomitable courage undampened. The man who had seen him yesterday, that Tom Dunn who had somehow recognized him, had seen in Jim Teal the ghost of the swaggering, laughing, fighting man he had followed across Chihuahua and Sonora in the swashbuckling red days of the great Pancho Villa. Now that same Tom Dunn and Add Ferguson were coming up the goat trail to lend a hand to a comrade.

The pseudo Jim Teal, at the head of the smuggling band, topped the mesa. Behind him came the others, one by one. There showed the white shirt of the man who had acted as undercover man. They rode up onto the grassy mesa, the last man to arrive being Cocaine Mike.

There followed the business of loosening saddle cinches, unloading packs, and the lighting of cigarettes. Men's voices talked in low tones. A bottle passed. A gritty laugh.

Cocaine Mike's mocking, taunting, ugly cursing at a mule was deliberate. Every man in that lawless cavalcade knew that Coke was baiting the man who called himself Teal. Teal's nerves were rubbed raw and he was in a black mood. Now Mose Clark's voice came, arguing some point with Teal. Teal, like a panther crouched and ready to fight, crazed by marijuana, abusing whoever came across his path as he bossed the job of unpacking and unsaddling, snarled: "I killed one man since morning. And I'll add more stiffs to the list. Careful with that pack, you two sons of the gutter. That's not barley in those sacks. Coke, herd those chinks over by the edge of the trail. What in hell is that man in the white shirt doing over by the upper trail?"

"Don't be so grouchy," interposed Mose. "He's on guard there, what else do ya suppose? Let him alone."

That explanation seemed to satisfy the ugly-tempered Teal. Cocaine Mike, moving quickly around with that easy gait of a boxer, was everywhere at once. Ignoring Teal, he did his job of under-boss. Mose sat down on the ground, nibbling at his flask, his fat body bathed in chilly sweat, his eyes watching Teal and Cocaine Mike.

Meanwhile up on the rim rock ledge the real Teal, the Teal who had been reborn of the old rollicking, swaggering machine-gun captain, watched with slitted eyes for the signal that would tell him that the tall Mexican with the scarred face had taken his post. Each second of waiting was weakening the wounded man. Each minute was an hour of torture. Take another pull at the old bottle. Fight back the pain and the sickness and the weariness that swept over his brain and body in nauseating waves. Perhaps something had happened to . . . there it was! God, there was the signal! There it showed against the moonlight! A white rag waving!

The wounded man swung the Lewis gun on its tripod. It ripped the night with staccato bark. As the echoes of it died, Skeeter's voice, not loud, not harsh, but clear and mocking and penetrating in its challenge, dropped through the stunned, paralyzed silence that gripped Mose Clark and his men.

"Hold everything, you scourings of hell! Move and this gun will mow you down. It's the law talking, you mangy rats. The law you've spit on and wiped your stinkin' feet on. The United States law, you spawn of hell! This mesa is United

States soil. You're not in Mexico, you tramps! And you'll take it in the guts in a holy second if you try to break back. This is Major Jim Teal that's telling it to you and he'd sooner make it your funeral service than take you alive. Mose, you filthy, cowardly, soft-bellied crook, it's time for you to say your prayers. The lying son of a mangy cur that calls himself Teal had better dig himself a hole and crawl into it and pull the hole in after him. Coke, you misbegotten whelp of the gutter, say your prayers! The rest of you rats that don't want your bellies pumped full of bullets, back over there where the Chinamen are. Lay down your guns and hope that my aim is as good as it used to be. The whole lousy, mangy, scurvy pack of you will go to prison or to hell and Major Jim Teal is just the right man to come to for your one-way tickets. I said Teal, you rats. Jim Teal! I got a badge pinned to my shirt and I'd like to see the color of the man's eyes that thinks he can hit it with a bullet. Coke, step out with your hands up!"

"I'll see you in hell, you cop!" Cocaine Mike emptied an automatic rifle at the rim rock. Skeeter's laugh mocked his futile effort.

There was a movement toward the trail they had just come up. Add Ferguson's rasping voice checked them.

"Stand back, you bums! Skeeter, you ol' hunk of cheese, me and Tom Dunn ain't so easy got rid of. We got the trail corked. Your other two *compadres* hold the other trail. Give us the word and we'll. . . ."

The rush came. Skeeter cut loose with the machine-gun. Men went down, cursing. The mesa was ripped with gunfire —groans, curses, screams—the Lewis gun rapping out its deadly tattoo.

The man who had palmed himself off as Teal was fighting desperately as he lay behind a dead mule. Mose Clark, like a fat, bewildered rabbit, sought shelter beside him. With a snarl, the marijuana-crazed man emptied a six-shooter into the flabby body. Mose, with a thin, screaming yelp, rolled over. The other man grinned horribly and used the bleeding, soggy body to shield his own.

Then something leaped on him. Cocaine Mike, his battered face twisted with fury, was on the man who had called himself Teal.

"Mose never called me a friend, but he done right by me. I'll take you, big boy!" His fists smashed with vicious jabs. The other man fought with fear-stricken fury.

The renegades, some knocked down by bullets, were begging for quarter. The frightened babble of the Chinamen mingled with their cries for mercy. Skeeter's machine-gun kicked up the dirt around them, driving them back, cowering, crawling, to the edge of the cliff.

In the moonlight Cocaine Mike and the man who had been the bodyguard for Mose fought hand to hand. Blood-smeared, reeling, knives ripping, they fought. Until only Cocaine Mike was on his feet, a ghastly, bloody, reeling thing on widespread legs, alone there, cursing the men who would not rally to his calls to fight.

"Fight, you devils! Fight, you dogs! Fight you . . . !"

He cursed them with every evil name a foul tongue can find to name a man, and then, when they would not rally, he emptied a gun into their huddled midst. Only when his second Luger was empty, when he stood there, snarling, sobbing, cursing, an empty gun in each hand, only then did he fall, a bullet hole between his eyes.

Major Jim Teal, a six-shooter in his hand, crawled painfully down from his perch to claim his victory on the blood-stained ground.

Tom Dunn and Add Ferguson, with the aid of the two

secret service men, the man with the scar and the man in the white shirt, had lined their prisoners up against the edge of the black chasm. They disarmed their sullen, scared crew of smugglers, throwing the confiscated guns over the edge of the cliff.

Wounded, his face ghastly in its smear of blood, Major Jim Teal stood over the dead bodies of Mose Clark, the pseudo Teal, and Cocaine Mike. From his pocket, Jim Teal pulled a bottle. Add and Tom came toward him.

"Boys . . . boys, have a little drink on Teal. James Teal. Now, by an act of Congress a gentleman, an officer of the United States Army, and the best judge of bad likker between Mexico and hell. Tom Dunn, you lousy, unmilitary bum. Add Ferguson, you damn' sheep-stealin' rebel. Drink with me, you sons, or I'll bust this bottle over you like the Congressman's wife christening a ship. I might have known you'd turn up like a couple of tramps after a hand-out. Crashing the gate like One-Eyed Connelly. Who slipped you the Annie Oakleys to my private circus? Drink hearty. And quit pawing a man. I'm all right. All I need is a shave and a bath and a nice, felt-lined coffin. And a month at the nearest Keely Cure. I never could stand hard likker. Never could. And that's the gospel. Three years' course and I'm flunkin' it. Can't hold my drinks like . . . like a gentleman. Hate the stuff. Hate the taste of it. Ask Tom. But orders said drink and I drank. Till I got the world's best skin full. If you need a drink, pinch me and it'll squirt out. My mother thinks I'm the rottenest drunk in the world. My best girl quit me, and no wonder. They didn't know, see, that I was after Mose Clark and these others that got my kid brother here on their lousy goat trail. Bumped the kid off when he tried to do his duty as a border officer. My kid brother. His grave is down there in the cañon. I got down there and buried him. Add, you old cow thief, gimme that bottle. I'm gettin' . . . sleepy."

With a queer sort of laugh Major Jim Teal went lurching into Tom Dunn's arms. Through the smeared blood and dirt on the unconscious man's cheeks were tears.

XIII

"Fiesta"

At the Rancho de Mañana there gathered a holiday crowd. There was music and laughter and bright colors. For this was the wedding *fiesta* day when María Teresa Dominguez should become the wife of Add Ferguson. María, tall, dark-eyed, beautiful in the gown that had been the wedding dress of her great grandmother in Spain, stood before a long mirror. Beside her stood a fair-haired, gray-eyed girl in a dove-colored gown, the bride of Major Jim Teal. The white-haired, handsome woman who fussed over the two was Jim Teal's mother, come all the way from Washington, D.C. for the wedding.

In one wing of the house there gathered *Don* Miguel Dominguez, Add Ferguson, and Jim Teal. *Don* Miguel was resplendent in black velvet and silver and scarlet. Add Ferguson was in formal evening clothes. Jim Teal was in the dress uniform of a United States Army officer, rank of lieutenant colonel.

"Mose Clark, you see," explained Add, "had stolen land and cattle near here. A whole grant. Thousands of acres and thousands of cattle, land and cattle belonging to *Don* Miguel's brother who was mysteriously murdered. I was raised by *Don* Miguel, educated in Arizona and California, and was like one of the family. Mose, when I returned from

France, had gotten hold of more land. He was robbing *Don* Miguel's range. And so I set out to get it back. I made a trip to Washington. Another trip to Mexico City. Then I came back here to the ranch. As a supposed border rustler, I got in touch with Mose. What cattle I sold him I stole from his own range. I paid duty on every head that ever crossed the border. And I made Mose Clark eat crow meat. *Don* Miguel wanted to fight him in a duel. It would be like a tiger licking a rabbit. I bled Mose through his pocketbook, which was his real heart. And that is the history of Add Ferguson, the toughest cow thief on the border. I'd hoped to tell the tale to Mose when I'd broken his bank, but a man can't ask too much of fate."

Add rose from his chair, a glass of old Spanish wine in his hand. *Don* Miguel's hand held a glass of the same rare old wine. Jim Teal grinned at his own glass of water.

"*Señores,*" said old *Don* Miguel gravely, "we drink to the two *señoritas* who soon will be the wives of two brave and gallant gentlemen. *¡Salud!*"

"*¡Salud!*" said Add Ferguson.

"*¡Salud!*" said Jim Teal, and their glasses touched.

THE BIG FIFTY

JOHNNY D. BOGGS

Young Coady McIlvain spends his days reading about the heroic exploits of the legendary heroes of the West, especially the glorious Buffalo Bill Cody. The harsh reality of frontier life in Kansas becomes brutally clear to Coady, however, when his father is scalped and he is taken prisoner by Comanches. When he is finally able to escape, Coady finds himself with a buffalo sharpshooter who he imagines is the living embodiment of his hero, Buffalo Bill. But real life is seldom like a dime novel, and Fate has more hard lessons in store for Coady—if he can stay alive to learn them.

PETER DAWSON

GHOST BRAND OF THE WISHBONES

Peter Dawson's fiction has retained its classic status among readers of many generations. This volume presents for the first time in paperback three of his most enduring short novels. The title tale opens with the daring robbery of an entire cattle train and gets only more exciting from there. "Hell's Half Acre" is filled with the chaos and danger that results from an all-out range war between cattle ranchers and the sheep raising syndicate. And in "Sagerock Sheriff," old Tom Platt faces his toughest challenge since he took office years ago. He has to find out—right away—if a man being sentenced to life in the penitentiary is really guilty of murder.

PETER DAWSON

LONE RIDER FROM TEXAS

The heart of the American West lives in Peter Dawson's stories, with characters who blaze a trail over a land of frontier dreams and across a country coming of age. Whether it tells of the attempt of an outlaw father to save the life of his son, who has become an officer of the law, or a shotgun guard who is forced to choose between a seemingly impossible love and involvement in a stagecoach robbery, each of these seven stories embodies the dramatic struggles that made the American frontier so unique and its people the stuff of legend.
